SPIRITS
of the
SEASON

SPIRITS
of the
SEASON

Christmas Hauntings

edited by
TANYA KIRK

This collection first published in 2018 by
The British Library
96 Euston Road
London NW1 2DB

Introduction and notes © Tanya Kirk 2018

Cataloguing in Publication Data
A catalogue record for this publication is available from the British Library

ISBN 978 0 7123 5252 9
eISBN 978 0 7123 6459 1

Frontispiece illustration by Enrique Bernardou, 2018

Text design and typesetting by Tetragon, London
Printed and bound by CPI Group (UK) Ltd, Croydon CR0 4YY

CONTENTS

INTRODUCTION

Nothing satisfies us on Christmas Eve but to hear each other tell authentic anecdotes about spectres. It is a genial, festive season, and we love to muse upon graves, and dead bodies, and murders, and blood.

JEROME K. JEROME

For centuries people have enjoyed the tradition of sharing ghost stories—an activity which crosses over many different languages and cultures. In 1918, Virginia Woolf wrote an essay in which she questioned the lure of the ghost narrative, asking 'how are we to account for the strange human craving for the pleasure of feeling afraid which is so much involved in our love of ghost stories?' The answer she suggests can tell us a lot about why they became a Christmas tradition in their own right: 'it is pleasant to be afraid when we are conscious that we are in no kind of danger'. For a time of year when those who can choose to stay indoors out of bad weather and with food, drink and comfort, the frisson of reading about a haunting can be a welcome contrast.

The association of ghosts with Christmastime probably dates back to early Christian beliefs that the anniversary of the birth of Christ had a calming effect on souls who were stuck in purgatory, and that therefore the day before, on Christmas Eve, they were at their most active. It's the same reason why ghosts are said to walk on Hallowe'en—the eve of All Saints' Day. Christmas Eve is also very close to the winter solstice—the longest night of the year. Some people have even theorised that in the 19th century, when ghost stories became hugely popular, the increased use of gas lamps over the darkest time of year could give a special enhancement to a reader's experience—the lamps emitted carbon monoxide if they weren't properly ventilated, and this caused headaches and even hallucinations.

What had originated as more of an oral tradition was first recorded in print in 1820, when American writer Washington Irving published a tale that referred to people gathering to tell ghost stories at Christmas. That the genre became immensely popular was the responsibility of another author—Charles Dickens. Dickens was a strong advocate for Christmas, and promoted it as a family holiday, perhaps as a reaction to his own poverty-stricken childhood. He loved the season and enjoyed walking the streets of London on Christmas Eve, people-watching. In 1843, his ghostly novella *A Christmas Carol* was published and proved hugely popular. The story tied into historical traditions of ghosts walking on Christmas Eve, as well as a strong message of atonement and redemption which the Victorian reading public approved of, and which was seen as suitable for the season. Dickens co-founded and began editing the magazine *Household Words* in 1850, moving on to a new journal, *All the Year Round*, in 1859. In the later years of *Household Words* he published special Christmas editions, filled with seasonal stories, poems and articles. His first Christmas at *All the Year Round*, he dedicated the whole Christmas issue to a series of ghost stories.

Ghost stories worked particularly well for the huge new magazine industry in the mid to late 19th century, and it led to a real golden age for the genre. The industrial revolution meant that printing was mechanised for the first time, and as a result reading matter became much more affordable and could be mass-produced. At the same time, literacy levels were on the rise, creating a new market for literature. Fiction periodicals functioned almost like the television of their day—offering light entertainment and requiring a large amount of content arranged into manageable chunks. The inclusion of soap opera-style serial stories ensured that the public kept buying new issues. Ghost stories were usually standalone rather than serials, and fitted in well as a way of varying the pace within a periodical. The special Christmas issues that Dickens introduced were designed to have a wider readership than normal, as people would buy them as gifts—so too many ongoing serial stories would not have worked well. Ghost stories, on the other hand, were perfect. In the latter half of the 19th century, many magazine titles started including ghost stories in their Christmas editions—*The Strand*, *Pall Mall Magazine*, *Blackwood's*, and *Cornhill*, among many others.

All but two of the stories in this volume first appeared in periodicals in the late 19th and early 20th century, mostly at Christmas. Today, some of the ghost stories from this golden age have remained famous and are frequently reprinted—but others have become unjustly obscure. These are some of my favourites.

TANYA KIRK

Lead Curator of Printed Heritage Collections 1601–1900,
British Library

THE FOUR-FIFTEEN EXPRESS

Amelia B. Edwards

First published in *Routledge's Christmas Annual* for 1867

Amelia Ann Blanford Edwards (1831–1892) was a polymath. As a child she wrote stories and poems which she illustrated herself. She then decided to aim for a career in music and learned the organ, went back to the idea of being a writer a few years later, and in later life became an influential Egyptologist. She was also an active supporter of women's suffrage. She published novels, children's books, poetry and travelogues, and was a regular contributor to Christmas periodicals, writing a number of ghost stories for them. Today she is remembered more for her contributions to archaeology than her stories, as she campaigned for more ethical methods in which historic sites were preserved rather than plundered.

THE EVENTS WHICH I AM ABOUT TO RELATE TOOK PLACE between nine and ten years ago. Sebastopol had fallen in the early Spring; the peace of Paris had been concluded since March; our commercial relations with the Russian empire were but recently renewed; and I, returning home after my first northward journey since the war, was well pleased with the prospect of spending the month of December under the hospitable and thoroughly English roof of my excellent friend Jonathan Jelf, Esquire, of Dumbleton Manor, Clayborough, East Anglia. Travelling in the interests of the well-known firm in which it is my lot to be a junior partner, I had been called upon to visit not only the capitals of Russia and Poland, but had found it also necessary to pass some weeks among the trading ports of the Baltic; whence it came that the year was already far spent before I again set foot on English soil, and that instead of shooting pheasants with him, as I had hoped, in October, I came to be my friend's guest during the more genial Christmastide.

My voyage over, and a few days given up to business in Liverpool and London, I hastened down to Clayborough with all the delight of a schoolboy whose holidays are at hand. My way lay by the Great East Anglian line as far as Clayborough station, where I was to be met by one of the Dumbleton carriages and conveyed across the remaining nine miles of country. It was a foggy afternoon, singularly warm for the fourth of December, and I had arranged to leave London by the 4.15 express. The early darkness of Winter had already closed in; the lamps were lighted in the carriages; a clinging damp dimmed the windows, adhered to the door-handles, and pervaded all the atmosphere; while the gas jets at the neighbouring bookstand diffused a luminous haze that only served to make the gloom of the terminus more visible. Having arrived some seven minutes before the starting of the train, and, by the connivance of the guard, taken sole possession of an empty compartment, I lighted my travelling lamp, made myself particularly snug, and settled down to the undisturbed enjoyment of a book and a cigar. Great, therefore, was my disappointment when, at the last moment, a gentleman came hurrying along the platform, glanced into my carriage, opened the locked door with a private key, and stepped in.

It struck me at the first glance that I had seen him before—a tall, spare man, thin-lipped, light-eyed, with an ungraceful stoop in the shoulders, and scant grey hair worn somewhat long upon the collar. He carried a light water-proof coat, an umbrella, and a large brown japanned deed-box, which last he placed under the seat. This done, he felt carefully in his breast-pocket, as if to make certain of the safety of his purse or pocket-book; laid his umbrella in the netting overhead; spread the water-proof across his knees; and exchanged his hat for a travelling cap of some Scotch material. By this time the train was moving out of the station, and into the faint grey of the wintry twilight beyond.

I now recognised my companion. I recognised him from the moment when he removed his hat and uncovered the lofty, furrowed and somewhat narrow brow beneath. I had met him, as I distinctly remembered, some three years before, at the very house for which, in all probability, he was now bound like myself. His name was Dwerrihouse; he was a lawyer by profession; and, if I was not greatly mistaken, was first cousin to the wife of my host. I knew also that he was a man eminently 'well to do,' both as regarded his professional and private means. The Jelfs entertained him with that sort of observant courtesy which falls to the lot of the rich relation; the children made much of him; and the old butler, albeit somewhat surly 'to the general,' treated him with deference. I thought, observing him by the vague mixture of lamplight and twilight, that Mrs. Jelf's cousin looked all the worse for the three years' wear and tear which had gone over his head since our last meeting. He was very pale, and had a restless light in his eye that I did not remember to have observed before. The anxious lines, too, about his mouth were deepened, and there was a cavernous hollow look about his cheeks and temples which seemed to speak of sickness or sorrow. He had glanced at me as he came in, but without any gleam of recognition in his face. Now he glanced again, as I fancied, somewhat doubtfully. When he did so for the third or fourth time, I ventured to address him.

'Mr. John Dwerrihouse, I think?'

'That is my name,' he replied.

'I had the pleasure of meeting you at Dumbleton about three years ago.'

Mr. Dwerrihouse bowed.

'I thought I knew your face,' he said. 'But your name, I regret to say—'

'Langford—William Langford. I have known Jonathan Jelf since we were boys together at Merchant Taylor's, and I generally spend a few weeks at Dumbleton in the shooting season. I suppose we are bound for the same destination?'

'Not if you are on your way to the Manor,' he replied. 'I am travelling upon business—rather troublesome business, too—whilst you, doubtless, have only pleasure in view.'

'Just so. I am in the habit of looking forward to this visit as to the brightest three weeks in all the year.'

'It is a pleasant house,' said Mr. Dwerrihouse.

'The pleasantest I know.'

'And Jelf is thoroughly hospitable.'

'The best and kindest fellow in the world!'

'They have invited me to spend Christmas week with them,' pursued Mr. Dwerrihouse, after a moment's pause.

'And you are coming?'

'I cannot tell. It must depend on the issue of this business which I have in hand. You have heard, perhaps, that we were about to construct a branch line from Blackwater to Stockbridge.'

I explained that I had been for some months away from England and had therefore heard nothing of the contemplated improvement.

Mr. Dwerrihouse smiled complacently.

'It will be an improvement,' he said; 'a great improvement. Stockbridge is a flourishing town, and only needs a more direct railway communication with the metropolis to become an important centre of commerce. This branch was my own idea. I brought the project before the board, and have myself superintended the execution of it up to the present time.'

'You are an East Anglian director, I presume?'

'My interest in the company,' replied Mr. Dwerrihouse, 'is threefold. I am a director; I am a considerable shareholder; and, as head of the firm of Dwerrihouse, Dwerrihouse, and Craik, I am the company's principal solicitor.'

Loquacious, self-important, full of his pet project, and apparently unable to talk on any other subject, Mr. Dwerrihouse then went on to tell of the opposition he had encountered and the obstacles he had overcome in the cause of the Stockbridge branch. I was entertained with a multitude of local details and local grievances. The rapacity of one squire; the impracticability of another; the indignation of the rector whose glebe was threatened; the culpable indifference of the Stockbridge townspeople, who could not be brought to see that their most vital interests hinged upon a junction with the Great East Anglian line; the spite of the local newspaper; and the unheard-of difficulties attending the Common question, were each and all laid before me with a circumstantiality that possessed the deepest interest for my excellent fellow-traveller, but none whatever for myself. From these, to my despair, he went on to more intricate matters: to the approximate expenses of construction per mile; to the estimates sent in by different contractors; to the probable traffic returns of the new line: to the provisional clauses of the new Act as enumerated in Schedule D of the company's last half-yearly report; and so on, and on, and on till my head ached, and my attention flagged, and my eyes kept closing in spite of every effort that I made to keep them open. At length I was roused by these words:—

'Seventy-five thousand pounds, cash down.'

'Seventy-five thousand pounds, cash down,' I repeated, in the liveliest tone I could assume. 'That is a heavy sum.'

'A heavy sum to carry here,' replied Mr. Dwerrihouse, pointing significantly to his breast-pocket; 'but a mere fraction of what we shall ultimately have to pay.'

'You do not mean to say that you have seventy-five thousand pounds at this moment upon your person?' I exclaimed.

'My good sir, have I not been telling you so for the last half hour?' said Mr. Dwerrihouse, testily. 'That money has to be paid over at half-past eight o'clock this evening, at the office of Sir Thomas's solicitors, on completion of the deed of sale.'

'But how will you get across by night from Blackwater to Stockbridge with seventy-five thousand pounds in your pocket?'

'To Stockbridge!' echoed the lawyer. 'I find I have made myself very imperfectly understood. I thought I had explained how this sum carries our new line only as far as Mallingford—this first stage, as it were, of our journey—and how our route from Blackwater to Mallingford lies entirely through Sir Thomas Liddell's property.'

'I beg your pardon,' I stammered. 'I fear my thoughts were wandering. So you only go as far as Mallingford tonight?'

'Precisely. I shall get a conveyance from the "Blackwater Arms." And you?'

'Oh, Jelf sends a trap to meet me at Clayborough. Can I be the bearer of any message from you?'

'You may say if you please, Mr. Langford, that I wished I could have been your companion all the way, and that I will come over if possible before Christmas.'

'Nothing more?'

Mr. Dwerrihouse smiled grimly.

'Well,' he said, 'you may tell my cousin that she need not burn the hall down in my honour *this* time, and that I shall be obliged if she will order the blue-room chimney to be swept before I arrive.'

'That sounds tragic. Had you a conflagration on the occasion of your last visit to Dumbleton?'

'Something like it. There had been no fire lighted in my bedroom since the spring, the flue was foul, and the rooks had built in it; so when I went up to dress for dinner, I found the room full of smoke, and the chimney on fire. Are we already at Blackwater?'

The train had gradually come to a pause while Mr. Dwerrihouse was speaking, and on putting my head out of the window, I could see the station some few hundred yards ahead. There was another train before us blocking the way, and the ticket-taker was making use of the delay to collect the Blackwater tickets. I had scarcely ascertained our position, when the ruddy-faced official appeared at our carriage door.

'Ticket, sir!' said he.

'I am for Clayborough,' I replied, holding out the tiny pink card.

He took it; glanced at it by the light of his little lantern; gave it back; looked, as I fancied, somewhat sharply at my fellow-traveller, and disappeared.

'He did not ask for yours,' I said with some surprise.

'They never do,' replied Mr. Dwerrihouse. 'They all know me; and of course, I travel free.'

'Blackwater! Blackwater!' cried the porter, running along the platform beside us, as we glided into the station.

Mr. Dwerrihouse pulled out his deed-box, put his travelling-cap in his pocket, resumed his hat, took down his umbrella, and prepared to be gone.

'Many thanks, Mr. Langford, for your society,' he said, with old-fashioned courtesy. 'I wish you a good evening.'

'Good evening,' I replied, putting out my hand.

But he either did not see it, or did not choose to see it, and, slightly lifting his hat, stepped out upon the platform. Having done this, he moved slowly away, and mingled with the departing crowd.

Leaning forward to watch him out of sight, I trod upon something which proved to be a cigar-case. It had fallen, no doubt, from the pocket of his water-proof coat, and was made of dark morocco leather, with a silver monogram upon the side. I sprang out of the carriage just as the guard came up to lock me in.

'Is there one minute to spare?' I asked eagerly. 'The gentleman who travelled down with me from town has dropped his cigar-case—he is not yet out of the station!'

'Just a minute and a half, sir,' replied the guard. 'You must be quick.'

I dashed along the platform as fast as my feet could carry me. It was a large station, and Mr. Dwerrihouse had by this time got more than half-way to the farther end.

I, however, saw him distinctly, moving slowly with the stream. Then, as I drew nearer, I saw that he had met some friend—that they were talking as they walked—that they presently fell back somewhat from the crowd, and stood aside in earnest conversation, I made straight for the spot where they were waiting. There was a vivid gas-jet just above their heads, and the light fell full upon their faces. I saw both distinctly—the face of Mr. Dwerrihouse and the face of his companion. Running, breathless, eager as I was, getting in the way of porters and passengers, and fearful every instant lest I should see the train going on without me, I yet observed that the new-comer was considerably younger and shorter than the director, that he was sandy-haired, mustachioed, small-featured, and dressed in a close-cut suit of Scotch tweed. I was now within a few yards of them. I ran against a stout gentleman—I was nearly knocked down by a luggage-truck—I stumbled over a carpet-bag—I gained the spot just as the driver's whistle warned me to return.

To my utter stupefaction they were no longer there. I had seen them but two seconds before—and they were gone! I stood still. I looked to right and left. I saw no sign of them in any direction. It was as if the platform had gaped and swallowed them.

'There were two gentlemen standing here a moment ago,' I said to a porter at my elbow; 'which way can they have gone?'

'I saw no gentlemen, sir,' replied the man.

The whistle shrilled out again. The guard, far up the platform, held up his arm, and shouted to me to 'Come on!'

'If you're going on by this train, sir,' said the porter, 'you must run for it.'

I did run for it, just gained the carriage as the train began to move, was shoved in by the guard, and left breathless and bewildered, with Mr. Dwerrihouse's cigar-case still in my hand.

It was the strangest disappearance in the world. It was like a transformation trick in a pantomime. They were there one moment—palpably there—talking—with the gaslight full upon their faces; and the next moment they were gone. There was no door near—no window—no staircase. It was a mere slip of barren platform, tapestried with big advertisements. Could anything be more mysterious?

It was not worth thinking about; and yet, for my life, I could not help pondering upon it—pondering, wondering, conjecturing, turning it over and over in my mind, and beating my brains for a solution of the enigma. I thought of it all the way from Blackwater to Clayborough. I thought of it all the way from Clayborough to Dumbleton, as I rattled along the smooth highway in a trim dog-cart drawn by a splendid black mare, and driven by the silentest and dapperest of East Anglian grooms.

We did the nine miles in something less than an hour, and pulled up before the lodge-gates just as the church clock was striking half-past seven. A couple of minutes more, and the warm glow of the lighted hall was flooding out upon the gravel; a hearty grasp was on my hand; and a clear jovial voice was bidding me 'Welcome to Dumbleton.'

'And now, my dear fellow,' said my host, when the first greeting was over, 'you have no time to spare. We dine at eight, and there are people coming to meet you; so you must just get the dressing business over as quickly as may be. By the way, you will meet some acquaintances. The Biddulphs are coming, and Prendergast (Prendergast, of the Skirmishers) is staying in the house. Adieu! Mrs. Jelf will be expecting you in the drawing-room.'

I was ushered to my room—not the blue room, of which Mr. Dwerrihouse had made disagreeable experience, but a pretty little bachelor's chamber, hung with a delicate chintz, and made cheerful by a blazing fire. I unlocked my portmanteau. I tried to be expeditious; but the memory of my railway adventure haunted me. I could not get free of it. I could not shake it off. It impeded me—it worried me—it tripped me up—it caused me to mislay my studs—to mis-tie my cravat—to wrench the buttons off my gloves. Worst of all, it made me so late that the party had all assembled before I reached the drawing-room. I had scarcely paid my respects to Mrs. Jelf when dinner was announced, and we paired off, some eight or ten couples strong, into the dining-room.

I am not going to describe either the guests or the dinner. All provincial parties bear the strictest family resemblance, and I am not aware that an East Anglian banquet offers any exception to the rule. There was the usual country baronet and his wife; there were the usual country parsons and their wives; there was the sempiternal turkey and haunch of venison. *Vanitas vanitatum.* There is nothing new under the sun.

I was placed about midway down the table. I had taken one rector's wife down to dinner, and I had another at my left hand. They talked across me, and their talk was about babies. It was dreadfully dull. At length there came a pause. The entrées had just been removed, and the turkey had come upon the scene. The conversation had all along been of the languidest, but at this moment it happened to have stagnated altogether. Jelf was carving the turkey. Mrs. Jelf looked as if she was trying to think of something to say. Everybody else was silent. Moved by an unlucky impulse, I thought I would relate my adventure.

'By the way, Jelf,' I began, 'I came down part of the way today with a friend of yours.'

'Indeed!' said the master of the feast, slicing scientifically into the breast of the turkey. 'With whom, pray?'

'With one who bade me tell you that he should, if possible, pay you a visit before Christmas.'

'I cannot think who that could be,' said my friend, smiling.

'It must be Major Thorp,' suggested Mrs. Jelf.

I shook my head.

'It was not Major Thorp,' I replied. 'It was a near relation of your own, Mrs. Jelf.'

'Then I am more puzzled than ever,' replied my hostess. 'Pray tell me who it was.'

'It was no less a person than your Cousin, Mr. John Dwerrihouse.'

Jonathan Jelf laid down his knife and fork. Mrs. Jelf looked at me in a strange, startled way, and said never a word.

'And he desired me to tell you, my dear madam, that you need not take the trouble to burn the Hall down in his honour this time; but only to have the chimney of the blue room swept before his arrival.'

Before I had reached the end of my sentence, I became aware of something ominous in the faces of the guests. I felt I had said something which I had better have left unsaid, and that for some unexplained reason my words had evoked a general consternation. I sat confounded, not daring to utter another syllable, and for at least two whole minutes there was dead silence round the table.

Then Captain Prendergast came to the rescue.

'You have been abroad for some months, have you not, Mr. Langford?' he said, with the desperation of one who flings himself into the breach. 'I heard you had been to Russia. Surely you have something to tell us of the state and temper of the country after the war?'

I was heartily grateful to the gallant Skirmisher for this diversion in my favour. I answered him, I fear, somewhat lamely; but he kept the conversation up, and presently one or two others joined in, and so the difficulty, whatever it might have been, was bridged over. Bridged over, but not repaired. A something, an awkwardness, a visible constraint remained. The guests hitherto had been simply dull; but now they were evidently uncomfortable and embarrassed.

The dessert had scarcely been placed upon the table when the ladies left the room. I seized the opportunity to drop into a vacant chair next to Captain Prendergast.

'In Heaven's name,' I whispered, 'what was the matter just now? What had I said?'

'You mentioned the name of John Dwerrihouse.'

'What of that? I had seen him not two hours before.'

'It is a most astounding circumstance that you should have seen him,' said Captain Prendergast. 'Are you sure it was he?'

'As sure as of my own identity. We were talking all the way between London and Blackwater. But why does that surprise you?'

'*Because*,' replied Captain Prendergast, dropping his voice to the lowest whisper—'*because John Dwerrihouse absconded three months ago, with seventy-five thousand pounds of the Company's money, and has never been heard of since.*'

John Dwerrihouse had absconded three months ago—and I had seen him only a few hours back. John Dwerrihouse had embezzled seventy-five thousand pounds of the Company's money—yet told me that he carried that sum upon his person. Were ever facts so strangely incongruous, so difficult to reconcile? How should he have ventured again into the light of day? How dared he show himself along the line? Above all, what had he been doing throughout those mysterious three months of disappearance?

Perplexing questions these. Questions which at once suggested themselves to the minds of all concerned, but which admitted of no easy solution. I could find no reply to them. Captain Prendergast had not even a suggestion to offer. Jonathan Jelf, who seized the first opportunity of drawing me aside and learning all that I had to tell, was more amazed and bewildered than either of us. He came to my room that night when all the guests were gone, and we talked the thing over from every point of view—without, it must be confessed, arriving at any kind of conclusion.

'I do not ask you,' he said, 'whether you can have mistaken your man. That is impossible.'

'As impossible as that I should mistake some stranger for yourself.'

'It is not a question of looks or voice, but of facts. That he should have alluded to the fire in the blue room is proof enough of John Dwerrihouse's identity. How did he look?'

'Older, I thought. Considerably older, paler, and more anxious.'

'He has had enough to make him look anxious, anyhow,' said my friend, gloomily; 'be he innocent or guilty.'

'I am inclined to believe he is innocent,' I replied. 'He showed no embarrassment when I addressed him, and no uneasiness when the guard came round. His conversation was open to a fault. I might almost say that he talked too freely of the business which he had in hand.'

'That again is strange; for I know no one more reticent on such subjects. He actually told you that he had the seventy-five thousand pounds in his pocket?'

'He did.'

'Humph! My wife has an idea about it, and she may be right—'

'What idea?'

'Well, she fancies—women are so clever, you know, at putting themselves inside people's motives—she fancies that he was tempted; that he did actually take the money; and that he has been concealing himself these three months in some wild part of the country—struggling possibly with his conscience all the time, and daring neither to abscond with his booty, nor to come back and restore it.'

'But now that he has come back?'

'That is the point. She conceives that he has probably thrown himself upon the Company's mercy; made restitution of the money; and, being forgiven, is permitted to carry the business through as if nothing whatever had happened.'

'The last,' I replied, 'is an impossible case. Mrs. Jelf thinks like a generous and delicate-minded woman; but not in the least like a board of railway directors. They would never carry forgiveness so far.'

'I fear not; and yet it is the only conjecture that bears a semblance of likelihood. However, we can run over to Clayborough tomorrow, and see if anything is to be learned. By the way, Prendergast tells me you picked up his cigar-case.'

'I did so, and here it is.'

Jelf took the cigar-case, examined it, and said at once that it was beyond doubt Mr. Dwerrihouse's property, and that he remembered to have seen him use it.

'Here, too, is his monogram on the side,' he added. 'A big J transfixing a capital D. He used to carry the same on his note paper.'

'It proves, at all events, that I was not dreaming.'

'Ay; but it is time you were asleep and dreaming now. I am ashamed to have kept you so long. Good night.'

'Good night, and remember that I am more than ready to go with you to Clayborough, or Blackwater, or London, or anywhere, if I can be of the least service.'

'Thanks! I know you mean it, old friend, and it may be that I shall put you to the test. Once more, good night.'

So we parted for that night, and met again in the breakfast-room at half-past eight next morning. It was a hurried, silent, uncomfortable meal. None of us had slept well, and all were thinking of the same subject. Mrs. Jelf had evidently been crying; Jelf was impatient to be off; and both Captain Prendergast and myself felt ourselves to be in the painful position of outsiders, who are involuntarily brought into a domestic trouble. Within twenty minutes after we had left the breakfast-table, the dog-cart was brought round, and my friend and I were on the road to Clayborough.

'Tell you what it is, Langford,' he said, as we sped along between the wintry hedges, 'I do not much fancy to bring up Dwerrihouse's name at Clayborough. All the officials know that he is my wife's relation, and the subject just now is hardly a pleasant one. If you don't much mind, we will take the 11.10 train to Blackwater. It's an important station, and we shall stand a far better chance of picking up information there than at Clayborough.'

So we took the 11.10, which happened to be an express, and, arriving at Blackwater about a quarter before twelve, proceeded at once to prosecute our inquiry.

We began by asking for the station-master—a big, blunt, business-like person, who at once averred that he knew Mr. John Dwerrihouse perfectly well, and that there was no director on the line whom he had seen and spoken to so frequently.

'He used to be down here two or three times a week, about three months ago,' said he, 'when the new line was first set afoot; but since then, you know, gentlemen—'

He paused, significantly.

Jelf flushed scarlet.

'Yes, yes,' he said hurriedly, 'we know all about that. The point now to be ascertained is whether anything has been seen or heard of him lately.'

'Not to my knowledge,' replied the station-master.

'He is not known to have been down the line any time yesterday, for instance?'

The station-master shook his head.

'The East Anglian, sir,' said he, 'is about the last place where he would dare to show himself. Why, there isn't a station-master, there isn't a guard, there isn't a porter, who doesn't know Mr. Dwerrihouse by sight as well as he knows his own face in the looking-glass; or who wouldn't telegraph for the police as soon as he had set eyes on him at any point along the line. Bless you, sir! there's been a standing order out against him ever since the twenty-fifth of September last.'

'And yet,' pursued my friend, 'a gentleman who travelled down yesterday from London to Clayborough by the afternoon express, testifies that he saw Mr. Dwerrihouse in the train, and that Mr. Dwerrihouse alighted at Blackwater station.'

'Quite impossible, sir,' replied the station-master, promptly.

'Why impossible?'

'Because there is no station along the line where he is so well known, or where he would run so great a risk. It would be just running his head into the lion's mouth. He would have been mad to come nigh Blackwater station; and if he had come, he would have been arrested before he left the platform.'

'Can you tell me who took the Blackwater tickets of that train?'

'I can, sir. It was the guard—Benjamin Somers.'

'And where can I find him?'

'You can find him, sir, by staying here, if you please, till one o'clock. He will be coming through with the up Express from Crampton, which stays at Blackwater for ten minutes.'

We waited for the up Express, beguiling the time as best we could by strolling along the Blackwater road till we came almost to the outskirts of the town, from which the station was distant nearly a couple of miles. By one o'clock we were back again upon the platform, and waiting for the train. It came punctually, and I at once recognised the ruddy-faced guard who had gone down with my train the evening before.

'The gentlemen want to ask you something about Mr. Dwerrihouse, Somers,' said the station-master, by way of introduction.

The guard flashed a keen glance from my face to Jelf's, and back again to mine.

'Mr. John Dwerrihouse, the late director?' said he, interrogatively.

'The same,' replied my friend. 'Should you know him if you saw him?'

'Anywhere, sir.'

'Do you know if he was in the 4.15 Express yesterday afternoon?'

'He was not, sir.'

'How can you answer so positively?'

'Because I looked into every carriage, and saw every face in that train, and I could take my oath that Mr. Dwerrihouse was not in it. This gentleman was,' he added, turning sharply upon me. 'I don't know that I ever saw him before in my life, but I remember his face perfectly. You nearly missed taking your seat in time at this station, sir, and you got out at Clayborough.'

'Quite true,' I replied; 'but do you not also remember the face of the gentleman who travelled down in the same carriage with me as far as here?'

'It was my impression, sir, that you travelled down alone,' said Somers, with a look of some surprise.

'By no means. I had a fellow-traveller as far as Blackwater, and it was in trying to restore him the cigar-case which he had dropped in the carriage, that I so nearly let you go on without me.'

'I remember your saying something about a cigar-case, certainly,' replied the guard, 'but—'

'You asked for my ticket just before we entered the station.'

'I did, sir.'

'Then you must have seen him. He sat in the corner next the very door to which you came.'

'No, indeed. I saw no one.'

I looked at Jelf. I began to think the guard was in the ex-director's confidence, and paid for his silence.

'If I had seen another traveller I should have asked for his ticket,' added Somers. 'Did you see me ask for his ticket, sir?'

'I observed that you did not ask for it, but he explained that by saying—'

I hesitated. I feared I might be telling too much, and so broke off abruptly.

The guard and the station-master exchanged glances. The former looked impatiently at his watch.

'I am obliged to go in four minutes more, sir,' he said.

'One last question, then,' interposed Jelf, with a sort of desperation. 'If this gentleman's fellow-traveller had been Mr. John Dwerrihouse, and he had been sitting in the corner next the door by which you took the tickets, could you have failed to see and recognise him?'

'No, sir; it would have been quite impossible.'

'And you are certain you did *not* see him?'

'As I said before, sir, I could take my oath I did not see him. And if it wasn't that I don't like to contradict a gentleman, I would say I could also take my oath that this gentleman was quite alone in the carriage the whole way from London to Clayborough. Why, sir,' he added, dropping his voice so as to be inaudible to the station-master, who had been called away to speak to some person close by, 'you expressly asked me to give you a compartment to yourself, and I did so. I locked you in, and you were so good as to give me something for myself.'

'Yes; but Mr. Dwerrihouse had a key of his own.'

'I never saw him, sir; I saw no one in the compartment but yourself. Beg pardon, sir, my time's up.'

And with this the ruddy guard touched his cap and was gone. In another minute the heavy panting of the engine began afresh, and the train glided slowly out of the station.

We looked at each other for some moments in silence. I was the first to speak.

'Mr. Benjamin Somers knows more than he chooses to tell,' I said.

'Humph! do you think so?'

'It must be. He could not have come to the door without seeing him. It's impossible.'

'There is one thing not impossible, my dear fellow.'

'What is that?'

'That you may have fallen asleep, and dreamt the whole thing.'

'Could I dream of a branch line that I had never heard of? Could I dream of a hundred and one business details that had no kind of interest for me? Could I dream of the seventy-five thousand pounds?'

'Perhaps you might have seen or heard some vague account of the affair while you were abroad. It might have made no impression upon you at the time, and might have come back to you in your dreams—recalled perhaps, by the mere names of the stations on the line.'

'What about the fire in the chimney of the blue room—should I have heard of that during my journey?'

'Well, no; I admit there is a difficulty about that point.'

'And what about the cigar-case?'

'Ay, by Jove! there is the cigar-case. That *is* a stubborn fact. Well, it's a mysterious affair, and it will need a better detective than myself, I fancy, to clear it up. I suppose we may as well go home.'

A week had not gone by when I received a letter from the Secretary of the East Anglian Railway Company, requesting the favour of my attendance at a special board meeting, not then many days distant. No reasons were alleged, and no apologies offered, for this demand upon my time; but they had heard, it was clear, of my inquiries about the missing director, and had a mind to put me through some sort of official examination upon the subject. Being still a guest at Dumbleton Hall, I had to go up to London for the purpose, and Jonathan Jelf accompanied me. I found the direction of the Great East Anglian line represented by a party of some twelve or fourteen gentlemen seated in solemn conclave round a huge green-baize table in a gloomy board-room, adjoining the London terminus.

Being courteously received by the chairman (who at once began by saying that certain statements of mine respecting Mr. John Dwerrihouse had come to the knowledge of the direction, and that they in consequence desired to confer with me on those points), we were placed at the table, and the inquiry proceeded in due form.

I was first asked if I knew Mr. John Dwerrihouse, how long I had been acquainted with him, and whether I could identify him at sight. I was then asked when I had seen him last. To which I replied, 'On the fourth of this present month, December, eighteen hundred and fifty-six.'

Then came the inquiry of where I had seen him on that fourth day of December; to which I replied that I met him in a first-class compartment of the 4.15 down-express; that he got in just as the train was leaving the London terminus, and that he alighted at

Blackwater station. The chairman then inquired whether I had held any communication with my fellow-traveller; whereupon I related, as I could remember it, the whole bulk and substance of Mr. John Dwerrihouse's diffuse information respecting the new branch line.

To all this the board listened with profound attention, while the chairman presided and the secretary took notes. I then produced the cigar-case. It was passed from hand to hand, and recognised by all. There was not a man present who did not remember that plain cigar-case with its silver monogram, or to whom it seemed anything less than entirely corroborative of my evidence.

When at length I had told all that I had to tell, the chairman whispered something to the secretary; the secretary touched a silver hand-bell; and the guard, Benjamin Somers, was ushered into the room. He was then examined as carefully as myself. He declared that he knew Mr. John Dwerrihouse perfectly well; that he could not be mistaken in him; that he remembered going down with the 4.15 express on the afternoon in question; that he remembered me; and that, there being one or two empty first-class compartments on that especial afternoon, he had, in compliance with my request, placed me in a carriage by myself. He was positive that I remained alone all the way in that compartment from London to Clayborough. He was ready to take his oath that Mr. Dwerrihouse was neither in that carriage with me, nor in any compartment of that train. He remembered distinctly to have examined my ticket at Blackwater; was certain that there was no one else at that time in the carriage; could not have failed to observe a second person, if there had been one; had that second person been Mr. John Dwerrihouse, should have quietly double-locked the door of the carriage, and have given information to the Blackwater station-master. So clear, so decisive, so ready, was Somers with this testimony, that the board looked fairly puzzled.

'You hear this person's statement, Mr. Langford,' said the chairman. 'It contradicts yours in every particular. What have you to say in reply?'

'I can only repeat what I said before. I am quite as positive of the truth of my own assertions as Mr. Somers can be of the truth of his.'

'You say that Mr. Dwerrihouse alighted at Blackwater, and that he was in possession of a private key. Are you sure that he had not alighted by means of that key before the guard came round for the tickets?'

'I am quite positive that he did not leave the carriage till the train had fairly entered the station, and the other Blackwater passengers alighted. I even saw that he was met there by a friend.'

'Indeed! Did you see that person distinctly?'

'Quite distinctly.'

'Can you describe his appearance?'

'I think so. He was short and very slight, sandy-haired, with a bushy moustache and beard, and he wore a closely-fitting suit of grey tweed. His age I should take to be about thirty-eight or forty.'

'Did Mr. Dwerrihouse leave the station in this person's company?'

'I cannot tell. I saw them walking together down the platform, and then I saw them standing aside under a gas-jet, talking earnestly. After that I lost sight of them quite suddenly; and just then my train went on, and I with it.'

The chairman and secretary conferred together in an under tone. The directors whispered to each other. One or two looked suspiciously at the guard. I could see that my evidence remained unshaken, and that, like myself, they suspected some complicity between the guard and the defaulter.

'How far did you conduct that 4.15 express on the day in question, Somers?' asked the chairman.

'All through, sir,' replied the guard; 'from London to Crampton.'

'How was it that you were not relieved at Clayborough? I thought there was always a change of guards at Clayborough.'

'There used to be, sir, till the new regulations came in force last Midsummer; since when, the guards in charge of Express trains go the whole way through.'

The chairman turned to the secretary.

'I think it would be as well,' he said, 'if we had the day-book to refer to upon this point.'

Again the secretary touched the silver hand-bell, and desired the porter in attendance to summon Mr. Raikes. From a word or two dropped by another of the directors, I gathered that Mr. Raikes was one of the under-secretaries.

He came—a small, slight, sandy-haired, keen-eyed man, with an eager, nervous manner, and a forest of light beard and moustache. He just showed himself at the door of the board-room, and being requested to bring a certain day-book from a certain shelf in a certain room, bowed and vanished.

He was there such a moment, and the surprise of seeing him was so great and sudden, that it was not till the door had closed upon him that I found voice to speak. He was no sooner gone, however, than I sprang to my feet.

'That person,' I said, 'is the same who met Mr. Dwerrihouse upon the platform at Blackwater!'

There was a general movement of surprise. The chairman looked grave, and somewhat agitated.

'Take care, Mr. Langford,' he said, 'take care what you say!'

'I am as positive of his identity as of my own.'

'Do you consider the consequences of your words? Do you consider that you are bringing a charge of the gravest character against one of the company's servants?'

'I am willing to be put upon my oath, if necessary. The man who came to that door a minute since, is the same whom I saw talking with Mr. Dwerrihouse on the Blackwater platform. Were he twenty times the company's servant, I could say neither more nor less.'

The chairman turned again to the guard.

'Did you see Mr. Raikes in the train, or on the platform?' he asked.

Somers shook his head.

'I am confident Mr. Raikes was not in the train,' he said; 'and I certainly did not see him on the platform.'

The chairman turned next to the secretary.

'Mr. Raikes is in your office, Mr. Hunter,' he said. 'Can you remember if he was absent on the fourth instant?'

'I do not think he was,' replied the secretary; 'but I am not prepared to speak positively. I have been away most afternoons myself lately, and Mr. Raikes might easily have absented himself if he had been disposed.'

At this moment the under-secretary returned with the day-book under his arm.

'Be pleased to refer, Mr. Raikes,' said the chairman, 'to the entries of the fourth instant, and see what Benjamin Somers' duties were on that day.'

Mr. Raikes threw open the cumbrous volume, and ran a practised eye and finger down some three or four successive columns of entries. Stopping suddenly at the foot of a page, he then read aloud that Benjamin Somers had on that day conducted the 4.15 express from London to Crampton.

The chairman leaned forward in his seat, looked the under-secretary full in the face, and said, quite sharply and suddenly—

'Where were *you*, Mr. Raikes, on the same afternoon?'

'*I*, sir?'

'You, Mr. Raikes. Where were you on the afternoon and evening of the fourth of the present month?'

'Here, sir—in Mr. Hunter's office. Where else should I be?'

There was a dash of trepidation in the under-secretary's voice as he said this; but his look of surprise was natural enough.

'We have some reason for believing, Mr. Raikes, that you were absent that afternoon without leave. Was this the case?'

'Certainly not, sir. I have not had a day's holiday since September. Mr. Hunter will bear me out in this.'

Mr. Hunter repeated what he had previously said on the subject, but added that the clerks in the adjoining office would be certain to know. Whereupon the senior clerk, a grave, middle-aged person, in green glasses, was summoned and interrogated.

His testimony cleared the under-secretary at once. He declared that Mr. Raikes had in no instance, to his knowledge, been absent during office hours since his return from his annual holiday in September.

I was confounded. The chairman turned to me with a smile, in which a shade of covert annoyance was scarcely apparent.

'You hear, Mr. Langford?' he said.

'I hear, sir; but my conviction remains unshaken.'

'I fear, Mr. Langford, that your convictions are very insufficiently based,' replied the chairman, with a doubtful cough. 'I fear that you "dream dreams," and mistake them for actual occurrences. It is a dangerous habit of mind, and might lead to dangerous results. Mr. Raikes here would have found himself in an unpleasant position, had he not proved so satisfactory an *alibi*.'

I was about to reply, but he gave me no time.

'I think, gentlemen,' he went on to say, addressing the board, 'that we should be wasting time to push this inquiry farther. Mr. Langford's

evidence would seem to be of an equal value throughout. The testimony of Benjamin Somers disproves his first statement, and the
testimony of the last witness disproves his second. I think we may
conclude that Mr. Langford fell asleep in the train on the occasion
of his journey to Clayborough, and dreamt an unusually vivid and
circumstantial dream—of which, however, we have now heard quite
enough.'

There are few things more annoying than to find one's positive
convictions met with incredulity. I could not help feeling impatience
at the turn that affairs had taken. I was not proof against the civil
sarcasm of the chairman's manner. Most intolerable of all, however,
was the quiet smile lurking about the corners of Benjamin Somers'
mouth, and the half-triumphant, half-malicious gleam in the eyes of
the under-secretary. The man was evidently puzzled, and somewhat
alarmed. His looks seemed furtively to interrogate me. Who was I?
What did I want? Why had I come there to do him an ill turn with
his employers? What was it to me whether or not he was absent
without leave?

Seeing all this, and perhaps more irritated by it than the thing
deserved, I begged leave to detain the attention of the board for a
moment longer. Jelf plucked me impatiently by the sleeve.

'Better let the thing drop,' he whispered. 'The chairman's right
enough. You dreamt it; and the less said now, the better.'

I was not to be silenced, however, in this fashion. I had yet something to say, and I would say it. It was to this effect:—That dreams
were not usually productive of tangible results, and that I requested
to know in what way the chairman conceived I had evolved from
my dream so substantial and well-made a delusion as the cigar-case
which I had had the honour to place before him at the commence-
ment of our interview.

'The cigar-case, I admit, Mr. Langford,' the chairman replied, 'is a very strong point in your evidence. It is your *only* strong point, however, and there is just a possibility that we may all be misled by a mere accidental resemblance. Will you permit me to see the case again?'

'It is unlikely,' I said, as I handed it to him, 'that any other should bear precisely this monogram, and also be in all other particulars exactly similar.'

The chairman examined it for a moment in silence, and then passed it to Mr. Hunter. Mr. Hunter turned it over and over, and shook his head.

'This is no mere resemblance,' he said. 'It is John Dwerrihouse's cigar-case to a certainty. I remember it perfectly. I have seen it a hundred times.'

'I believe I may say the same,' added the chairman. 'Yet how shall we account for the way in which Mr. Langford asserts that it came into his possession?'

'I can only repeat,' I replied, 'that I found it on the floor of the carriage after Mr. Dwerrihouse had alighted. It was in leaning out to look after him that I trod upon it; and it was in running after him for the purpose of restoring it that I saw—or believed I saw—Mr. Raikes standing aside with him in earnest conversation.'

Again I felt Jonathan Jelf plucking at my sleeve.

'Look at Raikes,' he whispered. 'Look at Raikes!'

I turned to where the under-secretary had been standing a moment before, and saw him, white as death, with lips trembling and livid, stealing towards the door.

To conceive a sudden, strange, and indefinite suspicion; to fling myself in his way; to take him by the shoulders as if he were a child, and turn his craven face, perforce, towards the board, were with me the work of an instant.

'Look at him!' I exclaimed. 'Look at his face! I ask no better witness to the truth of my words.'

The chairman's brow darkened.

'Mr. Raikes,' he said, sternly, 'if you know anything, you had better speak.'

Vainly trying to wrench himself from my grasp, the under-secretary stammered out an incoherent denial.

'Let me go!' he said. 'I know nothing—you have no right to detain me—let me go!'

'Did you, or did you not, meet Mr. John Dwerrihouse at Blackwater Station? The charge brought against you is either true or false. If true, you will do well to throw yourself upon the mercy of the board, and make full confession of all that you know.'

The under-secretary wrung his hands in an agony of helpless terror.

'I was away,' he cried. 'I was two hundred miles away at the time! I know nothing about it—I have nothing to confess—I am innocent—I call God to witness I am innocent!'

'Two hundred miles away!' echoed the chairman. 'What do you mean?'

'I was in Devonshire. I had three weeks' leave of absence—I appeal to Mr. Hunter—Mr. Hunter knows I had three weeks' leave of absence! I was in Devonshire all the time—I can prove I was in Devonshire!'

Seeing him so abject, so incoherent, so wild with apprehension, the directors began to whisper gravely among themselves; while one got quietly up, and called the porter to guard the door.

'What has your being in Devonshire to do with the matter?' said the chairman. 'When were you in Devonshire?'

'Mr. Raikes took his leave in September,' said the secretary; 'about the time when Mr. Dwerrihouse disappeared.'

'I never even heard that he had disappeared till I came back!'

'That must remain to be proved,' said the chairman. 'I shall at once put this matter in the hands of the police. In the meanwhile, Mr. Raikes, being myself a magistrate, and used to deal with these cases, I advise you to offer no resistance; but to confess while confession may yet do you service. As for your accomplice—'

The frightened wretch fell upon his knees.

'I had no accomplice!' he cried. 'Only have mercy upon me—only spare my life, and I will confess all! I didn't mean to harm him! I didn't mean to hurt a hair of his head. Only have mercy upon me, and let me go!'

The chairman rose in his place, pale and agitated. 'Good heavens!' he exclaimed, 'what horrible mystery is this? What does it mean?'

'As sure as there is a God in heaven,' said Jonathan Jelf, 'it means that murder has been done.'

'No—no—no!' shrieked Raikes, still upon his knees, and cowering like a beaten hound. 'Not murder! No jury that ever sat could bring it in murder. I thought I had only stunned him—I never meant to do more than stun him! Manslaughter—manslaughter—not murder!'

Overcome by the horror of this unexpected revelation, the chairman covered his face with his hand, and for a moment or two remained silent.

'Miserable man,' he said at length, 'you have betrayed yourself.'

'You bade me confess! You urged me to throw myself upon the mercy of the board!'

'You have confessed to a crime which no one suspected you of having committed,' replied the chairman, 'and which this board has no power either to punish or forgive. All that I can do for you is to advise you to submit to the law, to plead guilty, and to conceal nothing. When did you do this deed?'

The guilty man rose to his feet, and leaned heavily against the table. His answer came reluctantly, like the speech of one dreaming.

'On the twenty-second of September!'

On the twenty-second of September! I looked in Jonathan Jelf's face, and he in mine. I felt my own paling with a strange sense of wonder and dread. I saw his blanch suddenly, even to the lips.

'Merciful heaven!' he whispered, *'What was it, then, that you saw in the train?'*

What was it that I saw in the train? That question remains unanswered to this day. I have never been able to reply to it. I only know that it bore the living likeness of the murdered man, whose body had been lying some ten weeks under a rough pile of branches, and brambles, and rotting leaves, at the bottom of a deserted chalk-pit about half-way between Blackwater and Mallingford. I know that it spoke, and moved, and looked as that man spoke, and moved, and looked in life; that I heard, or seemed to hear, things related which I could never otherwise have learned; that I was guided, as it were, by that vision on the platform to the identification of the murderer; and that, a passive instrument myself, I was destined, by means of these mysterious teachings, to bring about the ends of justice. For these things I have never been able to account.

As for that matter of the cigar-case, it proved, on inquiry, that the carriage in which I travelled down that afternoon to Clayborough had not been in use for several weeks, and was, in point of fact, the same in which poor John Dwerrihouse had performed his last journey. The case had, doubtless, been dropped by him, and had lain unnoticed till I found it.

Upon the details of the murder I have no need to dwell. Those who desire more ample particulars may find them, and the written confession of Augustus Raikes, in the files of the 'Times' for 1856. Enough that the under-secretary, knowing the history of the new line, and following the negotiation step by step through all its stages, determined to waylay Mr. Dwerrihouse, rob him of the seventy-five thousand pounds, and escape to America with his booty.

In order to effect these ends he obtained leave of absence a few days before the time appointed for the payment of the money; secured his passage across the Atlantic in a steamer advertised to start on the twenty-third; provided himself with a heavily-loaded 'life-preserver,' and went down to Blackwater to await the arrival of his victim. How he met him on the platform with a pretended message from the board; how he offered to conduct him by a short cut across the fields to Mallingford; how, having brought him to a lonely place, he struck him down with the life-preserver, and so killed him; and how, finding what he had done, he dragged the body to the verge of an out-of-the-way chalk-pit, and there flung it in, and piled it over with branches and brambles, are facts still fresh in the memories of those who, like the connoisseurs in De Quincey's famous essay, regard murder as a fine art. Strangely enough, the murderer, having done his work, was afraid to leave the country. He declared that he had not intended to take the director's life, but only to stun and rob him; and that finding the blow had killed, he dared not fly for fear of drawing down suspicion upon his own head. As a mere robber he would have been safe in the States, but as a murderer he would inevitably have been pursued, and given up to justice. So he forfeited his passage, returned to the office as usual at the end of his leave, and locked up his ill-gotten thousands till a more convenient opportunity. In the meanwhile he had the satisfaction of finding that Mr. Dwerrihouse was universally believed to have absconded with the money, no one knew how or whither.

Whether he meant murder or not, however, Mr. Augustus Raikes paid the full penalty of his crime, and was hanged at the Old Bailey in the second week in January, 1857. Those who desire to make his further acquaintance may see him any day (admirably done in wax) in the Chamber of Horrors at Madame Tussaud's exhibition, in Baker Street. He is there to be found in the midst of a select society of ladies and gentlemen of atrocious memory, dressed in the close-cut tweed suit which he wore on the evening of the murder, and holding in his hand the identical life-preserver with which he committed it.

THE CURSE OF THE CATAFALQUES

F. Anstey

First published in *Cornhill Magazine*, August 1882

Thomas Anstey Guthrie (1856–1934) wrote under the name F Anstey—not as a corruption of the word 'fantasy', as people sometimes guess, but for a rather more mundane reason: his name included a typo in one of his first published pieces of writing. He was a trained (but never practising) lawyer, and became a successful novelist and comic writer for *Punch* magazine in the late 19th century. Although not well-known today, he's notable for having written a novel called *Vice Versa*, in which a father and son magically change places and have to live each other's lives—a premise which has inspired several later books and films.

I THINK I MAY SAFELY SAY THAT, UNTIL THE STRANGE EVENT which I am now about to relate, I had never been brought into close contact with anything of a supernatural character. I may have been so, of course; but if I was, the circumstance made no lasting impression upon me. In the Curse of the Catafalques, however, I experienced a horror, so weird, so altogether unusual, that I fear it will be some time before I can wholly forget it. Indeed, I have not been really well ever since.

I was not a success at home; in my anxiety to please a wealthy uncle upon whom I was practically dependent, I had submitted myself to a series of competitive examinations for a variety of professions, but had failed successively in all. I found afterwards, too late, that this was partly due to the fact that I had omitted to prepare myself by any particular course of study, which it would seem is almost indispensable to success in these intellectual contests.

This was the view which my uncle himself took of the case, and conceiving that I was by no means likely to retrieve myself by any severe degree of application in the future—in which he was perfectly right—he had me shipped out to Australia, where he had correspondents and friends who were to put things in my way.

They did put all manner of things in my way, and, as was only to be expected, I came to grief over every one of them. So at last, after giving a fair trial to every opening provided for me, I became convinced that my uncle had made a grave mistake in believing that I was suited for a colonial career. I resolved to return home and tell him so, and give him one more opportunity of repairing his error. He had failed to understand my capabilities, but I did not then (nor do I now) reproach him for that. It is a difficulty which I have felt myself.

I now come to the period at which my story begins. I had booked my passage home by one of the Orient Line steamships from Melbourne to London, and, going on board about an hour before the ship was to leave her moorings, I made my way at once to the state-room which I was to share with a fellow-passenger, and found the fellow-passenger there before me. My first view of him was not reassuring: he was a tall cadaverous young man of about my own age, and when I came in he was rolling restlessly upon the floor and uttering hollow groans in a really painful and distressing manner.

I did my best to encourage him. 'This will never do,' I said: 'if you're like this now, my good sir, what will you be when we're fairly started?—you must reserve yourself for that. And why roll? The ship will do all that for you by-and-by.'

He explained, with some annoyance, I thought, that he was suffering from mental agony—not sea-sickness. The possession of my fellow-creatures' secrets has always a certain degree of interest for me, while it seldom proves unremunerative; so by a little careful questioning I soon discovered what was troubling my companion, whose name, as I also learned, was Augustus McFadden.

His story was shortly this: He had lived all his life in the Colony, where he was doing very fairly, when an eccentric old aunt of his over in England happened to die. She left him nothing, but gave the bulk of her property to a young lady, the daughter of a baronet of ancient family, in whom she was interested. No conditions were attached to the gift, but the testatrix stated it to be her earnest desire that the lady should, if possible, accept the hand of her nephew Augustus, should he come over to England and offer it within a certain time, and she had also communicated, by letter, her wishes in this respect to McFadden shortly before her death.

'Chlorine's father,' said McFadden—'Chlorine is *her* name, you know' (I thought it was rather a bilious kind of name)—'Sir Paul Catafalque, wrote to me, inclosing his daughter's photograph, and formally inviting me in her name to come over and do my best to carry out the last wishes of the departed—he added that my aunt's executors would shortly forward me a packet, in which I should find certain explanations and directions for my guidance... I did not wait for its arrival—I felt that my poor aunt's wishes were sacred—the photograph was an eminently pleasing one—and so,' he added, with a heavy sigh, 'I wrote at once to Sir Paul, accepting the invitation—miserable wretch that I am, I pledged my honour to present myself as a suitor! and now, now here I am actually embarked on this desperate errand!'

Here he seemed inclined to begin to roll again, but I stopped him. 'Really,' I said, 'I think in your place, with a fair chance of obtaining a baronet's daughter of pleasing appearance with a large fortune, I should try to bear up.'

'You think so?' he groaned. 'You don't know all! After I had despatched that fatal letter, the packet with my aunt's instructions arrived. When I read the hideous revelations that packet contained, and knew the horrors to which I had unintentionally pledged myself, my hair stood on end (it is still on end—feel it)—but it was too late! Here I am, engaged to carry out a task from which my inmost soul recoils. If I dared but retract!'

'Then why in the name of common sense don't you retract?' I said. 'Write and say you have changed your mind, regret that a previous engagement deprives you of the pleasure of accepting—all that sort of thing.'

'I would,' he said, 'but I am ashamed—her photograph is that of a being whose contempt it would be agony to me to feel I had incurred. And, if I backed out of it now, she would despise me, wouldn't she?'

I owned that it was very likely indeed.

'You see my dilemma—I cannot retract; on the other hand, I dare not attempt to carry out my undertaking. The only thing that could at once save me and my honour would be my death on the voyage out—she would not suspect my cowardice then, my memory would be sacred to her!'

'Well,' I said, 'you can die on the voyage out if you like—there need be no difficulty about that. All you have to do is just to slip over the side some dark night when no one is looking at you. I tell you what,' I added (for I began to feel an odd sort of interest in the poor weak creature): 'if you don't find your nerve equal to it when it comes to the point, I'll give you a leg over myself!'

'I never intended to go as far as that,' he said, rather pettishly and without any sign of gratitude for my offer. 'It would be quite enough if she could be made to believe that I had died. I could live on here as before, happy in the thought that she was cherishing my memory, instead of scorning it. But then how can she be made to believe it? That's the difficulty.'

'Precisely,' I said; 'you can't very well write and inform her that you died on the voyage. You might do this, though—sail to England as you propose, and then seek her out under another name and break the news to her.'

'I might do that, to be sure,' he said, with some animation; 'I certainly should not be recognised—she has no photograph of me—I never have been photographed... but no,' he added with a shudder, 'it's no use—I can't do it, I dare not trust myself under that roof! I must find some other way. Listen,' he said, after a short pause; 'you have given me an idea—you are going to London… they live near it, at a place called Parson's Green. Can I ask a great favour from you? Will *you* seek them out and, as a fellow-voyager of mine, call upon her? I do not ask you to tell a positive untruth—but if in the course of the interview you could contrive to convey the impression that I had died on the passage home, you would be doing me a service I can never repay.'

'I should much prefer to do you a service that you *could* repay,' I could not help suggesting.

'She will not require strict proof. I could give you papers and things that would abundantly convince her you came from me. You will do me this great kindness—say that you will?'

I hesitated for some time; not so much from conscientious scruples, as from a disinclination to give myself so much trouble for an entire stranger, gratuitously—but McFadden used arguments that have always had considerable weight with me, and so at last I consented to execute this little commission for him—and a consideration.

'The only thing now is,' I said, when this was settled, 'how would you prefer to pass away? How would it be if I made you fall over and be devoured by a shark? That would be picturesque and striking, and I could do myself justice over the shark. I should make her weep considerably!'

'That will not do at all!' he said irritably. 'Chlorine is a girl of delicate sensibilities—it would disgust her to picture any suitor of hers spending his last conscious moments inside a beastly repulsive thing like a shark. I do not wish to be associated in her mind with anything so unpleasant. I will die, sir, of a low fever (of a non-infectious type), at sunset, gazing at her portrait with my fading eyesight, and breathing with my last gasp a tender prayer for her welfare—she will cry more over that, sir!'

'I think I could work that up very effectively—it ought to be touching,' I said; 'but if you are going to expire in my state-room, I think I ought to know a little more about you than I do now. We have a little time yet before we sail; perhaps you would not object to spend it in coaching me up in your life's history?'

He did more than that—he supplied me with several documents to study on the voyage, and even abandoned to me the whole of his travelling arrangements, which proved very complete and serviceable.

And then the 'All ashore' bell rang, and McFadden, as he bade me farewell, took from his pocket a bulky packet: 'You have saved me!' he said. 'Now I can banish every recollection of this miserable episode… I need preserve my poor aunt's directions no longer. Let them go, then, with the rest of it!' And, before I could prevent him, he had fastened a heavy jack-knife to the parcel, and dropped it through the cabin-light into the sea.

He went ashore, and I have never seen him or heard of him since; but during the voyage I began to think seriously over the affair, and the more I thought of the task I had undertaken, the less I liked it.

I was on my way to harrow up a poor young lady's feelings by a perfectly fictitious account of the death of this poor-spirited creature, who selfishly chose thus to spare his reputation.

It was not a pleasant commission, and had McFadden's terms been a degree less liberal I doubt if I could have brought myself to undertake it. But it struck me that Chlorine might prove not inconsolable under judiciously sympathetic treatment; and then she was wealthy, and lost none of her wealth by not marrying McFadden.

On the other hand, I had not a penny, while my prospects might not appear roseate in her parents' eyes.

I studied her photograph; it showed me a pale, pensive, but distinctly pretty face, without much strength of character, pointing to a plastic nature which it would not be difficult for a man of my personal advantages to win and subdue had I the recommendation, like McFadden, of an aunt's dying wishes.

In McFadden's place, favoured by the romance which invested the whole affair, Chlorine's money would have been mine in a month!

Then came the thought—why should I not procure myself these advantages?

Nothing was easier. I had only to present myself as Augustus McFadden (who was hitherto a mere name to them); the information I already had as to his past life would enable me to support the character respectably, and as it seemed that the baronet lived in great seclusion, I could contrive to keep out of the way of the few friends and relations I had in London until my position was secure.

The scheme gradually came to exert a strange fascination over me; it opened out a far more manly and honourable means of obtaining a livelihood than any I had previously contemplated.

It could injure no one—not McFadden, for he had given up all pretensions, while his regard for his reputation would be more completely gratified than ever; for I flattered myself that I should come nearer Chlorine's ideal of him than he himself could ever have done. He had resigned himself to be tearfully regretted for a brief period; he would be fondly, it might be madly, loved—by proxy, it is true—but then that was far more than he deserved.

Chlorine would regain a suitor instead of hearing of his decease, while his mere surname could make no possible difference to her.

And it was a distinct benefit to *me*; for with the aid of my assumed name and character success was almost a certainty.

So, after really less mental deliberation than might be expected, I made up my mind to personate the chicken-hearted McFadden—and if ever an unfortunate man was bitterly punished for a harmless, if not actually a pious, fraud, by a season of intense and protracted physical terror, I was that person!

II

After arriving in England, and before presenting myself in my new character at Parson's Green, I took one precaution, to assure myself that I was in no danger of throwing myself away in a fit of youthful impulsiveness. I went to Somerset House, and carefully examined a copy of the late Miss Petronia McFadden's last will and testament.

Nothing could have been more satisfactory; a sum of between forty and fifty thousand pounds was Chlorine's unconditionally, a marriage with McFadden was merely recommended, and there was nothing whatever in the will to prevent her property from passing under the entire control of a future husband.

After this I could no longer restrain my ardour; and so, one foggy afternoon about the middle of December, I found myself in a cab driving down the King's Road, Chelsea, on my way to the house in which I reckoned upon winning a comfortable independence.

We reached Parson's Green in time—a small, triangular plot, bordered on two of its sides by humble cottages and beerhouses, and on the third by some ancient mansions, gloomy and neglected looking, but not without traces of their former consequence.

The cab stopped before the gloomiest of them all, a square, grim house, with dull small-paned windows, uncurtained and heavy-sashed, flanked by two narrow and slightly projecting wings, and built of dingy brick faced with yellow stone. Some old scrollwork railings, with a corroded frame in the middle, which had once held an oil lamp, separated it from the road; inside was a semicircular patch of rank grass, and a damp gravel sweep led from the heavy gate to a square portico, supported by two wasted black wooden pillars.

As I pulled the pear-shaped bell handle, and heard the bell tinkling and jangling fretfully within, and when I glanced up at the dull house-front looming cheerless out of the fog-laden December twilight, my confidence failed me for the first time. I was almost inclined to give up the whole thing and run away; but before I had made up my mind a mouldy, melancholy butler came out and opened the gate, and my opportunity was gone for ever.

I remembered later that, as I walked up the gravel sweep, a wild and wailing scream pierced the heavy silence—it seemed half a lament, half a warning; but coming, as I believe it did, from one of the locomotives on the District Railway hard by, I attached no particular importance to it.

I followed the butler through a dank and chilly hall, where an antique lamp was glimmering inside its dusty stained-glass panes, up a broad carved staircase, and along tortuous panelled passages, until at last he ushered me into a long and rather low reception-room, scantily furnished with the tarnished mirrors and spindle-legged brocaded furniture of the last century.

A tall and meagre old man, with a long white beard and haggard, sunken black eyes, was sitting on one side of the high old-fashioned chimney-piece; opposite him was a limp little old lady, with a nervous, anxious expression, and dressed in trailing black robes relieved by a little yellow lace about the head and throat. I recognised at once that I was in the presence of Sir Paul Catafalque and his wife.

They both rose and advanced arm-in-arm to meet me, with a slow, stately solemnity. 'You are very welcome!' they said, in a faint hollow voice. 'We thank you for this proof of your chivalry and devotion. Such courage and self-sacrifice will have their reward!'

I did not quite understand how I could be considered to have given any proofs, as yet, of chivalry or devotion; but it was gratifying, of course, to find that they looked at matters in that light, and I begged them not to mention it.

And then, a slender figure, with a drooping head, a wan face, and large sad eyes, came softly down the dimly lighted room to me, and I met my destined bride for the first time.

I saw her eyes first anxiously raised to my face, and then resting upon it with a certain ineffable relief and satisfaction in them at the discovery that the accomplishment of Miss Petronia's wishes would not be personally distasteful.

I think that, upon the whole, I was myself slightly disappointed; her portrait had considerably flattered her; the real Chlorine was thinner and paler than I had imagined, while there was a settled, abstracted melancholy in her manner which seemed likely to render her society depressing.

I have always preferred a touch of archness and animation in womankind, and I should have greatly preferred to enter a more cheerful family; but, under all the circumstances, I felt scarcely in a position to be too particular.

For some days after my arrival I remained with the Catafalques as their honoured guest, every opportunity being afforded me for establishing nearer and dearer relations with the family.

But it was not a lively period; they went nowhere, no visitors ever called or dined, the days dragged slowly by in a dull and terrible monotony in that dim tomb of a house, which I found I was not expected to leave, except now and then when I contrived to steal out to smoke a pipe along the Putney road in the foggy evenings after dinner.

The diligence with which I had got up McFadden's antecedents enabled me to give perfectly satisfactory answers to most of the few questions that were put to me, and for the rest I drew on my imagination. But what puzzled me for some time was their general attitude to myself; there was something of tearful admiration in it, of gratitude, a touch of pity too as for some youthful martyr, blended with an anxious hope.

Now I was well aware that this was not the ordinary attitude of the parents of an heiress to an obscure and penniless suitor. I could only account for it at last by the supposition that there was some latent defect in Chlorine's temper or constitution which entitled the man who won her to commiseration; this explained, too, their evident anxiety to get rid of her. Anything of this kind would be a drawback of course, but forty or fifty thousand pounds would more than compensate for it—I could not expect *everything*.

I had more trouble in bringing Chlorine to confess that her heart was mine than I had counted upon at first, although my ultimate success was never for a moment doubtful. But she seemed to have an unaccountable shrinking from saying the word which bound us—a dread which she confessed was not for her own sake, but for mine. I thought such extreme self-depreciation very morbid, and devoted every energy to arguing her out of it.

And at last I succeeded; it evidently cost her a great effort. I believe she swooned immediately afterwards, but of this I cannot be certain, for I did not lose a moment in seeking Sir Paul and clenching the matter before Chlorine had time to repent.

His manner of receiving me certainly struck me as odd and scarcely encouraging. 'We must hope for the best, my boy,' he said with a rather dreary sigh. 'I own I am too selfish to try to deter you from your high purpose. You would probably prefer as little delay as possible.'

'I should,' I replied promptly, pleased with his discernment.

'Then leave all preliminaries to me: you shall be informed when the day and time have been settled. It will be necessary, as you are aware, to have your signature to this document, but I feel it my duty to warn you solemnly that by signing it you make your decision irrevocable. There is yet time if your courage fails you.'

After such an intimation as that, I need not say that I was in such a hurry to sign that I did not even trouble myself to make out the somewhat crabbed writing in which the terms of the agreement were set out. I presumed that since it was binding on me, the baronet would, as a man of honour, consider it equally conclusive on his side. Looking back on it all now, it seems simply extraordinary that I should have been so easily satisfied, have taken so little pains to find out exactly the position in which I was placing myself, but I fell an easy victim to a naturally confiding and unsuspicious disposition.

'Say nothing of this to Chlorine,' said Sir Paul, as I gave him back the document, 'until the final arrangements are made. She must not be needlessly distressed, poor child, before the time.'

This seemed strange, too, but I promised to obey, supposing that he knew best.

And so for some days after that I made no mention to Chlorine of the approaching day which was to unite us: we were much together, and I learnt to feel a personal esteem for her which was quite independent of her main attractions. Her low spirits, however, seemed constitutional, and I anticipated a dull and drizzly honeymoon.

One afternoon the baronet took me aside mysteriously. 'Prepare yourself, Augustus,' he said: 'it is all arranged. The event upon which our dearest hopes depend will take place tomorrow, in the Grey Chamber, and of course at midnight.'

This I thought a curious time and place for the ceremony, but I knew his eccentric love of retirement, and supposed he had procured some very special form of licence.

'You do not know the place,' he added: 'come with me and I will show it you, from the outside at least.'

So he led me up the broad staircase, and stopping before an immense door covered with black baize and studded with brass nails, which gave it a hideous resemblance to a coffin-lid, he pressed a spring and it fell slowly back, revealing a long dim gallery leading to a heavy oak door with cumbrous metal plates and fastenings.

'At twelve o'clock tomorrow night—Christmas Eve,' he said, under his voice, 'you will present yourself at the Grey Chamber—it is there that you must go through it.'

I wondered why he should choose such a place for it, it would have been more cheerful in the drawing-room, but it was evidently a fancy of his, and I did not care to oppose it—I was too happy. I hastened to Chlorine, and, with her father's permission, told her that the crowning moment of both our lives was fixed.

It had the most astonishing effect upon her—she fainted away, just as she had done at the moment of giving her consent. I thought such conduct hypersensitive, and as soon as I had succeeded in bringing her round I remonstrated with her seriously. 'It is highly creditable to your maidenly delicacy, my love,' I said, 'but it is hardly complimentary to *me*!'

'Do not think I doubt you, Augustus,' she said, 'but the ordeal is so terrible.'

'There are cases,' I said grimly, 'in which it has not proved absolutely fatal; the victim occasionally survives the ceremony, I believe.'

'I will try to hope so,' she said earnestly. I thought her insane, which alarmed me for the validity of the marriage. 'I am weak,

I know,' she resumed; 'but I shudder to think of you in that Grey Chamber, going through it all alone.'

My worst fears seemed confirmed: no wonder her parents were grateful to me for relieving them of such a responsibility. 'May I ask where *you* intend to be at the time?' I inquired.

'You will not think us unfeeling, Augustus,' she said. 'Papa thought that we should endeavour to forget our anxiety by seeking some distraction. So we are going to Madame Tussaud's directly after dinner.'

'If you forget your anxiety at Madame Tussaud's, while I am cooling my heels in the Grey Chamber,' I said, 'I don't quite see how any clergyman will see his way to performing the ceremony—they won't marry us separately, you know.'

This time it was her turn to be astonished. 'You are joking!' she cried: 'you cannot really believe we are to be married in the Grey Chamber?'

'Then where are we to be married?' I asked, in utter bewilderment. 'Hardly at Madame Tussaud's?'

She turned upon me with what seemed a sudden misgiving. 'Augustus, tell me,' she said anxiously; 'you have read your aunt's last message to you?'

Now, thanks to McFadden, this was my one weak point. I had *not* read it, and I felt myself upon delicate ground. It evidently related to business of importance which was to be transacted in this Grey Chamber, and, as the real McFadden clearly knew all about it, to confess ignorance would have been suicidal just then.

'Of course, darling, of course,' I said hastily; 'it was my silly joke—you are quite right, there is something I have to arrange in the Grey Chamber before I can call you mine. I did not think you knew. But, tell me, why does it make you so uneasy?' I added, thinking that it might be prudent to find out what particular formality was expected from me.

'I cannot help it,' she sighed; 'the test will be so searching; are you sure that you are prepared at all points? I overheard papa say that no precaution could be neglected… If this should come between us after all!'

It was all clear now; the baronet was not so easy to satisfy in the choice of a son-in-law as I had imagined; he had no intention after all of accepting me without some inquiry into my previous habits and prospects. With characteristic eccentricity he was going to make the examination more impressive by holding it in this ridiculous midnight interview.

I thought I could easily contrive to satisfy the baronet, and said as much to Chlorine, with the idea of consoling her. 'Why do you persist in treating me like a child, Augustus?' she said petulantly. 'They have tried to hide all from me, but at least I know that in the Grey Chamber you will have to encounter one far more formidable, far harder to satisfy, than poor dear papa.'

'I see you know all, dearest,' I said; 'I was wrong. I will not try to deceive you again. I *shall* have to encounter some one who is all you say he is, but don't be afraid, I shall come out of it with flying colours—you shall see!'

I said no more about it then; but I saw that matters were worse than I had thought. I should have to deal with some stranger, some exacting and suspicious friend or relation, perhaps; or, more probably, a keen family solicitor, who would put awkward questions, and even be capable of insisting on strict settlements.

Love, in my opinion, has nothing in common with Law. Law, with its offensively suspicious restraints, its indelicately premature provisions—I would have nothing to do with it. I would refuse to meet a family solicitor anywhere, and I resolved to tell Sir Paul so at the first convenient opportunity.

The opportunity came after dinner, when we had retired to the drawing-room. Lady Catafalque was dozing uneasily in an armchair behind a firescreen, and Chlorine, in the inner room, was playing funereal dirges in the darkness, pressing the notes of the old piano with a languid uncertain touch.

I drew a chair beside Sir Paul's, and began to broach the subject calmly and temperately. 'I find,' I said, 'we have not quite understood one another about this affair in the Grey Chamber. When I agreed to make that appointment there, I thought—well, it doesn't matter what I thought—what I want to say now is, that, while I was always ready to give you, as Chlorine's father, every information you could reasonably require, I feel a delicacy in discussing my private affairs with an entire stranger.'

'I don't in the least understand you,' he said. 'What are you talking about?'

I began all over again. 'In short,' I concluded, 'I don't recognise your solicitor's right to interfere in the matter, and I decline to meet him.'

'Did I ever ask you to meet a solicitor anywhere?' he said sternly. 'And do you mean to tell me now that you do not know what has to be done tomorrow in the Grey Chamber?'

I saw that I was wrong again; but, as I was so obviously supposed to be thoroughly acquainted with the real nature of this perplexing appointment, I dared not betray my ignorance. I stammered something to the effect that I was referring to something else, some other interview which I had fancied was intended from some words of Chlorine's.

'What Chlorine could have said to give you such an idea,' said the baronet, 'I have no notion—here she is, to answer for herself.'

The faint mournful music had died away whilst we were speaking, and, looking up, I saw Chlorine, a pale slight form framed in the archway between the two rooms.

Before her father could question her about the solicitor, however, she spoke, as if forced to do so by some irresistible hysterical excitement.

'Papa,' she said trembling; 'dearest mamma... Augustus... I can bear it no longer. All my life I have felt that we have lived this strange life under the shadow of some fearful Thing—a Thing which no home can possess and be a happy one. I never sought to know more than this—I dared not ask... But now, when I know that Augustus, to whom I have given my first, my only love, must shortly face this ghastly presence, I cannot rest till I know exactly what the danger is that threatens him. You need not fear to tell me all, I can bear to know the worst.'

Lady Catafalque awoke with a faint shriek, and began to wring her long mittened hands and moan feebly; Sir Paul seemed slightly discomposed and undecided. I began to feel exquisitely uncomfortable—Chlorine's words pointed to something infinitely more terrible than a mere solicitor.

'Poor girl!' said Sir Paul at last, 'we concealed the whole truth for your good, but perhaps the time has come when the truest kindness will be to reveal all... Augustus, break to her, as you best know how, the nature of the ordeal before you.'

It was precisely what I would have given worlds to know myself, and I stared at his gloomy old face with what I felt were glassy and meaningless eyes. At last I managed to suggest that the story would come less harshly from a parent's lips.

'So be it,' he said. 'Chlorine, my darling, take a chair, and, yes, take a cup of tea before I begin.' There was a little delay over this, the baronet being anxious that his daughter should be perfectly composed. No one thought about me, and I suffered tortures of suspense during the interval which I dared not betray.

At last Sir Paul was satisfied, and in a dull monotonous tone, and yet with a gloomy sort of pride and relish, too, at the exceptional nature of his affliction, he began his weird and almost incredible tale.

'For some centuries,' he said, 'our unhappy house has been afflicted with a Family Curse. One Humfrey de Catafalque, by his familiarity with the Black Art, as it was said, attracted to his service a kind of Familiar, a dread and supernatural Being. Living in bitter enmity with the whole of his relations, to whom he bore for some reason an undying grudge, he bequeathed this baleful Thing with refined malice to his descendants for ever, as an inalienable heirloom. It goes with the title. The head of the family for the time being is bound to assign it a secret apartment under his own roof, and as each member of our house succeeds to the ancestral rank and honours, he must seek an interview with the Curse (for by that name it has been called for generations). In that interview it is decided whether the spell is broken for ever, or whether the Curse is to continue its blighting influence, and hold him in miserable thraldom until he dies.'

'Then are you one of its thralls, papa?' faltered Chlorine.

'I am,' he said: 'I failed to quell it, as every Catafalque, however brave and resolute, has failed yet. It checks all my accounts. I have to go and tremble before it annually, and even habit has not been able to rob that awful Presence, with its cold withering eye, of all its terrors! I shall never get quite accustomed to it!'

Never in my wildest thoughts had I imagined anything one quarter so dreadful as this! I could not rest until I had satisfied myself that *I* was not affected by these alarming family disclosures.

'She's frightened,' I said diplomatically, 'she, ha, ha—she has got some idea *I* have to go through the same sort of thing, don't you see? Explain that to her... *I'm* not a Catafalque, Chlorine, so it—it doesn't interfere with me, eh? does it, Sir Paul?'

'You mean well, Augustus,' he said, 'but we must deceive her no longer—she shall know the worst. Yes, my poor child,' he went on, to Chlorine, whose eyes were wide with terror—like my own. 'Unhappily, although our beloved Augustus is, as he says, not a Catafalque himself, it does concern him—he, too, must deliver himself up at the appointed hour, and brave the malevolence of the Curse of the Catafalques!'

I could not say a word—the horror of the idea was altogether too much for me—I fell back on my chair in a state of speechless collapse.

'Not only all new baronets,' continued Sir Paul, 'but every one who would seek an alliance with the females of our race must also undergo this test. Perhaps it is in some degree owing to this necessity that, ever since Humfrey de Catafalque's diabolical bequest, every maiden of our house has died a spinster!' (Here Chlorine hid her face with a low wail.) 'It is true that in 1770 one suitor was found bold enough to face the ordeal! He was conducted to the chamber where the curse was then lodged, and left there. Next day they found him outside the door—a gibbering maniac!'

I writhed on my chair. 'Augustus!' cried Chlorine wildly, 'promise you will never permit the Curse to turn you into a gibbering maniac! If I saw you gibber, I should die!'

I was very near gibbering then. I dared not trust myself to speak.

'Do not be afraid,' said Sir Paul more cheerfully. 'Augustus is happily in no danger. All is smooth for him!' (I began to brighten a little at this.) 'His aunt Petronia had made a special study of these things, and had at last succeeded in discovering the master-word which alone can break the unhallowed spell. Her great interest in you, my child, and the reports she heard of her nephew's excellent character gave her the idea that he might be the instrument which would rid us of the ban for ever. Her belief was well founded. Augustus has nobly offered himself, and, with his aunt's instructions for his safeguard, failure is next to impossible.'

Those instructions were somewhere at the bottom of the Melbourne docks! I could bear no more: 'It's simply astonishing to me!' I said, 'that you can calmly allow this hideous Curse, as you call it, to have things all its own way up to the present, in the nineteenth century, and not six miles from Charing Cross!'

'What can I do, Augustus?' he said helplessly.

'Do? Anything!' I retorted wildly (I hardly knew what I said). 'Take it out for an airing (it must want an airing by this time): take it out—and lose it. Get both the archbishops to step in and lay it for you! Sell the house, and make the purchaser take it with the other fixtures, at a valuation. I wouldn't have such a thing in my house— it's not respectable! And I want you to understand one thing. My aunt never told me the whole truth. I knew there was some sort of a curse in the family—but I never dreamed it was as bad as *that!* I never intended to be shut up alone with it. And I shall not go near the Grey Chamber!'

'Not go near it!' they cried aghast.

'Not on any account!' I said, beginning to recover my firmness. 'If the Curse has any business with me, let it come down and settle it here before you all, in a straightforward manner. I hate mysteries. On second thoughts,' I added, fearing lest they might find means of acting on this suggestion, 'I won't meet it anywhere.'

'And why—why won't you meet it?' they asked breathlessly.

'Because,' I explained desperately, 'because I'm—I'm a Materialist' (I did not know I was anything of the sort, but I could not stay then to consider the point). 'How can I have any dealings with a preposterous supernatural something which reason forbids me to believe in?

There's my difficulty—it would be inconsistent, and—and extremely painful to both sides.'

'You forget,' said Sir Paul, 'that you are pledged—irrevocably pledged—you *must* meet it. And let me beg you, my dear boy, to be more careful what you say. The Curse knows all that passes beneath this roof. This shocking ribaldry may hereafter be terribly remembered against you!'

One short hour ago and I had counted Chlorine's fortune as virtually my own! Now I saw with feelings I cannot unveil in any magazine that the time had come to abandon all my pretensions. It was a terrible wrench—but I had no other course but to state what would effectually shatter my fondest hopes.

'I had no right to pledge myself,' I said, with quivering lips, 'under all the circumstances.'

'What circumstances?' they all three demanded at once.

'Well, in the first place, I'm a base impostor—I am, indeed, I assure you,' I said very earnestly: 'I'm not Augustus McFadden at all; my real name is of no consequence, but it's not that. McFadden himself is, I regret to say, no more!'

Now, why I could not tell the plain truth here has always been a mystery to me. I suppose I had been lying so long that it was difficult to break myself of the habit at so short a notice, but I certainly did mix things up to a hopeless extent.

'Yes,' I continued sorrowfully, 'he is dead—he fell overboard during the voyage and a shark seized him almost immediately. It was my melancholy privilege to see him pass away. For one brief moment I saw him between the jaws of the creature, pale but composed (I refer to McFadden, you understand, not the shark); he just glanced up at me, and then, with a smile the sweetness of which I shall never forget (it was McFadden's smile, of course, not the shark's), he—he desired to be kindly remembered to you all (he was always courteous, poor fellow). Directly after that he was gradually withdrawn from my horror-stricken view.'

In bringing the shark in at all I was acting contrary to my instructions, but I quite forgot them: all I could think of was how to escape making the acquaintance of the Curse of the Catafalques.

'Then, sir,' said the baronet haughtily, 'you have basely deceived us all!'

'That is what I was endeavouring to bring out,' I replied. 'You see it puts it quite out of my power to meet your family Curse; I do not feel myself entitled to intrude on it. So, if you will kindly let some one fetch a cab in a quarter of an hour—'

'Stop!' cried Chlorine. 'Augustus (I will call you by that name still), you must not go like this! It was for love of me that you stooped to deceit, and—and—Mr. McFadden is dead. If he were alive, it might be my duty to remain free for at least two years; but he lies within the shark, and—and—you have taught me to love you. You must stay—stay and brave the Curse—and we may yet be happy!'

How I blamed my folly in not telling the truth at first! 'When—when—I said McFadden was dead,' I explained hoarsely, 'I was not speaking quite correctly. It was another fellow the shark swallowed—in fact, it was another shark altogether. And McFadden is alive and well at Melbourne; but, feeling slightly alarmed at the Curse, he asked me to call and make his excuses. I have now done so, and will trespass no further on your kindness. So if you will tell somebody to bring a cab—'

'Pardon me,' said the baronet, 'we cannot part in this way. I always feared that your resolution would break down in some such way—it is only natural. Do you think we cannot see that these extraordinary stories are prompted by a sudden panic? I quite understand it,

Augustus. I cannot blame you for it; but to listen to you would be culpable weakness on my part. It will pass away—you will forget your fears tomorrow. You *must* forget them; for, remember, you have promised! I dare not let you run the danger of exciting the Curse by a deliberate insult. For your own sake, I shall take care that your solemn bond is not forfeited.'

I read beneath his words the innate selfishness which prompted them—the old man did not entirely believe me, and he was determined that he would not lose the smallest chance of escaping from the thraldom of his race by my means.

I raved, I protested, I implored—but all in vain; they would not believe a single word I said; they positively refused to release me; they insisted that, for my sake as well as their own, they were bound to insist upon my performing my engagement.

And, at last, Chlorine and her mother left the room with a little contempt in their pity for my unworthiness; and after that, Sir Paul conducted me to my room, and left me, as he said, to return to my senses.

III

What a night I passed! Tossing sleeplessly from side to side under the hearse-like canopy of my old-fashioned bedstead, I tortured my fevered brain with vain speculations as to the fate the morrow would bring me.

I was perfectly helpless—I saw no way out of it; they would not believe me; they were bent upon offering me up as a sacrifice to this private Moloch of theirs, the very vagueness of which made it doubly fearful. If I had only some idea what it was like to look at, I might not feel quite so afraid of it; the impalpable awfulness of the thing was what I found so terrible—the very thought of it made me fling myself about in an ecstasy of horror.

But by degrees I grew calmer and able to consider my position with something like composure, until, by daybreak, I had come to a final resolution.

As I was evidently bound to meet my fate, the wisest course was to do so with a good grace; then, if by some fortunate chance I came well out of it, my future was insured. Whereas, if I went on repudiating myself to the very last, I might in time arouse suspicions which the most successful encounter with the Curse would not dispel.

And then, after all, the affair might have been much exaggerated. By keeping my head, and exercising all my powers of cool impudence, I might surely manage to hoodwink this formidable relic of mediaeval superstition, which must have fallen rather behind the age by this time.

It might even turn out to be (though I confess I was not very sanguine as to this) as big a humbug as I was myself, and the interview resolve itself into a sort of augurs' meeting.

At all events, I resolved to see this mysterious business out, and trust to my customary good fortune to bring me safely through. I came down to breakfast something like my usual self, and I managed to reassure the family, in contradicting by word and deed my weakness of the night before.

From a mistaken consideration for me, they left me to myself for the whole of the day; and, although I was as determined as ever to make a bold fight for the fortune that I saw in danger of eluding me, I moped about that gloom-laden house with a depression that deepened every hour.

We dined almost in solemn silence; Sir Paul made no remark, except as he saw my hand approaching a decanter, when he would observe that I had need of a clear head and strong nerves that night, and warn me to beware of the brown sherry.

Chlorine and her mother stole apprehensive glances at me from time to time, and sighed heavily between the courses, their eyes brimming with unshed tears. It was not a lively meal.

It came to an end at last; the ladies rose, and Sir Paul and I sat brooding silently over the dessert. I think both of us felt a delicacy in beginning a conversation.

But before I could venture upon a safe remark, Lady Catafalque and Chlorine returned—dressed, to my unspeakable horror, in readiness to go out. Worse still, Sir Paul apparently intended to join them.

'It is now time to say farewell,' he said, in his hollow voice. 'You will need a season of self-preparation; you have more than three hours yet. At midnight you will go to the Grey Chamber. You will find the Curse prepared for you.'

'You are not all going!' I cried. I had never expected this. They were not a gay family to sit with; but even their company was better than my own.

'We must,' they said: 'it is one of the traditions connected with the Curse. No human being but one must be in the house during the night appointed for the interview. The servants have already left it, and we ourselves are about to pass the night at a private hotel, after a brief visit to Madame Tussaud's, to allay, if possible, our terrible anxiety.'

I believe at this I positively howled with terror—all the old fears came back with a sudden rush. 'Don't leave me all alone with it!' I cried. 'I shall go mad if you do!'

Sir Paul turned on his heel with a gesture of contempt, and his wife followed. Chlorine remained behind for one instant. I had never thought her so pretty before, as she looked at me with a yearning pity in her pale face.

'Augustus,' she said, 'show me I was not mistaken in you. I would spare you this if I could; but you know I cannot. Be brave, now, or you will lose me for ever!'

I felt a stronger determination to win her then than I had ever done before—her gentle appeal seemed to make a man of me once more; and, as I kissed the slender hand she held out to me, I vowed sincerely enough to prove myself worthy of her.

Almost immediately after that the heavy front door slammed behind them, the rusty old gate screeched like a banshee as it swung back with a hollow clang. I heard the carriage wheels grinding the slush, and knew that I was alone—shut up on Christmas Eve in that sombre house, with the Curse of the Catafalques for my only companion!

Somehow the generous ardour with which Chlorine had inspired me did not last very long. Before the clock struck nine I found myself shivering, and I drew up a clumsy old leathern armchair close to the fire, piled on the logs, and tried to overcome a horrible sensation of internal vacancy and look my situation fairly in the face.

However repugnant it might seem to one's ordinary common-sense ideas, there was no possible doubt that there was something of a supernatural order shut up in that great chamber, and also that, if I meant to win Chlorine, I should have to go up and have some kind of an interview with it.

If I could only have had some distinct idea of what this would be! What description of being should I find this Curse? Would it be aggressively ugly—like the bogie of my childish days? Or should I see an awful unsubstantial shape, draped in clinging black, with nothing visible but a pair of hollow burning eyes and one long, pale, bony hand? Really I could not decide which would be the more trying.

All the frightful stories I had ever read came crowding into my unwilling mind. One in particular of a Marshal Somebody, who, after much industry, succeeded in invoking an evil spirit, which came bouncing into the room, shaped like a gigantic ball with (I think) a hideous face in the middle of it, and the horrified marshal could not get rid of it until after hours of hard praying and persistent exorcism.

Only suppose the Curse should be something like that!

Then there was another appalling tale I had read in some magazine—a tale of a secret chamber, too, and almost a parallel case to my own, where the heir of a great house had to go in and meet a mysterious aged person with strange eyes and an evil smile, who wanted to shake hands with him. I determined that I would steadfastly refrain from shaking hands with the Curse of the Catafalques.

If I had only had McFadden's aunt's instructions I should have felt safer; but I had no hint even for my conduct, and besides I was an impostor, about to confront a power which knew nearly everything! For a moment the desperate thought occurred to me of confessing all, and sobbing out my deceit upon its bosom. But suppose it had no such thing as a bosom, what then?

By this time I had worked up my nerves to such a pitch of terror that it was absolutely necessary to brace them. I did brace them. I emptied all three of the decanters, but Sir Paul's cellar being none of the best, the only result was that I began to feel exceedingly unwell without gaining any perceptible moral courage.

I dared not smoke, though tobacco might soothe me. The Curse, being old-fashioned, might object to it, and I was anxious to do nothing to prejudice it against me.

So I simply sat there and shook. Every now and then I heard steps on the glistening path outside; sometimes a rapid tread of some happy person no doubt on his way to scenes of Christmas revelry, and little dreaming of the miserable wretch he passed; sometimes the slow, elephantine tramp of the Fulham policeman on his beat.

What if I called him in and gave the Curse into custody—say for putting me in bodily fear, or for being found on the premises under suspicious circumstances?

There was a boldness in thus cutting the knot which rather fascinated me; but most probably, I thought, the stolid officer would decline to interfere on some pretext, and, even if he did, Sir Paul would be deeply annoyed to hear of his Family Curse spending its Christmas in the cell of a police station. He would certainly consider it a piece of unpardonable bad taste on my part.

So one hour passed. A few minutes after ten I heard footsteps again and voices in low consultation, as of a band of men outside the railings. Could there be any indication without of the horrors those walls contained?

But the gaunt house front kept its secret. They were merely the waits.

They struck up the old carol, 'God rest you, merry gentleman, let nothing you dismay!' which, of course, was very appropriate, and followed it up with that most doleful of airs, 'The Mistletoe Bough,' which they gave with some wheeziness but intense feeling. At first I had a vague comfort in listening. I felt that I was not quite alone, and I even had a faint hope that the Curse might hear and be softened by the strains. Such things have been known to happen at this season of the year. But they did play so infernally that I was soon convinced that such music could only have an irritating effect, and I rushed to the window and beckoned to them to go away.

I had better have left it alone, for they took it as an encourage-ment, and played on yet more villainously, while one of the band remained at the gate for quite a quarter of an hour, ringing inces-santly, in the vain expectation of some gratuity.

This must have stirred the Curse up quite enough; but after they had gone there came a man with a barrel-organ, and his barrel-organ had been out in the weather for so long that it had become altogether demoralised, or, as it were, deranged. When he turned the handle it brayed out confused portions of its entire repertory all at once with a maddening effect. Even its owner seemed aware that there was something wrong, for he stopped occasionally, probably struck aghast at the din, but apparently he still hoped that by perseverance he would bring the instrument round, and Parson's Green being a quiet place for the experiment he remained there for some time, every fresh discord lessening my chances of success.

He went too at last, though not before he must have rendered the Curse absolutely rabid; and then, as the hour-hand stole on towards eleven, my excited fancy began to catch strange sounds echoing about the old house—sharp reports from the furniture, sighing moans in the windy passages, doors shutting, and, worse still, stealthy padding footsteps above and outside in the ghostly hall.

I sat there in a cold perspiration until I could really bear it no longer.

My nerves wanted more bracing than ever. I got out the spirit case, and after I had consumed several consecutive tumblers of brandy and water my fears began at last to melt rapidly away.

What a ridiculous bugbear I was making of the Thing after all! How did I know that I should not find this dreaded Curse as pleas-ant and gentlemanly a demon—or familiar, or whatever it was—as a man could wish to meet?

I would go up at once and wish it a merry Christmas. That would put it in a good temper. On the other hand, it might look as if I was afraid of it. Afraid! ha, ha! Why, for two straws I would go up and pull its nose for it, if it had a nose? At all events, I would go up to the door of the Grey Chamber, and defy it boldly—perhaps not exactly defy it, but just go as far as the corridor to get used to the neighbourhood.

I made my way with this object, rather unsteadily, up the dim and misty staircase, and opened the coffin-lid door which led to the corridor, down which I looked apprehensively.

The strange metal fittings on the massive door of the Grey Chamber seemed to be all flashing and sparkling with a mysterious pale light, like electricity, or perhaps phosphorus, and from under the door came a sullen red glow, while I heard within sounds like the roar of a mighty wind, above which rose at intervals peals of fiendish mirth, accompanied by a hideous dull clanking.

Evidently the Curse was getting up the steam to receive me.

I did not stay there long. It might dart out suddenly and catch me eavesdropping—a bad beginning of our acquaintance. I got back to the dining-room somehow, and found the fire out, and the time, which was just visible by the fast dimming lamp, a quarter to twelve.

Only fifteen more short minutes and, unless I gave up Chlorine and her money for ever, I must go up and knock at that awful door, and enter the presence of the frightful mystic Thing that was roaring and laughing and clanking inside.

I sat staring stupidly at the funereal black face of the clock, watching the long gold hand steal relentlessly on. In six minutes I should be beginning my desperate duel with one of the powers of darkness! It gave me a sick qualm as I thought of it, and still the time wore on.

I had but two precious minutes left, when the lamp gave a faint gurgling sob, like a death-rattle, and went out, leaving me in the dark alone.

If I lingered, the Curse might come down and fetch me, and the horror of this made me resolve to go up at once; punctuality might propitiate it.

I groped my way to the door, reached the hall, and stood there, swaying for a moment under the old stained-glass lantern. Then I began to be aware of the terrible fact that I was not in a condition to transact any business successfully—much less to go through an encounter with the Curse of the Catafalques! I had disregarded Sir Paul's well-meant warning at dinner—I was not my own master—I was lost!

I was endeavouring to get upstairs when the clock in the room below tolled twelve, and from without the faint peal and chime from distant steeples proclaimed that it was Christmas morning—my hour had come!

I made one more desperate effort to go up, and then—then, upon my word, I don't know how it was, but I happened to see my hat on the hat-rack below, and I did what I venture to think most men in my position would have done too.

I renounced my ingeniously elaborate scheme for ever; I rushed to the door (which was fortunately unbolted and unlocked), and the next moment I was making for the King's Road with an unsteady run, as if the Curse itself were at my heels.

There is little more to say; for weeks I lay in hiding, trembling every hour lest the outraged Curse should hunt me down at last; my belongings were all at Parson's Green, and for obvious reasons I dared not write or call for them, nor indeed have I seen any of the Catafalques since my ignominious flight.

I had been trapped and cruelly deceived—my hopes of an ample and assured income with a wife I could honestly love are fled for ever—but, although I regret this bitterly and sincerely, I am now resigned, for the price of success was too tremendous.

Perhaps there may be one or two who read this whose curiosity has been excited in the course of my strange and unhappy story, and who may feel a slight disappointment at not learning after all what the Curse's personal appearance is, and how it comports itself in its ghastly Grey Chamber. For myself, I have long ceased to feel any curiosity on the subject, but I can only suggest that full information as to these points would be easily obtained if any unmarried male person of unexceptionable recommendations were to call at Parson's Green and ask Sir Paul's permission to pay his addresses to his daughter.

I shall be very happy to allow my name to be used as a reference.

CHRISTMAS EVE ON
A HAUNTED HULK

Frank Cowper

First published in *Blackwood's Edinburgh Magazine*, January 1889

Frank Cowper (1849–1930) is perhaps one of the more unlikely ghost story writers included in this collection. He was a yachtsman who wrote both fiction and non-fiction about sailing, including a five-volume work called *Sailing Tours* which chronicles his circumnavigation of the British Isles, among other expeditions. He liked to sail alone, and popularised the idea of single-handed cruising. Perhaps this also helped to inspire this story.

I SHALL NEVER FORGET THAT NIGHT AS LONG AS I LIVE.

It was during the Christmas vacation 187—. I was staying with an old college friend who had lately been appointed the curate of a country parish, and had asked me to come and cheer him up, since he could not get away at that time.

As we drove along the straight country lane from the little wayside station; it forcibly struck me that a life in such a place must be dreary indeed. I have always been much influenced by local colour; above all things, I am depressed by a dead level, and here was monotony with a vengeance. On each side of the low hedges, lichen-covered and wind-cropped, stretched bare fields, the absolute level of the horizon being only broken at intervals by some mournful tree that pointed like a decrepit finger-post towards the east, for all its western growth was nipped and blasted by the roaring southwest winds. An occasional black spot, dotted against the grey distance, marked a hay-rick or labourer's cottage, while some two miles ahead of us the stunted spire of my friend's church stood out against the wintry sky, amid the withered branches of a few ragged trees. On our right hand stretched dreary wastes of mud, interspersed here and there with firmer patches of land, but desolate and forlorn, cut off from all communication with the mainland by acres of mud and thin streaks of brown water.

A few sea-birds were piping over the waste, and this was the only sound, except the grit of our own wheels and the steady step of the horse, which broke the silence.

'Not lively is it?' said Jones; and I couldn't say it was. As we drove 'up street,' as the inhabitants fondly called the small array of low houses which bordered the highroad, I noticed the lack-lustre expression of the few children and untidy women who were loitering about the doors of their houses.

There was an old tumble-down inn, with a dilapidated sign-board, scarcely held up by its rickety ironwork. A daub of yellow and red paint, with a dingy streak of blue, was supposed to represent the Duke's head, although what exalted member of the aristocracy was thus distinguished it would be hard to say. Jones inclined to think it was the Duke of Wellington; but I upheld the theory that it was the Duke of Marlborough, chiefly basing my arguments on the fact that no artist who desired to convey a striking likeness would fail to show the Great Duke in profile, whereas this personage was evidently depicted full face, and wearing a three-cornered hat.

At the end of the village was the church, standing in an untidy churchyard, and opposite it was a neat little house, quite new, and of that utilitarian order of architecture which will stamp the Victorian age as one of the least imaginative of eras. Two windows flanked the front door, and three narrow windows looked out overhead from under a slate roof; variety and distinction being given to the façade by the brilliant blending of the yellow bricks with red, so bright as to suggest the idea of their having been painted. A scrupulously clean stone at the front door, together with the bright green of the little palings and woodwork, told me what sort of landlady to expect, and I was not disappointed. A kindly featured woman, thin, cheery, and active, received us, speaking in that encouraging tone of half-compassionate, half-proprietary patronage, which I have observed so many women adopt towards lone beings of the opposite sex.

'You will find it precious dull, old man,' said Jones, as we were eating our frugal dinner. 'There's nothing for you to do, unless you care to try a shot at the duck over the mud flats. I shall be busy on and off nearly all tomorrow.'

As we talked, I could not help admiring the cheerful pluck with which Jones endured the terrible monotony of his life in this dreary place. His rector was said to be delicate, and in order to prolong a life, which no doubt he considered valuable to the Church, he lived with his family either at Torquay or Cannes in elegant idleness, quite unable to do any duty, but fully equal to enjoying the pleasant society of those charming places, and quite satisfied that he had done his duty when he sacrificed a tenth of his income to provide for the spiritual needs of his parish. There was no squire in the place; no 'gentlefolk,' as the rustics called them, lived nearer than five miles; and there was not a single being of his own class with whom poor Jones could associate. And yet he made no complaint. The nearest approach to one being the remark that the worst of it was, it was so difficult, if not impossible, to be really understood. 'The poor being so suspicious and ignorant, they look at everything from such a low standpoint, enthusiasm and freshness sink so easily into formalism and listlessness.'

The next day, finding that I really could be of no use, and feeling awkward and bored, as a man always is when another is actively doing his duty, I went off to the marshes to see if I could get any sport.

I took some sandwiches and a flask with me, not intending to return until dinner. After wandering about for some time, crossing dyke after dyke by treacherous rails more or less rotten, I found myself on the edge of a wide mere. I could see some duck out in the middle, and standing far out in the shallow water was a heron. They were all out of shot, and I saw I should do no good without a duck-punt.

I sat down on an old pile left on the top of the sea-wall, which had been lately repaired. The duck looked very tempting, but I doubted if I should do much good in broad daylight, even if I had a duck-punt, without a duck-gun. After sitting disconsolately for some time, I got up and wandered on.

The dreariness of the scene was most depressing: everything was brown and grey. Nothing broke the monotony of the wide-stretching mere; the whole scene gave me the impression of a straight line of interminable length, with a speck in the centre of it. That speck was myself.

At last, as I turned an angle in the sea-wall, I saw something lying above high-water mark, which looked like a boat.

Rejoiced to see any signs of humanity, I quickened my pace. It was a boat and, better still, a duck-punt. As I came nearer I could see that she was old and very likely leaky; but here was a prospect of adventure, and I was not going to be readily daunted. On examination, the old craft seemed more water-tight than I expected. At least she held water very well, arid if she kept it in, she must equally well keep it out. I turned her over to run the water out, and then dragging the crazy old boat over the line of sea-weed, launched her. But now a real difficulty met me. The paddles were nowhere to be seen. They had doubtless been taken away by the owner, and it would be little use searching for them. But a stout stick would do to punt her over the shallow water; and after some little search, I found an old stake which would answer well.

This was real luck. I had now some hope of bagging a few duck; at any rate, I was afloat, and could explore the little islets, which barely rose above the brown water. I might at least find some rabbits on them. I cautiously poled myself towards the black dots; but before I came within range, up rose first one, then another and another, like a string of beads, and the whole flight went, with outstretched necks and rapidly beating wings, away to my right, and seemed to pitch again beyond a low island some half-mile away. The heron had long ago taken himself off; so there was nothing to be done but pole across the mud in pursuit of the duck. I had not gone many yards when I found that I was going much faster than I expected, and soon saw the cause. The tide was falling, and I was being carried along with it. This would bring me nearer to my ducks, and I lazily guided the punt with the stake.

On rounding the island I found a new source of interest. The mere opened out to a much larger extent, and away towards my right I could see a break in the low land, as if a wide ditch had been cut through; while in this opening ever and anon dark objects rose up and disappeared again in a way I could not account for. The water seemed to be running off the mud-flats, and I saw that if I did not wish to be left high, but not dry, on the long slimy wastes, I must be careful to keep in the little channels or 'lakes,' which acted as natural drains to the acres of greasy mud.

A conspicuous object attracted my attention some mile or more towards the opening in the land. It was a vessel lying high up on the mud, and looking as if she was abandoned.

The ducks had pitched a hundred yards or so beyond the island, and I approached as cautiously as I could; but just as I was putting down the stake to take up my gun, there was a swift sound of beating wings and splashing water, and away my birds flew, low over the mud, towards the old hulk.

Here was a chance, I thought. If I could get on board and remain hidden, I might, by patiently waiting, get a shot. I looked at my watch; there was still plenty of daylight left, and the tide was only just beginning to leave the mud. I punted away, therefore, with renewed hope, and was not long in getting up to the old ship.

There was just sufficient water over the mud to allow me to approach within ten or twelve feet, but further I could not push the punt. This was disappointing; however, I noticed a deep lake ran round the other side, and determined to try my luck there. So with a slosh and a heave I got the flat afloat again, and made for the deeper water. It turned out quite successful, and I was enabled to get right under the square overhanging counter, while a little lane of water led alongside her starboard quarter. I pushed the nose of the punt into this, and was not long in clambering on board by the rusty irons of her fore-chains.

The old vessel lay nearly upright in the soft mud, and a glance soon told she would never be used again. Her gear and rigging were all rotten, and everything valuable had been removed. She was a brig of some two hundred tons, and had been a fine vessel, no doubt. To me there is always a world of romance in a deserted ship. The places she has been to, the scenes she has witnessed, the possibilities of crime, of adventure—all these thoughts crowd upon me when I see an old hulk lying deserted and forgotten—left to rot upon the mud of some lonely creek.

In order to keep my punt afloat as long as possible, I towed her round and moored her under the stern, and then looked over the bulwarks for the duck. There they were, swimming not more than a hundred and fifty yards away, and they were coming towards me. I remained perfectly concealed under the high bulwark, and could see them paddling and feeding in the greasy weed. Their approach was slow, but I could afford to wait. Nearer and nearer they came; another minute, and they would be well within shot. I was already congratulating myself upon the success of my adventure, and thinking of the joy of Jones at this large accession to his larder, when suddenly there was a heavy splash, and with a wild spluttering rush the whole pack rose out of the water, and went skimming over the mud towards the distant sea. I let off both barrels after them, and tried to console myself by thinking that I saw the feathers fly from one; but not a bird dropped, and I was left alone in my chagrin.

What could have caused the splash, that luckless splash, I wondered. There was surely no one else on board the ship, and certainly no one could get out here without mud-pattens or a boat. I looked round. All was perfectly still. Nothing broke the monotony of the grey scene—sodden and damp and lifeless. A chill breeze came up from the south-west, bringing with it a raw mist, which was blotting out the dark distance, and fast limiting my horizon. The day was drawing in, and I must be thinking of going home. As I turned round, my attention was arrested by seeing a duck-punt glide past me in the now rapidly falling water, which was swirling by the mud-bank on which the vessel lay. But there was no one in her. A dreadful thought struck me. It must be my boat, and how shall I get home? I ran to the stern and looked over. The duck-punt was gone.

The frayed and stranded end of the painter told me how it had happened. I had not allowed for the fall of the tide, and the strain of the punt, as the water fell away, had snapped the line, old and rotten as it was.

I ran to the bows, and jumping on to the bitts, saw my punt peacefully drifting away, some quarter of a mile off. It was perfectly evident I could not hope to get her again.

It was beginning to rain steadily. I could see that I was in for dirty weather, and became a little anxious about how I was to get back, especially as it was now rapidly growing dark. So thick was it that I could not see the low land anywhere, and could only judge of its position by remembering that the stern of the vessel pointed that way.

The conviction grew upon me that I could not possibly get away from this doleful old hulk without assistance, and how to get it, I could not for the life of me see. I had not seen a sign of a human being the whole day. It was not likely any more would be about at night. However, I shouted as loud as I could, and then waited to hear if there were any response. There was not a sound, only the wind moaned slightly through the stumps of the masts, and something creaked in the cabin.

Well, I thought, at least it might be worse. I shall have shelter for the night; while had I been left on one of these islands, I should have had to spend the night exposed to the pelting rain. Happy thought! Go below before it gets too dark, and see what sort of a berth can be got, if the worst comes to the worst. So thinking, I went to the booby-hatch, and found as I expected that it was half broken open, and any one could go below who liked.

As I stepped down the rotting companion, the air smelt foul and dank. I went below very cautiously, for I was not at all sure that the boards would bear me. It was fortunate I did so, for as I stepped off the lowest step the floor, gave way under my foot, and had I not been holding on to the stair-rail, I should have fallen through. Before going any further, I took a look round.

The prospect was not inviting. The light was dim; I could scarcely make out objects near me, all else was obscurity. I could see that the whole of the inside of the vessel was completely gutted. What little light there was came through the stern ports. A small round speck of light looked at me out of the darkness ahead, and I could see that the flooring had either all given way or been taken out of her. At my feet a gleam of water showed me what to expect if I should slip through the floor-joists. Altogether, a more desolate, gloomy, ghostly place it would be difficult to find.

I could not see any bunk or locker where I could sit down, and everything movable had been taken out of the hulk. Groping my way with increasing caution, I stepped across the joists, and felt along the side of the cabin. I soon came to a bulkhead. Continuing to grope, I came to an opening. If the cabin was dim, here was blackness itself. I felt it would be useless to attempt to go further, especially as a very damp foul odour came up from the bilge-water in her hold. As I stood looking into the darkness, a cold chilly shudder passed over me, and with a shiver I turned round to look at the cabin. My eyes had now become used to the gloom. A deeper patch of darkness on my right suggested the possibility of a berth, and groping my way over to it, I found the lower bunk was still entire. Here at least I could rest, if I found it impossible to get to shore. Having some wax vestas in my pocket, I struck a light and examined the bunk. It was better than I expected. If I could only find something to burn, I should be comparatively cheerful.

Before reconciling myself to my uncomfortable position, I resolved to see whether I could not get to the shore, and went up the rickety stairs again. It was raining hard, and the wind had got up. Nothing could be more dismal. I looked over the side and lowered myself down from the main-chains, to see if it were possible to walk over the mud. I found I could not reach the mud at all; and fearful of being unable to climb back if I let go, I clambered up the side again and got on board.

It was quite clean. I must pass the night here. Before going below I once more shouted at the top of my voice, more to keep up my own spirits than with any hope of being heard, and then paused to listen. Not a sound of any sort replied. I now prepared to make myself as comfortable as I could.

It was a dreary prospect. I would rather have spent the night on deck than down below in that foul cabin; but the drenching driving rain, as well as the cold, drove me to seek shelter below. It seemed so absurd to be in the position of a shipwrecked sailor, within two or three miles of a prosy country hamlet, and in a landlocked harbour while actually on land, if the slimy deep mud could be called land. I had not many matches left, but I had my gun and cartridges. The idea occurred to me to fire off minute-guns. 'That's what I ought to do, of course. The red flash will be seen in this dark night,' for it was dark now and no mistake. Getting up on to the highest part of the vessel, I blazed away. The noise sounded to me deafening; surely the whole countryside would be aroused. After firing off a dozen cartridges, I waited. But the silence only seemed the more oppressive, and the blackness all the darker. 'It's no good; I'll turn in,' I thought, dejectedly.

With great difficulty I groped my way to the top of the companion ladder, and bumped dismally down the steps. If only I had a light I should be fairly comfortable, I thought. 'Happy thought, make a "spit-devil!"' as we used when boys to call a little cone of damp gun powder.

I got out my last two cartridges, and emptying the powder carefully into my hand, I moistened it, and worked it up to a paste. I then placed it on the smooth end of the rail, and lighted it. This was brilliant: at least so it seemed by contrast with the absolute blackness around me. By its light I was able to find my way to the bunk, and it lasted just long enough for me to arrange myself fairly comfortably for the night. By contriving a succession of matches, I was enabled to have enough light to see to eat my frugal supper; for I had kept a little sherry and a few sandwiches to meet emergencies, and it was a fortunate thing I had. The light and the food made me feel more cheery, and by the time the last match had gone out, I felt worse might have happened to me by a long way.

As I lay still, waiting for sleep to come, the absurdity of the situation forced itself upon me. Here was I, to all intents and purposes as much cut off from all communication with the rest of the world as if I were cast away upon a desert island. The chances were that I should make some one see or hear me the next day. Jones would be certain to have the country searched, and at the longest I should only endure the discomfort of one night, and get well laughed at for my pains; but meanwhile I was absolutely severed from all human contact, and was as isolated as Robinson Crusoe, only 'more so,' for I had no other living thing whatever to share my solitude. The silence of the place was perfect; and if silence can woo sleep, sleep ought very soon to have come. But when one is hungry and wet, and in a strange uncanny kind of place, besides being in one's clothes, it is a very difficult thing to go to sleep. First, my head was too low; then, after resting it on my arms, I got cramp in them. My back seemed all over bumps; when I turned on my side, I appeared to have got a rather serious enlargement of the hip-joint; and I found my damp clothes smell very musty. After sighing and groaning for some time, I sat up for change of position, and nearly fractured my skull in so doing, against the remains of what had once been a berth above me. I didn't dare to move in the inky blackness, for I had seen sufficient to know that I might very easily break my leg or my neck in the floorless cabin.

There was nothing for it but to sit still, or lie down and wait for daylight. I had no means of telling the time. When I had last looked at my watch, before the last match had gone out, it was not more than six o'clock; it might be now about eight, or perhaps not so late. Fancy twelve long hours spent in that doleful black place, with nothing in the world to do to pass away the time! I *must* go to sleep; and so, full of this resolve, I lay down again.

I suppose I went to sleep. All I can recollect, after lying down, is keeping my mind resolutely turned inwards, as it were, and fixed upon the arduous business of counting an imaginary and interminable flock of sheep pass one by one through an ideal gate. This meritorious method of compelling sleep had, no doubt, been rewarded; but I have no means of knowing how long I slept, and I cannot tell at what hour of the night the following strange circumstances occurred—for occur they certainly did—and I am as perfectly convinced that I was the oral witness to some ghastly crime, as I am that I am writing these lines. I have little doubt I shall be laughed at, as Jones laughed at me—be told that I was dreaming, that I was overtired and nervous. In fact, so accustomed have I become to this sort of thing, that I now hardly ever tell my tale; or, if I do, I put it in the third person, and then I find people believe it, or at least take much more interest in it. I suppose the reason is, that people cannot bring themselves to think so strange a thing could have happened to such a prosy everyday sort of man as myself, and they cannot divest their minds of the idea that I am—well, to put it mildly—'drawing on my imagination for facts.' Perhaps, if the tale appears in print, it will be believed, as a facetious friend of mine once said to a newly married couple, who had just seen the announcement of their marriage in the 'Times,' 'Ah, didn't know you were married till you saw it in print!'

Well, be the time what it may have been, all I know is that the next thing I can remember after getting my five-hundredth sheep through the gate is, that I heard two most horrible yells ring through the darkness. I sat bolt-upright; and as a proof that my senses were 'all there,' I did not bring my head this time against the berth overhead, remembering to bend it outwards so as to clear it.

There was not another sound. The silence was as absolute as the darkness. 'I must have been dreaming,' I thought; but the sounds were ringing in my ears, and my heart was beating with excitement. There must have been some reason for this. I never was 'taken this way' before. I could not make it out, and felt very uncomfortable. I sat there listening for some time. No other sound breaking the deathly stillness, and becoming tired of sitting, I lay down again. Once more I set myself to get my interminable flocks through that gate, but I could not help myself listening.

There seemed to me a sound growing in the darkness, a something gathering in the particles of the air, as if molecules of the atmosphere were rustling together, and with stilly movement were whispering something. The wind had died down, and I would have gone on deck if I could move; but it was hazardous enough moving about in the light: it would have been madness to attempt to move in that blackness. And so I lay still and tried to sleep.

But now there was a sound, indistinct, but no mere fancy; a muffled sound, as of some movement in the forepart of the ship.

I listened intently and gazed into the darkness.

What was the sound? It did not seem like rats. It was a dull, shuffling kind of noise, very indistinct, and conveying no clue whatever as to its cause. It lasted only for a short time. But now the cold damp air seemed to have become more piercingly chilly. The raw iciness seemed to strike into the very marrow of my bones, and my teeth chattered. At the same time a new sense seemed to be assailed: the foul odour which I had noticed arising from the stagnant water in the bilge appeared to rise into more objectionable prominence, as if it had been stirred.

'I cannot stand this,' I muttered, shivering in horrible aversion at the disgusting odour; 'I will go on deck at all hazards.'

Rising to put this resolve in execution, I was arrested by the noise beginning again. I listened. This time I distinctly distinguished two separate sounds: one, like a heavy soft weight being dragged along with difficulty; the other like the hard sound of boots on boards.

Could there be others on board after all? If so, why had they made no sound when I clambered on deck, or afterwards, when I shouted and fired my gun?

Clearly, if there were people, they wished to remain concealed, and my presence was inconvenient to them. But how absolutely still and quiet they had kept! It appeared incredible that there should be any one. I listened intently. The sound had ceased again, and once more the most absolute stillness reigned around. A gentle swishing, wobbling, lapping noise seemed to form itself in the darkness. It increased, until I recognised the chattering and bubbling of water. 'It must be the tide which is rising,' I thought; 'it has reached the rudder, and is eddying round the stern-post.' This also accounted, in my mind, for the other noises, because, as the tide surrounded the vessel, and she thus became water-borne, all kinds of sounds might be produced in the old hulk as she resumed her upright position.

However, I could not get rid of the chilly horrid feeling those two screams had produced, combined with the disgusting smell, which was getting more and more obtrusive. It was foul, horrible, revolting, like some carrion, putrid and noxious. I prepared to take my chances of damage, and rose up to grope my way to the companion ladder.

It was a more difficult job than I had any idea of. I had my gun, it was true, and with it I could feel for the joists; but when once I let go of the edge of the bunk I had nothing to steady me, and nearly went headlong at the first step. Fortunately I reached back in time to prevent my fall; but this attempt convinced me that I had better endure the strange horrors of the unknown, than the certain miseries of a broken leg or neck.

I sat down, therefore, on the bunk.

Now that my own movements had ceased, I became aware that the shuffling noise was going on all the time. 'Well,' thought I, 'they may shuffle. They won't hurt me, and I shall go to sleep again.' So reflecting, I lay down, holding my gun, ready to use as a club if necessary.

Now it is all very well to laugh at superstitious terrors. Nothing is easier than to obtain a cheap reputation for brilliancy, independence of thought, and courage, by deriding the fear of the supernatural when comfortably seated in a drawing-room well lighted, and with company. But put those scoffers in a like situation with mine, and I don't believe they would have been any more free from a feeling the reverse of bold, mocking, and comfortable, than I was.

I had read that most powerful ghost-story, 'The Haunted and the Haunters,' by the late Lord Lytton, and the vividness of that weird tale had always impressed me greatly. Was I actually now to experience in my own person, and with no possibility of escape, the trying ordeal that bold ghost-hunter went through, under much more favourable circumstances? He at least had his servant with him. He had fuel and a light, and above all, he could get away when he wanted to. I felt I could face any number of spiritual manifestations, if only I had warmth and light. But the icy coldness of the air was eating into my bones, and I shivered until my teeth chattered.

I could not get to sleep. I could not prevent myself listening, and at last I gave up the contest, and let myself listen. But there seemed now nothing to listen to. All the time I had been refusing to let my ears do their office, by putting my handkerchief over one ear, and lying on my arm with the other, a confused noise appeared to reach me, but the moment I turned round and lay on my back, everything seemed quiet. 'It's only my fancy after all; the result of cold and want of a good dinner. I will go to sleep.' But in spite of this I lay still, listening a little longer. There was the sound of trickling water against the broad bilge of the old hulk, and I knew the tide was rising fast:

my thoughts turned to the lost canoe, and to reproaching myself
with my stupidity in not allowing enough rope, or looking at it more
carefully. Suddenly I became all attention again. An entirely different
sound now arrested me. It was distinctly a low groan, and followed
almost immediately by heavy blows—blows which fell on a soft
substance, and then more groans, and again those sickening blows.

'There must be men here. Where are they? And what is it?' I sat
up, and strained my eyes towards where the sound came from. The
sounds had ceased again. Should I call out, and let the man or men
know that I was here? What puzzled me was the absolute darkness.
How could any one see to hit an object, or do anything else in this
dense obscurity? It appalled me. Anything might pass at an inch's
distance, and I could not tell who or what it was. But how could
anything human find its way about, any more than I could? Perhaps
there was a solid bulkhead dividing the forecastle from me. But it
would have to be very sound, and with no chink whatever, to prevent
a gleam or ray of light finding its way out somewhere. I could not
help feeling convinced that the whole hull was open from one end
to the other. Was I really dreaming after all? To convince myself that
I was wide awake, I felt in my pockets for my note-book, and pulling
out my pencil, I opened the book, and holding it in my left hand,
wrote as well as I could, by feel alone: 'I am wide awake; it is about
midnight—Christmas eve, 187—.' I found I had got to the bottom
of the page, so I shut the book up, resolving to look at it the next
morning. I felt curious to see what the writing looked like by daylight.

But all further speculation was cut short by the shuffling and
dragging noise beginning again. There was no doubt the sounds
were louder, and were coming my way.

I never in all my life felt so uncomfortable—I may as well at
once confess it—so frightened. There, in that empty hull, over that

boardless floor, over these rotting joists, somebody or something was dragging some heavy weight. What, I could form no conjecture; only the shrieks, the blows, the groans, the dull thumping sounds, compelled me to suspect the worst,—to feel convinced that I was actually within some few feet of a horrible murder then being committed. I could form no idea of who the victim was, or who was the assassin. That I actually heard the sounds I had no doubt; that they were growing louder and more distinct I felt painfully aware. The horror of the situation was intense. If only I could strike a light, and see what was passing close there—but I had no matches. I could hear a sound as of some one breathing slowly, stertorously, then a dull groan. And once more the cruel sodden blows fell again, followed by a drip, drip, and heavy drop in the dank water below, from which the sickening smell rose, pungent, reeking, horrible.

The dragging shuffling noise now began again. It came quite close to me, so close that I felt I had only to put out my hand to touch the thing. Good heavens! was it coming to my bunk? The thing passed, and all the time the dull drip, as of some heavy drops, fell into the water below. It was awful. All this time I was sitting up, and holding my gun by its barrel, ready to use it if I were attacked. As the sound passed me at the closest, I put out the gun involuntarily; but it touched nothing, and I shuddered at the thought that *there was no floor over which the weight could be drawn.*

I must be dreaming some terribly vivid dream. It could not be real. I pinched myself. I felt I was pinching myself. It was no dream. The sweat poured off my brow, my teeth chattered with the cold. It was terrific in its dreadful mystery.

And now the sounds altered. The noises had reached the companion ladder. Something was climbing them with difficulty. The old stairs creaked. Bump, thump, the thing was dragged up the steps with many pauses, and at last it seemed to have reached the deck. A long pause now followed. The silence grew dense around. I dreaded the stillness—the silence that made itself be heard almost more than the sounds. What new horror would that awful quiet bring forth? What terror was still brooding in the depths of that clinging darkness—darkness that could be felt?

The absolute silence was broken,—horribly broken,—by a dull drip from the stairs, and then the dragging began again. Distant and less distinct, but the steps were louder. They came nearer—over my head—the old boards creaked, and the weight was dragged right over me. I could hear it above my head: for the steps stopped, and two distinct raps, followed by a third heavier one, sounded so clearly above me, that it seemed almost as if it was something striking the rotten woodwork of the berth over my head. The sounds were horribly suggestive of the elbows and head of a body being dropped on the deck.

And now, as if the horrors had not been enough, a fresh ghastliness was added. So close were the raps above me that I involuntarily moved, as if I had been struck by what caused them. As I did so, I felt something drop on to my head and slowly trickle over my forehead: it was too horrible! I sprang up in my disgust, and with a wild cry I stepped forward, and instantly fell between the joists into the rank water below.

The shock was acute. Had I been asleep and dreaming before, this must inevitably have roused me up. I found myself completely immersed in water, and, for a moment, was absolutely incapable of thinking. As it was pitch-dark and my head had gone under, I could not tell whether I was above water or not, as I felt the bottom and struggled and splashed on to my legs. It was only by degrees I knew I must be standing with my head out of the foul mixture, because

I was able to breathe easily, although the wet running down from my hair dribbled into my mouth as I stood shivering and gasping.

It was astonishing how a physical discomfort overcame a mental terror. Nothing could be more miserable than my present position, and my efforts were at once directed to getting out of this dreadful place. But let any one who has ever had the ill-luck to fall out of bed in his boyhood try and recollect his sensations. The bewildering realisation that he is not in bed, that he does not know where he is, which way to go, or what to do to get back again; everything he touches seems strange, and one piece of furniture much the same as any other. I well remember such an accident, and how, having rolled under the bed before I was wide awake, I could not for the life of me understand why I could not get up, what it was that kept me down. I had not the least idea which way to get out, and kept going round and round in a circle under my bed for a long time, and should probably have been doing it until daylight, had not my sighs and groans awoke my brother, who slept in the same room, and who came to my help.

If, then, one is so utterly at fault in a room every inch of which one knows intimately, how much more hopeless was my position at the bottom of this old vessel, half immersed in water, and totally without any clue which could help me to get out! I had not the least idea which was the ship's stern or which her stem, and every movement I made with my feet only served to unsteady me, as the bottom was all covered with slime, and uneven with the great timbers of the vessel.

My first thought on recovering my wits was to stretch my arms up over my head, and I was relieved to find that I could easily reach the joists above me. I was always fairly good at gymnastics, and I had not much difficulty in drawing myself up and sitting on the joist, although the weight of my wet clothes added to my exertions considerably. Having so far succeeded, I sat and drained, as it were, into the water below. The smell was abominable. I never disliked myself so much, and I shivered with cold.

As I could not get any wetter, I determined to go on deck somehow, but where was the companion ladder? I had nothing to guide me. Strange to say, the reality of my struggles had almost made me forget the mysterious phenomena I had been listening to. But now, as I looked round, my attention was caught by a luminous patch which quivered and flickered on my right, at what distance from me I could not tell. It was like the light from a glow-worm, only larger and changing in shape; sometimes elongated like a lambent oval, and then it would sway one way or another, as if caught in a draught of air. While I was looking at it and wondering what could cause it, I heard the steps over my head; they passed above me, and then seemed to grow louder on my left. A creeping dread again came over me. If only I could get out of this horrible place—but where were the stairs? I listened. The footfall seemed to be coming down some steps; then the companion ladder must be on my left. But if I moved that way I should meet the thing, whatever it was, that was coming down. I shuddered at the thought. However, I made up my mind. Stretching out my hand very carefully, I felt for the next joist, reached it, and crawled across. I stopped to listen. The steps were coming nearer. My hearing had now become acute; I could almost tell the exact place of each footfall. It came closer—closer,—quite close, surely—on the very joist on which I was sitting. I thought I could feel the joist quiver, and involuntarily moved my hand to prevent the heavy tread falling on it. The steps passed on, grew fainter, and ceased, as they drew near the pale lambent light. One thing I noticed with curious horror, and that was, that although the thing must have passed between me and the light, yet it was never for a moment obscured, which it must have been had any body or substance passed between, and yet I was certain that the steps went directly from me to it.

It was all horribly mysterious; and what had become of the other sound—the thing that was being dragged? An irresistible shudder passed over me; but I determined to pursue my way until I came to something. It would never do to sit still and shiver there.

After many narrow escapes of falling again, I reached a bulkhead, and cautiously feeling along it, I came to an opening. It was the companion ladder. By this time my hands, by feeling over the joists, had become dry again. I felt along the step to be quite sure that it was the stairs, and in so doing I touched something wet, sticky, clammy. Oh, horror! what was it? A cold shiver shook me nearly off the joist, and I felt an unutterable sense of repulsion to going on. However, the fresher air which came down the companion revived me, and, conquering my dread, I clambered on to the step. It did not take long to get up-stairs and stand on the deck again.

I think I never in all my life experienced such a sense of joy as I did on being out of that disgusting hole. It was true I was soaking wet, and the night wind cut through me like a knife; but these were things I could understand, and were matter of common experience. What I had gone through might only be a question of nerves, and had no tangible or visible terror; but it was none the less very dreadful, and I would not go through such an experience again for worlds. As I stood cowering under the lee of the bulwark, I looked round at the sky. There was a pale light as if of daybreak away in the east, and it seemed as if all my troubles would be over with the dawn. It was bitterly cold. The wind had got round to the north, and I could faintly make out the low shore astern.

While I stood shivering there, a cry came down the wind. At first I thought it was a sea-bird, but it sounded again. I felt sure it was a human voice. I sprang up on to the taffrail, and shouted at the top of my lungs, then paused. The cry came down clearer and distinct. It was Jones's voice—had he heard me? I waved my draggled pocket-handkerchief and shouted again. In the silence which followed, I caught the words, 'We are coming.' What joyful words! Never did a shipwrecked mariner on a lonely isle feel greater delight. My misery would soon be over. Anyhow, I should not have to wait long.

Unfortunately the tide was low, and was still falling. Nothing but a boat could reach me, I thought, and to get a boat would take some time. I therefore stamped up and down the deck to get warm; but I had an instinctive aversion for the companion ladder, and the deep shadows of the forepart of the vessel.

As I turned round in my walk, I thought I saw something moving over the mud. I stopped. It was undoubtedly a figure coming towards me. A voice hailed me in gruff accents—

'Lily, ahoy! Be any one aboard?'

Was any one aboard? What an absurd question! and here had I been shouting myself hoarse. However, I quickly reassured him, and then understood why my rescuer did not sink in the soft mud. He had mud-pattens on. Coming up as close as he could, he shouted to me to keep clear, and then threw first one, then the other, clattering wooden board on to the deck. I found them, and under the instructions of my friend, I did not take long in putting them on. The man was giving me directions as to how to manage; but I did not care how much wetter I got, and dropped over the side into the slime. Sliding and straddling, I managed to get up to my friend, and then together we skated, as it were, to the shore—although skating very little represents the awkward splashes and slips I made on my way to land. I found quite a little crowd awaiting me on the bank; but

Jones, with ready consideration, hurried me off to a cart he had in a lane near, and drove me home.

I told him the chief points of the adventure on our way; but did not say anything of the curious noises. It is odd how shy a man feels at telling what he knows people will never believe. It was not until the evening of the next day that I began to tell him, and then only after I was fortified by an excellent dinner, and some very good claret. Jones listened attentively. He was far too kindly and well-bred to laugh at me; but I could see he did not believe one word as to the reality of the occurrence. 'Very strange!' 'How remarkable!' 'Quite extraordinary!' he kept saying, with evident interest. But I was sure he put it all down to my fatigue and disordered imagination. And so, to do him justice, has everybody else to whom I have told the tale since.

The fact is, we cannot, in this prosaic age, believe in anything the least approaching the supernatural. Nor do I. But nevertheless I am as certain as I am that I am writing these words, that the thing did really happen, and will happen again, may happen every night for all I know, only I don't intend to try and put my belief to the test. I have a theory which of course will be laughed at, and as I am not in the least scientific, I cannot bolster it up by scientific arguments. It is this: As Mr. Edison has now discovered that by certain simple processes human sounds can be reproduced at any future date, so accidentally, and owing to the combination of most curious coincidences, it might happen that the agonised cries of some suffering being, or the sounds made by one at a time when all other emotions are as nothing compared to the supreme sensations of one committing some awful crime, could be impressed on the atmosphere or surface of an enclosed building, which could be reproduced by a current of air passing into that building under the same atmospheric conditions. This is the vague explanation I have given to myself.

However, be the explanation what it may, the facts are as I have stated them. Let those laugh who did not experience them. To return to the end of the story. There were two things I pointed out to Jones as conclusive that I was not dreaming. One was my pocket-book. I showed it him, and the words were quite clear—only, of course, very straggling. This is a facsimile of the writing, but I cannot account for the date being 1837—

I am to be awake it is about midnight Christmas Eve 1857

The other point was the horrible stains on my hands and clothes. A foul-smelling dark chocolate stain was on my hair, hands, and clothes. Jones said, of course, this was from the rust off the mouldering iron-work, some of which no doubt had trickled down, owing to the heavy rain, through the defective caulking of the deck. The fact is, there is nothing that an ingenious mind cannot explain; but the question is, Is the explanation the right one?

I could easily account for the phosphorescent light. The water was foul and stagnant, and it was no doubt caused by the same gases which produce the well-known ignis-fatuus or Will-o'-the-wisp.

We visited the ship, and I recovered my gun. There were the same stains on the deck as there were on my clothes; and curiously enough they went in a nearly straight line over the place where I lay, from the top of the companion to the starboard bulwark. We carefully examined the forepart of the ship: it was as completely gutted as the rest of her. Jones was glad to get on deck again, as the atmosphere was very unpleasant, and I had no wish to stay.

At my request Jones made every inquiry he could about the old hulk. Not much was elicited. It bore an evil name, and no one would go on board who could help it. So far it looked as if it were credited with being haunted. The owner, who had been the captain of her, had died about three years before. He bore an ill reputation; but as he had left his money to the most influential farmer in the district, the country-people were unwilling to talk against him.

I went with Jones to call on the farmer, and asked him point-blank if he had ever heard whether a murder had been committed on board the Lily. He stared at me, and then laughed. 'Not as I know of' was all his answer—and I never got any nearer than that.

I feel that this is all very unsatisfactory. I wish I could give some thrilling and sensational explanation. I am sorry I cannot. My imagination suggests many, as no doubt it will to each of my readers who possesses that faculty; but I have only written this to tell the actual facts, not to add to our superabundant fiction.

If ever I come across any details bearing upon the subject, I will not fail to communicate them at once.

The vessel I found was the Lily of Goole, owned by one Master Gad Earwaker, and built in 1801.

THE CHRISTMAS SHADRACH

Frank R. Stockton

First published in *The Century*, December 1891

Frank Richard Stockton (1834–1902) was born in Philadelphia, Pennsylvania, the son of a Methodist minister. He trained as a wood-engraver but became a hugely successful writer of novels and magazine fiction in the last two decades of his life. He is sometimes called America's first writer of science fiction, and was as well-known as his contemporary Mark Twain during their lifetimes. He struggled with his success, evidently feeling that the popular fiction he churned out for American magazines, despite providing him with financial stability, didn't allow him full creative independence. This story is supernatural rather than ghostly, and very enjoyable.

WHENEVER I MAKE A CHRISTMAS PRESENT I LIKE IT TO MEAN something, not necessarily my sentiments toward the person to whom I give it, but sometimes an expression of what I should like that person to do or to be. In the early part of a certain winter not very long ago I found myself in a position of perplexity and anxious concern regarding a Christmas present which I wished to make.

The state of the case was this. There was a young lady, the daughter of a neighbour and old friend of my father, who had been gradually assuming relations toward me which were not only unsatisfactory to me, but were becoming more and more so. Her name was Mildred Bronce. She was between twenty and twenty-five years of age, and as fine a woman in every way as one would be likely to meet in a lifetime. She was handsome, of a tender and generous disposition, a fine intelligence, and a thoroughly well-stocked mind. We had known each other for a long time, and when fourteen or fifteen Mildred had been my favourite companion. She was a little younger than I, and I liked her better than any boy I knew. Our friendship had continued through the years, but of late there had been a change in it; Mildred had become very fond of me, and her fondness seemed to have in it certain elements which annoyed me.

As a girl to make love to no one could be better than Mildred Bronce; but I had never made love to her,—at least not earnestly,— and I did not wish that any permanent condition of loving should be established between us. Mildred did not seem to share this opinion, for every day it became plainer to me that she looked upon me as a lover, and that she was perfectly willing to return my affection.

But I had other ideas upon the subject. Into the rural town in which my family passed the greater part of the year there had recently come a young lady, Miss Janet Clinton, to whom my soul went out of my own option. In some respects, perhaps, she was not the equal of Mildred, but she was very pretty, she was small, she had a lovely mouth, was apparently of a clinging nature, and her dark eyes looked into mine with a tingling effect that no other eyes had ever produced. I was in love with her because I wished to be, and the consciousness of this fact caused me a proud satisfaction. This affair was not the result of circumstances, but of my own free will.

I wished to retain Mildred's friendship, I wished to make her happy; and with this latter intent in view I wished very much that she should not disappoint herself in her anticipations of the future.

Each year it had been my habit to make Mildred a Christmas present, and I was now looking for something to give her which would please her and suit my purpose.

When a man wishes to select a present for a lady which, while it assures her of his kind feeling toward her, will at the same time indicate that not only has he no matrimonial inclinations in her direction, but that it would be entirely unwise for her to have any such inclinations in his direction; that no matter with what degree of fondness her heart is disposed to turn toward him, his heart does not turn toward her, and that, in spite of all sentiments induced by long association and the natural fitness of things, she need never expect to be to him anything more than a sister, he has, indeed, a difficult task before him. But such was the task which I set for myself.

Day after day I wandered through the shops. I looked at odd pieces of jewellery and bric-à-brac, and at many a quaint relic or bit of art work which seemed to have a meaning, but nothing had the meaning I wanted. As to books, I found none which satisfied me; not one which was adapted to produce the exact impression that I desired.

One afternoon I was in a little basement shop kept by a fellow in a long overcoat, who, so far as I was able to judge, bought curiosities but never sold any. For some minutes I had been looking at a beautifully decorated saucer of rare workmanship for which there was no cup to match, and for which the proprietor informed me no cup could now be found or manufactured. There were some points in the significance of an article of this sort, given as a present to a lady, which fitted to my purpose, but it would signify too much: I did not wish to suggest to Mildred that she need never expect to find a cup. It would be better, in fact, if I gave her anything of this kind, to send her a cup and saucer entirely unsuited to each other, and which could not, under any conditions, be used together.

I put down the saucer, and continued my search among the dusty shelves and cases.

'How would you like a paper-weight?' the shopkeeper asked. 'Here is something a little odd,' handing me a piece of dark-coloured mineral nearly as big as my fist, flat on the under side and of a pleasing irregularity above. Around the bottom was a band of arabesque work in some dingy metal, probably German silver. I smiled as I took it.

'This is not good enough for a Christmas present,' I said. 'I want something odd, but it must have some value.'

'Well,' said the man, 'that has no real value, but there is a peculiarity about it which interested me when I heard of it, and so I bought it. This mineral is a piece of what the iron-workers call shadrach. It is a portion of the iron or iron ore which passes through the smelting-furnaces without being affected by the great heat, and so they have given it the name of one of the Hebrew youths who was cast into the fiery furnace by Nebuchadnezzar, and who came out unhurt. Some people think there is a sort of magical quality about this shadrach, and that it can give out to human beings something of its power to keep their minds cool when they are in danger of being overheated. The old gentleman who had this made was subject to fits of anger, and he thought this piece of shadrach helped to keep him from giving way to them. Occasionally he used to leave it in the house of a hot-tempered neighbour, believing that the testy individual would be cooled down for a time, without knowing how the change had been brought about. I bought a lot of things of the old gentleman's widow, and this among them. I thought I might try it some time, but I never have.'

I held the shadrach in my hand, ideas concerning it rapidly flitting through my mind. Why would not this be a capital thing to give to Mildred? If it should, indeed, possess the quality ascribed to it; if it should be able to cool her liking for me, what better present could I give her? I did not hesitate long.

'I will buy this,' I said; 'but the ornamentation must be of a better sort. It is now too cheap and tawdry-looking.'

'I can attend to that for you,' said the shopkeeper. 'I can have it set in a band of gold or silver filigree-work like this, if you choose.'

I agreed to this proposition, but ordered the band to be made of silver, the cool tone of that metal being more appropriate to the characteristics of the gift than the warmer hues of gold.

When I gave my Christmas present to Mildred she was pleased with it; its oddity struck her fancy.

'I don't believe anybody ever had such a paper-weight as that,' she said, as she thanked me. 'What is it made of?'

I told her, and explained what shadrach was; but I did not speak of its presumed influence over human beings, which, after all, might be nothing but the wildest fancy. I did not feel altogether at my ease, as I added that it was merely a trifle, a thing of no value except as a reminder of the season.

'The fact that it is a present from you gives it value,' she said, as she smilingly raised her eyes to mine.

I left her house—we were all living in the city then—with a troubled conscience. What a deception I was practising upon this noble girl, who, if she did not already love me, was plainly on the point of doing so. She had received my present as if it indicated a warmth of feeling on my part, when, in fact, it was the result of a desire for a cooler feeling on her part.

But I called my reason to my aid, and I showed myself that what I had given Mildred—if it should prove to possess any virtue at all—was, indeed, a most valuable boon. It was something which would prevent the waste of her affections, the wreck of her hopes. No kindness could be truer, no regard for her happiness more sincere, than the motives which prompted me to give her the shadrach.

I did not soon again see Mildred, but now as often as possible I visited Janet. She always received me with a charming cordiality, and if this should develop into warmer sentiments I was not the man to wish to cool them. In many ways Janet seemed much better suited to me than Mildred. One of the greatest charms of this beautiful girl was a tender trustfulness, as if I were a being on whom she could lean and to whom she could look up. I liked this; it was very different from Mildred's manner: with the latter I had always been well satisfied if I felt myself standing on the same plane.

The weeks and months passed on, and again we were all in the country; and here I saw Mildred often. Our homes were not far apart, and our families were very intimate. With my opportunities for frequent observation I could not doubt that a change had come over her. She was always friendly when we met, and seemed as glad to see me as she was to see any other member of my family, but she was not the Mildred I used to know. It was plain that my exist-ence did not make the same impression on her that it once made. She did not seem to consider it important whether I came or went; whether I was in the room or not; whether I joined a party or stayed away. All this had been very different. I knew well that Mildred had been used to consider my presence as a matter of much impor-tance, and I now felt sure that my Christmas shadrach was doing its work. Mildred was cooling toward me. Her affection, or, to put it more modestly, her tendency to affection, was gently congealing into friendship. This was highly gratifying to my moral nature, for every day I was doing my best to warm the soul of Janet. Whether or not I succeeded in this I could not be sure. Janet was as tender and trustful and charming as ever, but no more so than she had been months before.

Sometimes I thought she was waiting for an indication of an increased warmth of feeling on my part before she allowed the temperature of her own sentiments to rise. But for one reason and another I delayed the solution of this problem. Janet was very fond of company, and although we saw a great deal of each other, we were not often alone. If we two had more frequently walked, driven, or rowed together, as Mildred and I used to do, I think Miss Clinton would soon have had every opportunity of making up her mind about the fervour of my passion.

The summer weeks passed on, and there was no change in the things which now principally concerned me, except that Mildred seemed to be growing more and more indifferent to me. From having seemed to care no more for me than for her other friends, she now seemed to care less for me than for most people. I do not mean that she showed a dislike, but she treated me with a sort of indifference which I did not fancy at all. This sort of thing had gone too far, and there was no knowing how much further it would go. It was plain enough that the shadrach was overdoing the business.

I was now in a state of much mental disquietude. Greatly as I desired to win the love of Janet, it grieved me to think of losing the generous friendship of Mildred—that friendship to which I had been accustomed for the greater part of my life, and on which, as I now discovered, I had grown to depend.

In this state of mind I went to see Mildred. I found her in the library writing. She received me pleasantly, and was sorry her father was not at home, and begged that I would excuse her finishing the note on which she was engaged, because she wished to get it into the post-office before the mail closed. I sat down on the other side of the table, and she finished her note, after which she went out to give it to a servant.

Glancing about me, I saw the shadrach. It was partly under a litter of papers, instead of lying on them. I took it up, and was looking at it when Mildred returned. She sat down and asked me if I had heard of the changes that were to be made in the time-table of the railroad. We talked a little on the subject, and then I spoke of the shadrach, saying carelessly that it might be interesting to analyse the bit of metal; there was a little knob which might be filed off without injuring it in the least.

'You may take it,' she said, 'and make what experiments you please. I do not use it much; it is unnecessarily heavy for a paper-weight.'

From her tone I might have supposed that she had forgotten that I had given it to her. I told her that I would be very glad to borrow the paper-weight for a time, and, putting it into my pocket, I went away, leaving her arranging her disordered papers on the table, and giving quite as much regard to this occupation as she had given to my little visit.

I could not feel sure that the absence of the shadrach would cause any diminution in the coolness of her feelings toward me, but there was reason to believe that it would prevent them from growing cooler. If she should keep that shadrach she might in time grow to hate me. I was very glad that I had taken it from her.

My mind easier on this subject, my heart turned more freely toward Janet, and, going to her house, the next day I was delighted to find her alone. She was as lovely as ever, and as cordial, but she was flushed and evidently annoyed.

'I am in a bad humour today,' she said, 'and I am glad you came to talk to me and quiet me. Dr. Gilbert promised to take me to drive this afternoon, and we were going over to the hills where they find the wild rhododendron. I am told that it is still in blossom up there, and I want some flowers ever so much—I am going to paint them. And besides, I am crazy to drive with his new horses; and now he sends me a note to say that he is engaged.'

This communication shocked me, and I began to talk to her about Dr. Gilbert. I soon found that several times she had been driving with this handsome young physician, but never, she said, behind his new horses, nor to the rhododendron hills.

Dr. Hector Gilbert was a fine young fellow, beginning practice in town, and one of my favourite associates. I had never thought of him in connection with Janet, but I could now see that he might make a most dangerous rival. When a young and talented doctor, enthusiastic in his studies, and earnestly desirous of establishing a practice, and who, if his time were not fully occupied, would naturally wish that the neighbours would think that such were the case, deliberately devotes some hours on I know not how many days to driving a young lady into the surrounding country, it may be supposed that he is really in love with her. Moreover, judging from Janet's present mood, this doctor's attentions were not without encouragement.

I went home; I considered the state of affairs; I ran my fingers through my hair; I gazed steadfastly upon the floor. Suddenly I rose. I had had an inspiration; I would give the shadrach to Dr. Gilbert.

I went immediately to the doctor's office, and found him there. He too was not in a very good humour.

'I have had two old ladies here nearly all the afternoon, and they have bored me to death,' he said. 'I could not get rid of them because I found they had made an appointment with each other to visit me today and talk over a hospital plan which I proposed some time ago and which is really very important to me, but I wish they had chosen some other time to come here. What is that thing?'

'That is a bit of shadrach,' I said, 'made into a paper-weight.' And then I proceeded to explain what shadrach is, and what peculiar properties it must possess to resist the power of heat, which melts other metal apparently of the same class; and I added that I thought it might be interesting to analyse a bit of it and discover what fire-proof constituents it possessed.

'I should like to do that,' said the doctor, attentively turning over the shadrach in his hand. 'Can I take off a piece of it?'

'I will give it to you,' said I, 'and you can make what use of it you please. If you do analyse it I shall be very glad indeed to hear the results of your investigations.'

The doctor demurred a little at taking the paper-weight with such a pretty silver ring around it, but I assured him that the cost of the whole affair was trifling, and I should be gratified if he would take it. He accepted the gift, and was thanking me, when a patient arrived, and I departed.

I really had no right to give away this paper-weight, which, in fact, belonged to Mildred, but there are times when a man must keep his eyes on the chief good, and not think too much about other things. Besides, it was evident that Mildred did not care in the least for the bit of metal, and she had virtually given it to me.

There was another point which I took into consideration. It might be that the shadrach might simply cool Dr. Gilbert's feelings toward me, and that would be neither pleasant nor advantageous. If I could have managed matters so that Janet could have given it to him, it would have been all right. But now all that I could do was to wait and see what would happen. If only the thing would cool the doctor in a general way, that would help. He might then give more thought to his practice and his hospital ladies, and let other people take Janet driving.

About a week after this I met the doctor; he seemed in a hurry, but I stopped him. I had a curiosity to know if he had analysed the shadrach, and asked him about it.

'No,' said he; 'I haven't done it. I haven't had time. I knocked off a piece of it, and I will attend to it when I get a chance. Good day.'

Of course if the man was busy he could not be expected to give his mind to a trifling matter of that sort, but I thought that he need not have been so curt about it. I stood gazing after him as he walked rapidly down the street. Before I resumed my walk I saw him enter the Clinton house. Things were not going on well. The shadrach had not cooled Dr. Gilbert's feelings toward Janet.

But because the doctor was still warm in his attentions to the girl I loved, I would not in the least relax my attentions to her. I visited her as often as I could find an excuse to do so. There was generally some one else there, but Janet's disposition was of such gracious expansiveness that each one felt obliged to be satisfied with what he got, much as he may have wished for something different.

But one morning Janet surprised me. I met her at Mildred's house, where I had gone to borrow a book of reference. Although I had urged her not to put herself to so much trouble, Mildred was standing on a little ladder looking for the book, because, she said, she knew exactly what I wanted, and she was sure she could find the proper volume better than I could. Janet had been sitting in a window-seat reading, but when I came in she put down her book and devoted herself to conversation with me. I was a little sorry for this, because Mildred was very kindly engaged in doing me a service, and I really wanted to talk to her about the book she was looking for. Mildred showed so much of her old manner this morning that I would have been very sorry to have her think that I did not appreciate her returning interest in me. Therefore, while under other circumstances I would have been delighted to talk to Janet, I did not wish to give her so much of my attention then. But Janet Clinton was a girl who insisted on people attending to her when she wished them to do so, and, having stepped through an open door into the garden, she presently called me to her. Of course I had to go.

'I will not keep you a minute from your fellow student,' she said, 'but I want to ask a favour of you.' And into her dark, uplifted eyes there came a look of tender trustfulness clearer than any I had yet seen there. 'Don't *you* want to drive me to the rhododendron hills?' she said. 'I suppose the flowers are all gone by this time, but I have never been there, and I should like ever so much to go.'

I could not help remarking that I thought Dr. Gilbert was going to take her there.

'Dr. Gilbert, indeed!' she said with a little laugh. 'He promised once, and didn't come, and the next day he planned for it it rained. I don't think doctors make very good escorts, anyway, for you can't tell who is going to be sick just as you are about to start on a trip. Besides there is no knowing how much botany I should have to hear, and when I go on a pleasure-drive I don't care very much about studying things. But of course I don't want to trouble you.'

'Trouble!' I exclaimed. 'It will give me the greatest delight to take you that drive or any other, and at whatever time you please.'

'You are always so good and kind,' she said, with her dark eyes again upraised. 'And now let us go in and see if Mildred has found the book.'

I spoke the truth when I said that Janet's proposition delighted me. To take a long drive with that charming girl, and at the same time to feel that she had chosen me as her companion, was a greater joy than I had yet had reason to expect; but it would have been a more satisfying joy if she had asked me in her own house and not in Mildred's; if she had not allowed the love which I hoped was growing up between her and me to interfere with the revival of the old friendship between Mildred and me.

But when we returned to the library Mildred was sitting at a table with a book before her, opened at the passage I wanted.

'I have just found it,' she said with a smile. 'Draw up a chair, and we will look over these maps together. I want you to show me how he travelled when he left his ship.'

'Well, if you two are going to the pole,' said Janet, with her prettiest smile, 'I will go back to my novel.'

She did not seem in the least to object to my geographical researches with Mildred, and if the latter had even noticed my willingness to desert her at the call of Janet, she did not show it. Apparently she was as much a good comrade as she had ever been. This state of things was gratifying in the highest degree. If I could be loved by Janet and still keep Mildred as my friend, what greater earthly joys could I ask?

The drive with Janet was postponed by wet weather. Day after day it rained, or the skies were heavy, and we both agreed that it must be in the bright sunshine that we would make this excursion. When we should make it, and should be alone together on the rhododendron hill, I intended to open my soul to Janet.

It may seem strange to others, and at the time it also seemed strange to me, but there was another reason besides the rainy weather which prevented my declaration of love to Janet. This was a certain nervous anxiety in regard to my friendship for Mildred. I did not in the least waver in my intention to use the best endeavours to make the one my wife, but at the same time I was oppressed by a certain alarm that in carrying out this project I might act in such a way as to wound the feelings of the other.

This disposition to consider the feelings of Mildred became so strong that I began to think that my own sentiments were in need of control. It was not right that while making love to one woman I should give so much consideration to my relations with another. The idea struck me that in a measure I had shared the fate of those who had thrown the Hebrew youths into the fiery furnace. My heart had not been consumed by the flames, but in throwing the shadrach into what I supposed were Mildred's affections it was quite possible that I had been singed by them. At any rate my conscience told me that under the circumstances my sentiments toward Mildred were too warm; in honestly making love to Janet I ought to forget them entirely.

It might have been a good thing, I told myself, if I had not given away the shadrach, but kept it as a gift from Mildred. Very soon after I reached this conclusion it became evident to me that Mildred was again cooling in my direction as rapidly as the mercury falls after sunset on a September day. This discovery did not make my mercury fall; in fact, it brought it for a time nearly to the boiling-point. I could not imagine what had happened. I almost neglected Janet, so anxious was I to know what had made this change in Mildred.

Weeks passed on, and I discovered nothing, except that Mildred had now become more than indifferent to me. She allowed me to see that my companionship did not give her pleasure.

Janet had her drive to the rhododendron hills, but she took it with Dr. Gilbert and not with me. When I heard of this it pained me, though I could not help admitting that I deserved the punishment; but my surprise was almost as great as my pain, for Janet had recently given me reason to believe that she had a very small opinion of the young doctor. In fact, she had criticised him so severely that I had been obliged to speak in his defence. I now found myself in a most doleful quandary, and there was only one thing of which I could be certain—I needed cooling toward Mildred if I still allowed myself to hope to marry Janet.

One afternoon I was talking to Mr. Bronce in his library, when, glancing toward the table used by his daughter for writing purposes, I was astounded to see, lying on a little pile of letters, the Christmas shadrach. As soon as I could get an opportunity I took it in my hand and eagerly examined it. I had not been mistaken. It was the paper-weight I had given Mildred. There was the silver band around it, and there was the place where a little piece had been knocked off by the doctor. Mildred was not at home, but I determined that I would wait and see her. I would dine with the Bronces; I would spend the evening; I would stay all night; I would not leave the house until I had had this mystery explained. She returned in about half an hour and greeted me in the somewhat stiff manner she had adopted of late; but when she noticed my perturbed expression and saw that I held the shadrach in my hand, she took a seat by the table, where for some time I had been waiting for her, alone.

'I suppose you want to ask me about that paper-weight,' she remarked.

'Indeed I do,' I replied. 'How in the world did you happen to get it again?'

'Again?' she repeated satirically. 'You may well say that. I will explain it to you. Some little time ago I called on Janet Clinton, and on her writing-desk I saw that paper-weight. I remembered it perfectly. It was the one you gave me last Christmas and afterward borrowed off me, saying that you wanted to analyse it, or something of the sort. I had never used it very much, and of course was willing that you should take it, and make experiments with it if you wanted to, but I must say that the sight of it on Janet Clinton's desk both shocked and angered me. I asked her where she got it, and she told me a gentleman had given it to her. I did not need to waste any words in inquiring who this gentleman was, but I determined that she should not rest under a mistake in regard to its proper ownership, and told her plainly that the person who had given it to her had previously given it to me; that it was mine, and he had no right to give it to any one else. "Oh, if that is the case," she exclaimed, "take it, I beg of you. I don't care for it, and, what is more, I don't care any more for the man who gave it to me than I do for the thing itself." So I took it and brought it home with me. Now you know how I happened to have it again.'

For a moment I made no answer. Then I asked her how long it had been since she had received the shadrach from Janet Clinton.

'Oh, I don't remember exactly,' she said; 'it was several weeks ago.'

Now I knew everything; all the mysteries of the past were revealed to me. The young doctor, fervid in his desire to please the woman he loved, had given Janet this novel paper-weight. From that moment she had begun to regard his attentions with apathy, and finally—her nature was one which was apt to go to extremes—to dislike him. Mildred repossessed herself of the shadrach, which she took, not as a gift from Janet, but as her rightful property, presented to her by me. And this horrid little object, probably with renewed power, had cooled, almost frozen indeed, the sentiments of that dear girl toward me. Then, too, had the spell been taken from Janet's inclinations, and she had gone to the rhododendron hills with Dr. Gilbert.

One thing was certain. *I* must have that shadrach.

'Mildred,' I exclaimed, 'will you not give me this paper-weight? Give it to me for my own?'

'What do you want to do with it?' she asked sarcastically. 'Analyse it again?'

'Mildred,' said I, 'I did not give it to Janet. I gave it to Dr. Gilbert, and he must have given it to her. I know I had no right to give it away at all, but I did not believe that you would care; but now I beg that you will let me have it. Let me have it for my own. I assure you solemnly I will never give it away. It has caused trouble enough already.'

'I don't exactly understand what you mean by trouble,' she said, 'but take it if you want it. You are perfectly welcome.' And picking up her gloves and hat from the table she left me.

As I walked home my hatred of the wretched piece of metal in my hand increased with every step. I looked at it with disgust when I went to bed that night, and when my glance lighted upon it the next morning I involuntarily shrank from it, as if it had been an evil thing. Over and over again that day I asked myself why I should keep in my possession something which would make my regard for Mildred grow less and less; which would eventually make me care for her not at all? The very thought of not caring for Mildred sent a pang through my heart.

My feelings all prompted me to rid myself of what I looked upon as a calamitous talisman, but my reason interfered. If I still wished to marry Janet it was my duty to welcome indifference to Mildred.

In this mood I went out, to stroll, to think, to decide; and that I might be ready to act on my decision I put the shadrach into my pocket. Without exactly intending it I walked toward the Bronce place, and soon found myself on the edge of a pretty pond which lay at the foot of the garden. Here, in the shade of a tree, there stood a bench, and on this lay a book, an ivory paper-cutter in its leaves as marker.

I knew that Mildred had left that book on the bench; it was her habit to come to this place to read. As she had not taken the volume with her, it was probable that she intended soon to return. But then the sad thought came to me that if she saw me there she would not return. I picked up the book; I read the pages she had been reading. As I read I felt that I could think the very thoughts that she thought as she read. I was seized with a yearning to be with her, to read with her, to think with her. Never had my soul gone out to Mildred as at that moment, and yet, heavily dangling in my pocket, I carried—I could not bear to think of it. Seized by a sudden impulse, I put down the book; I drew out the shadrach, and, tearing off the silver band, I tossed the vile bit of metal into the pond.

'There!' I cried. 'Go out of my possession, out of my sight! You shall work no charm on me. Let nature take its course, and let things happen as they may.' Then, relieved from the weight on my heart and the weight in my pocket, I went home.

Nature did take its course, and in less than a fortnight from that day the engagement of Janet and Dr. Gilbert was announced. I had done nothing to prevent this, and the news did not disturb my peace of mind; but my relations with Mildred very much disturbed it. I had hoped that, released from the baleful influence of the shadrach, her friendly feelings toward me would return, and my passion for her had now grown so strong that I waited and watched, as a wrecked mariner waits and watches for the sight of a sail, for a sign that she had so far softened toward me that I might dare to speak to her of my love. But no such sign appeared.

I now seldom visited the Bronce house; no one of that family, once my best friends, seemed to care to see me. Evidently Mildred's feelings toward me had extended themselves to the rest of the household. This was not surprising, for her family had long been accustomed to think as Mildred thought.

One day I met Mr. Bronce at the post-office, and, some other gentlemen coming up, we began to talk of a proposed plan to introduce a system of water-works into the village, an improvement much desired by many of us.

'So far as I am concerned,' said Mr. Bronce, 'I am not now in need of anything of the sort. Since I set up my steam-pump I have supplied my house from the pond at the end of my garden with all the water we can possibly want for every purpose.'

'Do you mean,' asked one of the gentlemen, 'that you get your drinking-water in that way?'

'Certainly,' replied Mr. Bronce. 'The basin of the pond is kept as clean and in as good order as any reservoir can be, and the water comes from an excellent, rapid-flowing spring. I want nothing better.'

A chill ran through me as I listened. The shadrach was in that pond. Every drop of water which Mildred drank, which touched her, was influenced by that demoniacal paper-weight, which, without knowing what I was doing, I had thus bestowed upon the whole Bronce family.

When I went home I made diligent search for a stone which might be about the size and weight of the shadrach, and having repaired to a retired spot I practised tossing it as I had tossed the bit of metal into the pond. In each instance I measured the distance which I had thrown the stone, and was at last enabled to make a very fair estimate of the distance to which I had thrown the shadrach when I had buried it under the waters of the pond.

That night there was a half-moon, and between eleven and twelve o'clock, when everybody in our village might be supposed to be in bed and asleep, I made my way over the fields to the back of the Bronce place, taking with me a long fish-cord with a knot in it, showing the average distance to which I had thrown the practice stone. When I reached the pond I stood as nearly as possible in the place by the bench from which I had hurled the shadrach, and to this spot I pegged one end of the cord. I was attired in an old tennis suit, and, having removed my shoes and stockings, I entered the water, holding the roll of cord in my hand. This I slowly unwound as I advanced toward the middle of the pond, and when I reached the knot I stopped, with the water above my waist.

I had found the bottom of the pond very smooth, and free from weeds and mud, and I now began feeling about with my bare feet, as I moved from side to side, describing a small arc; but I discovered nothing more than an occasional pebble no larger than a walnut.

Letting out some more of the cord, I advanced a little farther into the centre of the pond, and slowly described another arc. The water was now nearly up to my armpits, but it was not cold, though if it had been I do not think I should have minded it in the ardour of my search. Suddenly I put my foot on something hard and as big as my fist, but in an instant it moved away from under my foot; it must have been a turtle. This occurrence made me shiver a little, but I did not swerve from my purpose, and, loosing the string a little more, I went farther into the pond. The water was now nearly up to my chin, and there was something weird, mystical, and awe-inspiring in standing thus in the depths of this silent water, my eyes so near its gently rippling surface, fantastically lighted by the setting moon, and tenanted by nobody knew what cold and slippery creatures. But from side to side I slowly moved, reaching out with my feet in every direction, hoping to touch the thing for which I sought.

Suddenly I set my right foot upon something hard and irregular. Nervously I felt it with my toes. I patted it with my bare sole. It was as big as the shadrach! It felt like the shadrach. In a few moments I was almost convinced that the direful paper-weight was beneath my foot.

Closing my eyes, and holding my breath, I stooped down into the water, and groped on the bottom with my hands. In some way I had moved while stooping, and at first I could find nothing. A sensation of dread came over me as I felt myself in the midst of the dark solemn water,—around me, above me, everywhere,—almost suffocated, and apparently deserted even by the shadrach. But just as I felt that I could hold my breath no longer my fingers touched the thing that had been under my foot, and, clutching it, I rose and thrust my head out of the water. I could do nothing until I had taken two or three long breaths; then, holding up the object in my hand to the light of the expiring moon, I saw that it was like the shadrach; so like, indeed, that I felt that it must be it.

Turning, I made my way out of the water as rapidly as possible, and, dropping on my knees on the ground, I tremblingly lighted the lantern which I had left on the bench, and turned its light on the thing I had found. There must be no mistake; if this was not the shadrach I would go in again. But there was no necessity for reentering the pond; it *was* the shadrach.

With the extinguished lantern in one hand and the lump of mineral evil in the other, I hurried home. My wet clothes were sticky and chilly in the night air. Several times in my haste I stumbled over clods and briers, and my shoes, which I had not taken time to tie, flopped up and down as I ran. But I cared for none of these discomforts; the shadrach was in my power.

Crossing a wide field I heard, not far away, the tramping of hoofs, as of a horseman approaching at full speed. I stopped and looked in the direction of the sound. My eyes had now become so accustomed to the dim light that I could distinguish objects somewhat plainly, and I quickly perceived that the animal that was galloping toward me was a bull. I well knew what bull it was; this was Squire Starling's pasture-field, and that was his great Alderney bull, Ramping Sir John of Ramapo II.

I was well acquainted with that bull, renowned throughout the neighbourhood for his savage temper and his noble pedigree—son of Ramping Sir John of Ramapo I., whose sire was the Great Rodolphin, son of Prince Maximus of Granby, one of whose daughters averaged eighteen pounds of butter a week, and who, himself, had killed two men.

The bull, who had not perceived me when I crossed the field before, for I had then made my way with as little noise as possible, was now bent on punishing my intrusion upon his domains, and bellowed as he came on. I was in a position of great danger. With my flopping shoes it was impossible to escape by flight; I must stand and defend myself. I turned and faced the furious creature, who was not twenty feet distant, and then, with all my strength, I hurled the shadrach, which I held in my right hand, directly at his shaggy forehead. My ability to project a missile was considerable, for I had held, with credit, the position of pitcher in a base-ball nine, and as the shadrach struck the bull's head with a great thud he stopped as if he had suddenly run against a wall.

I do not know that actual and violent contact with the physical organism of a recipient accelerates the influence of a shadrach upon the mental organism of said recipient, but I do know that the contact of my projectile with that bull's skull instantly cooled the animal's fury. For a few moments he stood and looked at me, and then his interest in me as a man and trespasser appeared to fade away, and, moving slowly from me, Ramping Sir John of Ramapo II. began to crop the grass.

I did not stop to look for the shadrach; I considered it safely disposed of. So long as Squire Starling used that field for a pasture, connoisseurs in mineral fragments would not be apt to wander through it, and when it should be ploughed, the shadrach, to ordinary eyes no more than a common stone, would be buried beneath the sod. I awoke the next morning refreshed and happy, and none the worse for my wet walk.

'Now,' I said to myself, 'nature shall truly have her own way. If the uncanny comes into my life and that of those I love, it shall not be brought in by me.'

About a week after this I dined with the Bronce family. They were very cordial, and it seemed to me the most natural thing in the world to be sitting at their table. After dinner Mildred and I walked together in the garden. It was a charming evening, and we sat down on the bench by the edge of the pond. I spoke to her of some passages in the book I had once seen there.

'Oh, have you read that?' she asked with interest.

'I have seen only two pages of it,' I said, 'and those I read in the volume you left on this bench, with a paper-cutter in it for a marker. I long to read more and talk with you of what I have read.'

'Why, then, didn't you wait? You might have known that I would come back.'

I did not tell her that I knew that because I was there she would not have come. But before I left the bench I discovered that hereafter, wherever I might be, she was willing to come and to stay.

Early in the next spring Mildred and I were married, and on our wedding-trip we passed through a mining district in the mountains. Here we visited one of the great ironworks, and were both much interested in witnessing the wonderful power of man, air, and fire over the stubborn king of metals.

'What is this substance?' asked Mildred of one of the officials who was conducting us through the works.

'That,' said the man, 'is what we call shad—'

'My dear,' I cried, 'we must hurry away this instant or we shall lose the train. Come; quick; there is not a moment for delay.' And with a word of thanks to the guide I seized her hand and led her, almost running, into the open air.

Mildred was amazed.

'Never before,' she exclaimed, 'have I seen you in such a hurry. I thought the train we decided to take did not leave for at least an hour.'

'I have changed my mind,' I said, 'and think it will be a great deal better for us to take the one which leaves in ten minutes.'

NUMBER NINETY

B. M. Croker

First published in *Chapman's Magazine of Fiction*, December 1895

Bithia Mary Croker (née Sheppard) (*c.*1848–1920) was born in Ireland but lived in India for 14 years, accompanying her husband who was in the army. Whilst there, she started writing to pass the time and eventually became a prolific novelist, writing books often set in India or Ireland. Her first novel, *Proper Pride*, achieved notoriety when the Prime Minister William Ewart Gladstone was spotted reading it.

'To LET FURNISHED, FOR A TERM OF YEARS, AT A VERY LOW rental, a large old-fashioned family residence, comprising eleven bed-rooms, four reception-rooms, dressing-rooms, two staircases, complete servants' offices, ample accommodation for a Gentleman's establishment, including six-stall stable, coach-house, etc.'

The above advertisement referred to number ninety. For a period extending over some years this notice appeared spasmodically in various daily papers. Occasionally you saw it running for a week or a fortnight at a stretch, as if it were resolved to force itself into consideration by sheer persistency. Sometimes for months I looked for it in vain. Other ignorant folk might possibly fancy that the effort of the house agent had been crowned at last with success—that it was let, and no longer in the market.

I knew better. I knew that would never, never find a tenant as long as oak and ash endured. I knew that it was passed on as a hopeless case, from house-agent to house-agent. I knew that it would never be occupied, save by rats—and, more than this, I knew the reason why!

I will not say in what square, street, or road number ninety may be found, nor will I divulge to human being its precise and exact locality, but this I'm prepared to state, that it is positively in existence, is in London, and is still empty.

Twenty years ago, this very Christmas, my friend John Hollyoak (civil engineer) and I were guests at a bachelor's party; partaking, in company with eight other celibates, of a very *recherché* little dinner, in the neighbourhood of Piccadilly. Conversation became very brisk as the champagne circulated, and many topics were started, discussed, and dismissed.

They (I say *they* advisedly, as I myself am a man of few words) talked on an extraordinary variety of subjects.

I distinctly recollect a long argument on mushrooms—mushrooms, murders, racing, cholera; from cholera we came to sudden death, from sudden death to churchyards, and from churchyards, it was naturally but a step to ghosts.

On this last topic the arguments became fast and furious, for the company was divided into two camps. The larger, 'the opposition,' who scoffed, sneered, and snapped their fingers, and laughed with irritating contempt at the very name of ghosts, was headed by John Hollyoak; the smaller party, who were dogged, angry, and prepared to back their opinions to any extent, had for their leader our host, a bald-headed man of business, whom I certainly would have credited (as I mentally remarked) with more sense.

The believers in the supernatural obtained a hearing, so far as to relate one or two blood-curdling, first or second-hand experiences, which, when concluded, instead of being received with an awestruck and respectful silence, were pooh-poohed, with shouts of laughter, and taunting suggestions that were by no means complimentary to the intelligence, or sobriety, of the victims of superstition. Argument and counter-argument waxed louder and hotter, and there was every prospect of a very stormy conclusion to the evening's entertainment.

John Hollyoak, who was the most vehement, the most incredulous, the most jocular, and the most derisive of the anti-ghost faction, brought matters to a climax by declaring that nothing would give him greater pleasure than to pass a night in a haunted house—and the worse its character, the better he would be pleased!

His challenge was instantly taken up by our somewhat ruffled host, who warmly assured him that his wishes could be easily satisfied, and that he would be accommodated with a night's lodging in a haunted house within twenty-four hours—in fact, in a house of such a desperate reputation, that even the adjoining mansions stood vacant.

He then proceeded to give a brief outline of the history of number ninety. It had once been the residence of a well-known county family, but what evil events had happened therein tradition did not relate.

On the death of the last owner—a diabolical-looking aged person, much resembling the typical wizard—it had passed into the hands of a kinsman, resident abroad, who had no wish to return to England, and who desired his agents to let it, if they could—a most significant proviso!

Year by year went by, and still this 'Highly desirable family mansion' could find no tenant, although the rent was reduced, and reduced, and again reduced, to almost zero!

The most ghastly whispers were afloat—the most terrible experiences were actually proclaimed on the housetops!

No tenant would remain, even *gratis*; and for the last ten years, this, 'handsome, desirable town family residence' had been the abode of rats by day, and something else by night—so said the neighbours.

Of course it was the very thing for John, and he snatched up the gauntlet on the spot. He scoffed at its evil repute, and solemnly promised to rehabilitate its character within a week.

It was in vain that he was solemnly warned—that one of his fellow guests gravely assured him 'that he would not pass a night in number ninety for ninety thousand pounds—it would be the price of his reason.'

'You value your reason at a very high figure,' replied John, with an indulgent smile. 'I will venture mine for nothing.'

'Those laugh who win,' put in our host sharply. 'You have not been through the wood yet though your name is Hollyoak! I invite all present to dine with me in three days from this; and then, if our friend here has proved that he has got the better of the spirits, we will all laugh together. Is that a bargain?'

This invitation was promptly accepted by the whole company; and then they fell to making practical arrangements for John's lodgings for the next night.

I had no actual hand—or, more properly speaking, tongue—in this discussion, which carried us on till a late hour; but nevertheless, the next night at ten o'clock—for no ghost with any self respect would think of appearing before that time—I found myself standing, as John's second, on the steps of the notorious abode; but I was not going to remain; the hansom that brought us was to take me back to my respectable chambers.

This ill-fated house was large, solemn-looking, and gloomy. A heavy portico frowned down on neighbouring bare-faced hall-doors. The caretaker (an army pensioner, bravest of the brave in daylight) was prudently awaiting us outside with a key, which said key he turned in the lock, and admitted us into a great echoing hall, black as Erebus, saying as he did so: 'My missus has haired the bed, and made up a good fire in the first front, sir. Your things is all laid hout, and (dubiously to John) I hope you'll have a comfortable night, sir.'

'No, sir! Thank you, sir! Excuse me, I'll not come in! Good-night!' and with the words still on his lips, he clattered down the steps with most indecent haste, and—vanished.

'And of course you will not come in either?' said John. 'It is not in the bond, and I prefer to face them alone!' and he laughed contemptuously, a laugh that had a curious echo, it struck me at the time. A laugh strangely repeated, with an unpleasant mocking emphasis. 'Call for me, alive or dead, at eight o'clock tomorrow morning!' he added, pushing me forcibly out into the porch, and closing the door with a heavy, reverberating clang, that sounded half-way down the street.

I did call for him the next morning as desired, with the army pensioner, who stared at his common-place, self-possessed appearance, with an expression of respectful astonishment.

'So it was all humbug, of course,' I said, as he took my arm, and we set off for our club.

'You shall have the whole story whenever we have had something to eat,' he replied somewhat impatiently. 'It will keep till after breakfast—I'm famishing!'

I remarked that he looked unusually grave as we chatted over our broiled fish and omelette, and that occasionally his attention seemed wandering, to say the least of it. The moment he had brought out his cigar-case and lit up he turned to me and said:

'I see you are just quivering to know my experience, and I won't keep you on tenter-hooks any longer. In four words—I have seen them!'

I am (as before hinted) a silent man. I merely looked at him with widely-parted mouth and staring interrogative eyes.

I believe I had best endeavour to give the narrative without comment, and in John Hollyoak's own way. This is, as well as I can recollect, his experience word for word:—

'I proceeded upstairs, after I had shut you out, lighting my way by a match, and found the front room easily, as the door was ajar, and it was lit up by a roaring and most cheerful-looking fire, and two wax candles. It was a comfortable apartment, furnished with old-fashioned chairs and tables, and the traditional four-poster. There were numerous doors, which proved to be cupboards; and when I had executed a rigorous search in each of these closets and locked them, and investigated the bed above and beneath, sounded the walls, and bolted the door, I sat down before the fire, lit a cigar, opened a book, and felt that I was going to be master of the situation, and most thoroughly and comfortably "at home." My novel proved absorbing. I read on greedily, chapter after chapter, and so interested was I, and amused—for it was a lively book—that I positively lost sight of my whereabouts, and fancied myself reading in my own chamber! There was not a sound—not even a mouse in wainscot. The coals dropping from the grate occasionally broke the silence, till a neighbouring church-clock slowly boomed twelve! *"The hour!"* I said to myself, with a laugh, as I gave the fire a rousing poke, and commenced a fresh chapter; but ere I had read three pages I had occasion to pause and listen. What was that distinct sound now coming nearer and nearer? "Rats, of course," said Common-sense—"it was just the house for vermin." Then a longish silence. Again a stir, sounds approaching, as if apparently caused by many feet passing down the corridor—high heeled shoes, the sweeping switch of silken trains! Of course it was all imagination, I assured myself—or rats! Rats were capable of making such curious improbable noises!

'Then another silence. No sound but cinders and the ticking of my watch, which I had laid upon the table.

'I resumed my book, rather ashamed, and a little indignant with myself for having neglected it, and calmly dismissed my late interruption as "rats—nothing but rats."

'I had been reading and smoking for some time in a placid and highly incredulous frame of mind, when I was somewhat rudely startled by a loud single knock at my room door. I took no notice of

it, but merely laid down my novel and sat tight. Another knock more
imperious this time. After a moment's mental deliberation I arose,
armed myself with the poker, prepared to brain any number of rats,
and threw the door open with a violent swing that strained its very
hinges, and beheld, to my amazement, a tall powdered footman in
a laced scarlet livery, who, making a formal inclination of his head,
astonished me still further by saying:

"'Dinner is ready!"

"'I'm not coming!" I replied, without a moment's hesitation, and
thereupon I slammed the door in his face, locked it, and resumed
my seat, also my book; but reading was a farce; my ears were aching
for the next sound.

'It came soon—rapid steps running up the stairs, and again a
single knock. I went over to the door, and once more discovered the
tall footman, who repeated, with a studied courtesy:

"'Dinner is ready, and the company are waiting!"

"'I told you I was not coming. Be off, and be hanged to you!" I
cried again, shutting the door violently.

'This time I did not make even a pretence at reading, I merely sat
and waited for the next move.

'I had not long to sit. In ten minutes I heard a third loud summons.
I rose, went to the door, and tore it open. There, as I expected, was
the servant again, with his parrot speech:

"'Dinner is ready, the company are waiting, and the master says
you must come!"

"'All right, then, I'll come," I replied, wearied by reason of his
importunity, and feeling suddenly fired with a desire to see the end
of the adventure.

'He accordingly led the way downstairs, and I followed him,
noting as I went the gilt buttons on his coat, and his splendidly

turned calves, also that the hall and passages were now brilliantly illuminated, and that several liveried servants were passing to and fro, and that from—presumably—the dining room, there issued a buzz of tongues, loud volleys of laughter, many hilarious voices, and a clatter of knives and forks. I was not left much time for speculation, as in another second I found myself inside the door, and my escort announced me in a stentorian voice as "Mr. Hollyoak."

'I could hardly credit my senses, as I looked round and saw about two dozen people, dressed in a fashion of the last century, seated at the table, which was loaded with gold and silver plate, and lighted up by a blaze of wax candles in massive candelabra.

'A swarthy elderly gentleman, who presided at the head of the board, rose deliberately as I entered. He was dressed in a crimson coat, braided with silver. He wore a peruke, had the most piercing black eyes I ever encountered, made me the finest bow I ever received in all my life, and with a polite wave of a taper hand, indicated my seat—a vacant chair between two powdered and patched beauties, with overflowing white shoulders and necks sparkling with diamonds.

'At first I was fully convinced that the whole affair was a superbly-matured practical joke. Everything looked so real, so truly flesh and blood, so complete in every detail; but I gazed around in vain for one familiar face.

'I saw young, old, and elderly; handsome and the reverse. On all faces there was a similar expression—reckless, hardened defiance, and something else that made me shudder, but that I could not classify or define.

'Were they a secret community? Burglars or coiners? But no; in one rapid glance I noticed that they belonged exclusively to the upper stratum of society—bygone society. The jabber of talking had momentarily ceased, and the host, imperiously hammering the table with a knife-handle, said in a singularly harsh grating voice:

"'Ladies and gentlemen, permit me to give you a toast! 'Our guest!'" looking straight at me with his glittering coal-black eyes.

'Every glass was immediately raised. Twenty faces were turned towards mine, when, happily, a sudden impulse seized me. I sprang to my feet and said:

"'Ladies and gentlemen, I beg to thank you for your kind hospitality, but before I accept it, allow me to say grace!"

'I did not wait for permission, but hurriedly repeated a Latin benediction. Ere the last syllable was uttered, in an instant there was a violent crash, an uproar, a sound of running, of screams, groans and curses, and then utter darkness.

'I found myself standing alone by a big mahogany table which I could just dimly discern by the aid of a street-lamp that threw its meagre rays into the great empty dining-room from the other side of the area.

'I must confess that I felt my nerves a little shaken by this instantaneous change from light to darkness—from a crowd of gay and noisy companions, to utter solitude and silence. I stood for a moment trying to recover my mental balance. I rubbed my eyes hard to assure myself that I was wide awake, and then I placed this very cigar-case in the middle of the table, as a sign and token that I had been downstairs—which cigar-case I found exactly where I left it this morning—and then went and groped my way into the hall and regained my room.

'I met with no obstacle *en route*. I saw no one, but as I closed and double-locked my door I distinctly heard a low laugh outside the keyhole—a sort of suppressed, malicious titter, that made me furious.

'I opened the door at once. There was nothing to be seen. I waited and listened—dead silence. I then undressed and went to bed, resolved that a whole army of footmen would fail to allure me once more to that festive board. I was determined not to lose my night's rest—ghosts or no ghosts.

'Just as I was dozing off I remember hearing the neighbouring clock chime two. It was the last sound I was aware of; the house was now as silent as a vault. My fire burnt away cheerfully. I was no longer in the least degree inclined for reading, and I fell fast asleep and slept soundly till I heard the cabs and milk-carts beginning their morning career.

'I then rose, dressed at my leisure, and found you, my good, faithful friend, awaiting me, rather anxiously, on the hall-door steps.

'I have not done with that house yet. I'm determined to find out who these people are, and where they come from. I shall sleep there again tonight, and so shall "Crib," my bulldog; and you will see that I shall have news for you tomorrow morning—if I am still alive to tell the tale,' he added with a laugh.

In vain I would have dissuaded him. I protested, argued, and implored. I declared that rashness was not courage; that he had seen enough; that I, who had seen nothing, and only listened to his experiences, was convinced that number ninety was a house to be avoided.

I might just as well have talked to my umbrella! So, once more, I reluctantly accompanied him to his previous night's lodging. Once more I saw him swallowed up inside the gloomy, forbidding-looking, re-echoing hall.

I then went home in an unusually anxious, semi-excited, nervous state of mind; and I, who generally outrival the Seven Sleepers, lay wide awake, tumbling and tossing hour after hour, a prey to the most foolish ideas—ideas I would have laughed to scorn in daylight.

More than once I was certain that I heard John Hollyoak distractedly calling me; and I sat up in bed and listened intently. Of course it was fancy, for the instant I did so, there was no sound.

At the first gleam of winter dawn, I rose, dressed, and swallowed a cup of good strong coffee to clear my brain from the misty notions it had harboured during the night. And then I invested myself in my warmest topcoat and comforter, and set off for number ninety. Early as it was—it was but half-past seven—I found the army pensioner was before me, pacing the pavement with a countenance that would have made a first-rate frontispiece for 'Burton's Anatomy of Melancholy'—a countenance the reverse of cheerful.

I was not disposed to wait for eight o'clock. I was too uneasy, and too impatient for further particulars of the dinner-party. So I rang with all my might, and knocked with all my main.

No sound within—no answer! But John was always a heavy sleeper. I was resolved to arouse him all the same, and knocked and rang, and rang and knocked, incessantly for fully ten minutes.

I then stooped down and applied my eye to the keyhole; I looked steadily into the aperture, till I became accustomed to the darkness, and then it seemed to me that another eye—a very strange, fiery eye—was glaring into mine from the other side of the door!

I removed my eye and applied my mouth instead, and shouted with all the power of my lungs (I did not care a straw if passers-by took me for an escaped lunatic):

'John! John! Hollyoak!'

How his name echoed and re-echoed up through that great empty house! 'He must hear *that*,' I said to myself as I pressed my ear closely against the lock, and listened with throbbing suspense.

The echo of 'Hollyoak' had hardly died away when I swear that I distinctly heard a low, sniggering, mocking laugh—*that* was my only answer—that; and a vast unresponsive silence.

I was now quite desperate. I shook the door frantically, with all my strength. I broke the bell; in short, my behaviour was such that it excited the curiosity of a policeman, who crossed the road to know 'What was up?'

'I want to get in!' I panted, breathless with my exertions.

'You'd better stay where you are!' said Bobby; 'the outside of this house is the best of it! There are terrible stories—'

'But there is a gentleman inside it!' I interrupted impatiently. 'He slept there last night, and I can't wake him. He has the key!'

'Oh, you can't *wake* him!' returned the policeman gravely. 'Then we must get a locksmith!'

But already the thoughtful pensioner had procured one; and already a considerable and curious crowd surrounded the steps.

After five minutes of (to me) maddening delay, the great heavy door was opened and swung slowly back, and I instantly rushed in, followed less precipitately by the policeman and pensioner.

I had not far to seek John Hollyoak! He and his dog were lying at the foot of the stairs, both stone dead!

THE SHADOW

E. Nesbit

First published as The Portent of the Shadow
in *Black & White*, 23 December 1905

Edith Nesbit (married name Bland) (1858–1924) was a ground-breaking children's author who led an unconventional life. In her late teens, she eloped with her fiancé's colleague Hubert Bland and became pregnant. She married Bland but he fathered children by at least two other women, one of whom was Nesbit's close friend Alice who ended up living with them in a *ménage à trois*. Nesbit and Bland were also socialists and active in the Fabian Society, and she took the bohemian step of not wearing corsets and cutting her hair short. Nesbit was inspired to write fiction by having spent time recounting her unhappy schooldays for the *Girls' Own Paper*. She went on to develop a working relationship with *The Strand* magazine and other periodicals, serialising several fantasy novels for children, as well as many ghost stories.

THIS IS NOT AN ARTISTICALLY ROUNDED-OFF GHOST STORY, and nothing is explained in it, and there seems to be no reason why any of it should have happened. But that is no reason why it should not be told. You must have noticed that all the real ghost stories you have ever come close to, are like this in these respects—no explanation, no logical coherence. Here is the story.

There were three of us and another, but she had fainted suddenly at the second extra of the Christmas dance, and had been put to bed in the dressing-room next to the room which we three shared. It had been one of those jolly, old-fashioned dances where nearly everybody stays the night, and the big country house is stretched to its utmost containing—guests harbouring on sofas, couches, settles, and even mattresses on floors. Some of the young men actually, I believe, slept on the great dining-table. We had talked of our partners, as girls will, and then the stillness of the manor house, broken only by the whisper of the wind in the cedar branches, and the scraping of their harsh fingers against our window panes, had pricked us to such a luxurious confidence in our surroundings of bright chintz and candle-flame and fire-light, that we had dared to talk of ghosts—in which, we all said, we did not believe one bit. We had told the story of the phantom coach, and the horribly strange bed, and the lady in the sacque, and the house in Berkeley Square.

We none of us believed in ghosts, but my heart, at least, seemed to leap to my throat and choke me there, when a tap came to our door—a tap faint, not to be mistaken.

'Who's there?' said the youngest of us, craning a lean neck towards the door. It opened slowly, and I give you my word the instant of suspense that followed is still reckoned among my life's least confident moments. Almost at once the door opened fully, and Miss Eastwich, my aunt's housekeeper, companion and general stand-by looked in on us.

We all said 'Come in,' but she stood there. She was, at all normal hours, the most silent woman I have ever known. She stood and looked at us, and shivered a little. So did we—for in those days corridors were not warmed by hot-water pipes, and the air from the door was keen.

'I saw your light,' she said at last, 'and I thought it was late for you to be up—after all this gaiety. I thought perhaps—' her glance turned towards the door of the dressing-room.

'No,' I said, 'she's fast asleep.' I should have added a good-night, but the youngest of us forestalled my speech. She did not know Miss Eastwich as we others did; did not know how her persistent silence had built a wall round her—a wall that no one dared to break down with the commonplaces of talk, or the littlenesses of mere human relationship. Miss Eastwich's silence had taught us to treat her as a machine; and as other than a machine we never dreamed of treating her. But the youngest of us had seen Miss Eastwich for the first time that day. She was young, crude, ill-balanced, subject to blind, calf-like impulses. She was also the heiress of a rich tallow-chandler, but that has nothing to do with this part of the story. She jumped up from the hearth-rug, her unsuitably rich silk lace-trimmed dressing-gown falling back from her thin collar-bones, and ran to the door and put an arm round Miss Eastwich's prim, lisse-encircled neck. I gasped. I should as soon have dared to embrace Cleopatra's Needle. 'Come in,' said the youngest of us—'come in and get warm. There's lots of cocoa left.' She drew Miss Eastwich in and shut the door.

The vivid light of pleasure in the housekeeper's pale eyes went through my heart like a knife. It would have been so easy to put an arm round her neck, if one had only thought she wanted an arm there. But it was not I who had thought that—and indeed, my arm might not have brought the light evoked by the thin arm of the youngest of us.

'Now,' the youngest went on eagerly, 'you shall have the very biggest, nicest chair, and the cocoa-pot's here on the hob as hot as hot—and we've all been telling ghost stories, only we don't believe in them a bit; and when you get warm you ought to tell one too.'

Miss Eastwich—that model of decorum and decently done duties, tell a ghost story!

'You're sure I'm not in your way,' Miss Eastwich said, stretching her hands to the blaze. I wondered whether housekeepers have fires in their rooms even at Christmas time. 'Not a bit'—I said it, and I hope I said it as warmly as I felt it. 'I—Miss Eastwich—I'd have asked you to come in other times—only I didn't think you'd care for girls' chatter.'

The third girl, who was really of no account, and that's why I have not said anything about her before, poured cocoa for our guest. I put my fleecy Madeira shawl round her shoulders. I could not think of anything else to do for her, and I found myself wishing desperately to do something. The smiles she gave us were quite pretty. People can smile prettily at forty or fifty, or even later, though girls don't realise this. It occurred to me, and this was another knife-thrust, that I had never seen Miss Eastwich smile—a real smile, before. The pale smiles of dutiful acquiescence were not of the same blood as this dimpling, happy, transfiguring look.

'This is very pleasant,' she said, and it seemed to me that I had never before heard her real voice. It did not please me to think that at the cost of cocoa, a fire, and my arm round her neck, I might have heard this new voice any time these six years.

'We've been telling ghost stories,' I said. 'The worst of it is, we don't believe in ghosts. No-one one knows has ever seen one.'

'It's always what somebody told somebody, who told somebody you know,' said the youngest of us, 'and you can't believe that, can you?'

'What the soldier said, is not evidence,' said Miss Eastwich. Will it be believed that the little Dickens quotation pierced one more keenly than the new smile or the new voice?

'And all the ghost stories are so beautifully rounded off—a murder committed on the spot—or a hidden treasure, or a warning… I think that makes them harder to believe. The most horrid ghost-story I ever heard was one that was quite silly.'

'Tell it.'

'I can't—it doesn't sound anything to tell. Miss Eastwich ought to tell one.'

'Oh do,' said the youngest of us, and her salt cellars loomed dark, as she stretched her neck eagerly and laid an entreating arm on our guest's knee.

'The only thing that I ever knew of was—was hearsay,' she said slowly, 'till just the end.'

I knew she would tell her story, and I knew she had never before told it, and I knew she was only telling it now because she was proud, and this seemed the only way to pay for the fire and the cocoa, and the laying of that arm round her neck.

'Don't tell it,' I said suddenly. 'I know you'd rather not.'

'I daresay it would bore you,' she said meekly, and the youngest of us, who, after all, did not understand everything, glared resentfully at me.

'We should just *love* it,' she said. 'Do tell us. Never mind if it isn't a real, proper, fixed up story. I'm certain anything *you* think ghostly would be quite too beautifully horrid for anything.'

Miss Eastwich finished her cocoa and reached up to set the cup on the mantelpiece.

'It can't do any harm,' she said half to herself, 'they don't believe in ghosts, and it wasn't exactly a ghost either. And they're all over twenty—they're not babies.'

There was a breathing time of hush and expectancy. The fire crackled and the gas suddenly glared higher because the billiard lights had been put out. We heard the steps and voices of the men going along the corridors.

'It is really hardly worth telling,' Miss Eastwich said doubtfully, shading her faded face from the fire with her thin hand.

We all said 'Go on—oh, go on—do!'

'Well,' she said, 'twenty years ago—and more than that—I had two friends, and I loved them more than anything in the world. And they married each other—'

She paused, and I knew just in what way she had loved each of them. The youngest of us said—

'How awfully nice for you. Do go on.'

She patted the youngest's shoulder, and I was glad that I had understood, and that the youngest of all hadn't. She went on.

'Well, after they were married, I did not see much of them for a year or two; and then he wrote and asked me to come and stay, because his wife was ill, and I should cheer her up, and cheer him up as well; for it was a gloomy house, and he himself was growing gloomy too.'

I knew, as she spoke, that she had every line of that letter by heart.

'Well, I went. The address was in Lee, near London; in those days there were streets and streets of new villa-houses growing up round old brick mansions standing in their own grounds, with red walls round, you know, and a sort of flavour of coaching days, and post chaises, and Blackheath highwaymen about them. He had said the house was gloomy, and it was called "The Firs," and I imagined my cab going through a dark, winding shrubbery, and drawing up in front of one of these sedate, old, square houses. Instead, we drew up in front of a large, smart villa, with iron railings, gay encaustic tiles leading from the iron gate to the stained-glass-panelled door, and for shrubbery only a few stunted cypresses and aucubas in the tiny front garden. But inside it was all warm and welcoming. He met me at the door.'

She was gazing into the fire, and I knew she had forgotten us. But the youngest girl of all still thought it was to us she was telling her story.

'He met me at the door,' she said again, 'and thanked me for coming, and asked me to forgive the past.'

'What past?' said that high priestess of the *inàpropos*, the youngest of all.

'Oh—I suppose he meant because they hadn't invited me before, or something,' said Miss Eastwich worriedly, 'but it's a very dull story, I find, after all, and—'

'Do go on,' I said—then I kicked the youngest of us, and got up to rearrange Miss Eastwich's shawl, and said in blatant dumb show, over the shawled shoulder: 'Shut up, you little idiot—'

After another silence, the housekeeper's new voice went on.

'They were very glad to see me, and I was very glad to be there. You girls, now, have such troops of friends, but these two were all

I had—all I had ever had. Mabel wasn't exactly ill, only weak and excitable. I thought he seemed more ill than she did. She went to bed early and before she went, she asked me to keep him company through his last pipe, so we went into the dining-room and sat in the two arm chairs on each side of the fireplace. They were covered with green leather I remember. There were bronze groups of horses and a black marble clock on the mantelpiece—all wedding-presents. He poured out some whisky for himself, but he hardly touched it. He sat looking into the fire. At last I said:—

'"What's wrong? Mabel looks as well as you could expect."

'He said, "yes—but I don't know from one day to another that she won't begin to notice something wrong. That's why I wanted you to come. You were always so sensible and strong-minded, and Mabel's like a little bird on a flower."

'I said yes, of course, and waited for him to go on. I thought he must be in debt, or in trouble of some sort. So I just waited. Presently he said:

'"Margaret, this is a very peculiar house—" he always called me Margaret. You see we'd been such old friends. I told him I thought the house was very pretty, and fresh, and homelike—only a little too new—but that fault would mend with time. He said:—

'"It *is* new: that's just it. We're the first people who've ever lived in it. If it were an old house, Margaret, I should think it was haunted."

'I asked if he had seen anything. "No," he said, "not yet."

'"Heard then?" said I.

'"No—not heard either," he said, "but there's a sort of feeling: I can't describe it—I've seen nothing and I've heard nothing, but I've been so near to seeing and hearing, just near, that's all. And something follows me about—only when I turn round, there's never anything, only my shadow. And I always feel that I *shall* see the thing next minute—but I never do—not quite—it's always just not visible."

'I thought he'd been working rather hard—and tried to cheer him up by making light of all this. It was just nerves, I said. Then he said he had thought I could help him, and did I think anyone he had wronged could have laid a curse on him, and did I believe in curses. I said I didn't—and the only person anyone could have said he had wronged forgave him freely, I knew, if there was anything to forgive. So I told him this too.'

It was I, not the youngest of us, who knew the name of that person, wronged and forgiving.

'So then I said he ought to take Mabel away from the house and have a complete change. But he said No; Mabel had got everything in order, and he could never manage to get her away just now without explaining everything—"and, above all," he said, "she mustn't guess there's anything wrong. I daresay I shan't feel quite such a lunatic now you're here."

'So we said good-night.'

'Is that all the story?' said the third girl, striving to convey that even as it stood it was a good story.

'That's only the beginning,' said Miss Eastwich. 'Whenever I was alone with him he used to tell me the same thing over and over again, and at first when I began to notice things, I tried to think that it was his talk that had upset my nerves. The odd thing was that it wasn't only at night—but in broad daylight—and particularly on the stairs and passages. On the staircase the feeling used to be so awful that I have had to bite my lips till they bled to keep myself from running upstairs at full speed. Only I knew if I did I should go mad at the top. There was always something behind me—exactly as he had said—something that one could just not see. And a sound that one could just not hear. There was a long corridor at the top of the house. I have sometimes almost seen something—you know how one sees things without looking—but if I turned round, it seemed as if the thing drooped and melted into my shadow. There was a little window at the end of the corridor.

'Downstairs there was another corridor, something like it, with a cupboard at one end and the kitchen at the other. One night I went down into the kitchen to heat some milk for Mabel. The servants had gone to bed. As I stood by the fire, waiting for the milk to boil, I glanced through the open door and along the passage. I never could keep my eyes on what I was doing in that house. The cupboard door was partly open; they used to keep empty boxes and things in it. And, as I looked, I knew that now it was not going to be "almost" any more. Yet I said, "Mabel?" not because I thought it could be Mabel who was crouching down there, half in and half out of the cupboard. The thing was grey at first, and then it was black. And when I whispered, "Mabel," it seemed to sink down till it lay like a pool of ink on the floor, and then its edges drew in, and it seemed to flow, like ink when you tilt up the paper you have spilt it on; and it flowed into the cupboard till it was all gathered into the shadow there. I saw it go quite plainly. The gas was full on in the kitchen. I screamed aloud, but even then, I'm thankful to say, I had enough sense to upset the boiling milk, so that when he came downstairs three steps at a time, I had the excuse for my scream of a scalded hand. The explanation satisfied Mabel, but next night he said:—

'"Why didn't you tell me? It was that cupboard. All the horror of the house comes out of that. Tell me—have you seen anything yet? Or is it only the nearly seeing and nearly hearing still?"

'I said, "You must tell me first what you've seen." He told me, and his eyes wandered, as he spoke, to the shadows by the curtains, and I turned up all three gas lights, and lit the candles on the mantelpiece. Then we looked at each other and said we were both mad, and thanked God that Mabel at least was sane. For what he had seen was what I had seen.

'After that I hated to be alone with a shadow, because at any moment I might see something that would crouch, and sink, and lie like a black pool, and then slowly draw itself into the shadow that was nearest. Often that shadow was my own. The thing came first at night, but afterwards there was no hour safe from it. I saw it at dawn and at noon, in the dusk and in the firelight, and always it crouched and sank, and was a pool that flowed into some shadow and became part of it. And always I saw it with a straining of the eyes—a pricking and aching. It seemed as though I could only just see it, as if my sight, to see it, had to be strained to the uttermost. And still the sound was in the house—the sound that I could just not hear. At last, one morning early, I did hear it. It was close behind me, and it was only a sigh. It was worse than the thing that crept into the shadows.

'I don't know how I bore it. I couldn't have borne it, if I hadn't been so fond of them both. But I knew in my heart that, if he had no-one to whom he could speak openly, he would go mad, or tell Mabel. His was not a very strong character; very sweet, and kind, and gentle, but not strong. He was always easily led. So I stayed on and bore up, and we were very cheerful, and made little jokes, and tried to be amusing when Mabel was with us. But when we were alone, we did not try to be amusing. And sometimes a day or two would go by without our seeing or hearing anything, and we should perhaps have fancied that we had fancied what we had seen and heard—only there was always the feeling of there being something about the house, that one could just not hear and not see. Sometimes we used to try

not to talk about it, but generally we talked of nothing else at all. And
the weeks went by, and Mabel's baby was born. The nurse and the
doctor said that both mother and child were doing well. He and I sat
late in the dining-room that night. We had neither of us seen or heard
anything for three days; our anxiety about Mabel was lessened. We
talked of the future—it seemed then so much brighter than the past.
We arranged that, the moment she was fit to be moved, he should
take her away to the sea, and I should superintend the moving of
their furniture into the new house he had already chosen. He was
gayer than I had seen him since his marriage—almost like his old
self. When I said good-night to him, he said a lot of things about my
having been a comfort to them both. I hadn't done anything much,
of course, but still I am glad he said them.

'Then I went upstairs, almost for the first time without the feeling
of something following me. I listened at Mabel's door. Everything
was quiet. I went on towards my own room, and in an instant I felt
that there *was* something behind me. I turned. It was crouching there;
it sank, and the black fluidness of it seemed to be sucked under the
door of Mabel's room.

'I went back. I opened the door a listening inch. All was still. And
then I heard a sigh close behind me. I opened the door and went in.
The nurse and the baby were asleep. Mabel was asleep too—she
looked so pretty—like a tired child—the baby was cuddled up into
one of her arms with its tiny head against her side. I prayed then
that Mabel might never know the terrors that he and I had known.
That those little ears might never hear any but pretty sounds, those
clear eyes never see any but pretty sights. I did not dare to pray for
a long time after that. Because my prayer was answered. She never
saw, she never heard anything more in this world. And now I could
do nothing more for him or for her.

'When they had put her in her coffin, I lighted wax candles round her, and laid the horrible white flowers that people will send near her, and then I saw he had followed me. I took his hand to lead him away.

'At the door we both turned. It seemed to us that we heard a sigh. He would have sprung to her side, in I don't know what mad, glad hope. But at that instant we both saw it. Between us and the coffin, first grey, then black, it crouched an instant, then sank and liquefied—and was gathered together and drawn till it ran into the nearest shadow. And the nearest shadow was the shadow of Mabel's coffin. I left the next day. His mother came. She had never liked me.'

Miss Eastwich paused. I think she had quite forgotten us.

'Didn't you see him again?' asked the youngest of us all.

'Only once,' Miss Eastwich answered, 'and something black crouched then between him and me. But it was only his second wife, crying beside his coffin. It's not a cheerful story is it? And it doesn't lead anywhere. I've never told anyone else. I think it was seeing his daughter that brought it all back.'

She looked towards the dressing-room door.

'Mabel's baby?'

'Yes—and exactly like Mabel, only with his eyes.'

The youngest of all had Miss Eastwich's hands, and was petting them.

Suddenly the woman wrenched her hands away, and stood at her gaunt height, her hands clenched, eyes straining. She was looking at something that we could not see, and I know what the man in the Bible meant when he said: 'The hair of my flesh stood up.'

What she saw seemed not quite to reach the height of the dressing-room door handle. Her eyes followed it down, down—widening and widening. Mine followed them—all the nerves of them seemed strained to the uttermost—and I almost saw—or did I quite see? I can't be certain. But we all heard the long-drawn, quivering sigh. And to each of us it seemed to be breathed just behind us.

It was I who caught up the candle—it dripped all over my trembling hand—and was dragged by Miss Eastwich to the girl who had fainted during the second extra. But it was the youngest of all whose lean arms were round the housekeeper when we turned away, and that have been round her many a time since, in the new home where she keeps house for the youngest of us.

The doctor who came in the morning said that Mabel's daughter had died of heart disease—which she had inherited from her mother. It was that that had made her faint during the second extra. But I have sometimes wondered whether she may not have inherited something from her father. I have never been able to forget the look on her dead face.

THE KIT-BAG

Algernon Blackwood

First published in *Pall Mall Magazine*, December 1908

Algernon Henry Blackwood (1869–1951) established a new kind
of weird fiction, describing supernatural encounters in which the
natural world possesses sinister powers. He was born into a wealthy
family, the son of a man who had been a playboy known as 'Beauty
Blackwood' but who had been converted into a deeply conserva-
tive and evangelical Christian during the Crimean War. Blackwood
rebelled against his upbringing, becoming interested in mysticism
and involved in The Hermetic Order of the Golden Dawn, an occult
group that also included Bram Stoker, Arthur Machen and Aleister
Crowley as members. His most famous story is 'The Willows', in
which two men on a canoeing trip up the Danube stop on an island
covered with willows. Blackwood sets up a sense of impending doom
by making each natural element on the island seem increasingly
malevolent, until it seems that a mystical force is actually attacking
the friends.

In addition to fiction exploring the darker side of nature,
Blackwood was famed for ghost stories, and in fact featured on the
BBC's first ever television programme, *Picture Page*, relating a ghost
story at the broadcast from Alexandra Palace on 2 November 1936.
He later made regular appearances on both television and radio, and
became known as 'The Ghost Man'.

WHEN THE WORDS 'NOT GUILTY' SOUNDED THROUGH the crowded court-room that dark December afternoon, Arthur Wilbraham, the great criminal K.C., and leader for the triumphant defence, was represented by his junior: but Johnson, his private secretary, carried the verdict across to his chambers like lightning.

'It's what we expected, I think,' said the barrister, without emotion; 'and, personally, I am glad the case is over.' There was no particular sign of pleasure that his defence of John Turk, the murderer, on a plea of insanity, had been successful, for no doubt he felt, as everybody who had watched the case felt, that no man had ever better deserved the gallows.

'I'm glad too,' said Johnson. He had sat in the court for ten days watching the face of the man who had carried out with callous detail one of the most brutal and cold-blooded murders of recent years.

The counsel glanced up at his secretary. They were more than employer and employed; for family and other reasons, they were friends. 'Ah, I remember; yes,' he said with a kind smile, 'and you want to get away for Christmas? You're going to skate and ski in the Alps, aren't you? If I was your age I'd come with you.'

Johnson laughed shortly. He was a young man of twenty-six, with a delicate face like a girl's. 'I can catch the morning boat now,' he said; 'but that's not the reason I'm glad the trial is over. I'm glad it's over because I've seen the last of that man's dreadful face. It positively haunted me. That white skin, with the black hair brushed low over the forehead, is a thing I shall never forget, and the description of the way the dismembered body was crammed and packed with lime into that—'

'Don't dwell on it, my dear fellow,' interrupted the other, looking at him curiously out of his keen eyes, 'don't think about it. Such pictures have a trick of coming back when one least wants them.' He paused a moment. 'Now go,' he added presently, 'and enjoy your holiday. I shall want all your energy for my Parliamentary work when you get back. And don't break your neck ski-ing.'

Johnson shook hands and took his leave. At the door he turned suddenly.

'I knew there was something I wanted to ask you,' he said. 'Would you mind lending me one of your kit-bags? It's too late to get one tonight, and I leave in the morning before the shops are open.'

'Of course; I'll send Henry over with it to your rooms. You shall have it the moment I get home.'

'I promise to take great care of it,' said Johnson gratefully, delighted to think that within thirty hours he would be nearing the brilliant sunshine of the high Alps in winter. The thought of that criminal court was like an evil dream in his mind.

He dined at his club and went on to Bloomsbury, where he occupied the top floor in one of those old, gaunt houses in which the rooms are large and lofty. The floor below his own was vacant and unfurnished, and below that were other lodgers whom he did not know. It was cheerless, and he looked forward heartily to a change. The night was even more cheerless: it was miserable, and few people were about. A cold, sleety rain was driving down the streets before the keenest east wind he had ever felt. It howled dismally among the big, gloomy houses of the great squares, and when he reached his rooms he heard it whistling and shouting over the world of black roofs beyond his windows.

In the hall he met his landlady, shading a candle from the draughts with her thin hand. 'This come by a man from Mr. Wilbr'im's, sir.'

She pointed to what was evidently the kit-bag, and Johnson thanked her and took it upstairs with him. 'I shall be going abroad in the morning for ten days, Mrs. Monks,' he said. 'I'll leave an address for letters.'

'And I hope you'll 'ave a merry Christmas, sir,' she said, in a raucous, wheezy voice that suggested spirits, 'and better weather than this.'

'I hope so too,' replied her lodger, shuddering a little as the wind went roaring down the street outside.

When he got upstairs he heard the sleet volleying against the window-panes. He put his kettle on to make a cup of hot coffee, and then set about putting a few things in order for his absence. 'And now I must pack—such as my packing is,' he laughed to himself, and set to work at once.

He liked the packing, for it brought the snow mountains so vividly before him, and made him forget the unpleasant scenes of the past ten days. Besides, it was not elaborate in nature. His friend had lent him the very thing—a stout canvas kit-bag, sack-shaped, with holes round the neck for the brass bar and padlock. It was a bit shapeless, true, and not much to look at, but its capacity was unlimited, and there was no need to pack carefully. He shoved in his water-proof coat, his fur cap and gloves, his skates and climbing boots, his sweaters, snow-boots, and ear-caps; and then on the top of these he piled his woollen shirts and underwear, his thick socks, puttees, and knickerbockers. The dress-suit came next, in case the hotel people dressed for dinner, and then, thinking of the best way to pack his white shirts, he paused a moment to reflect. 'That's the worst of these kit-bags,' he mused vaguely, standing in the centre of the sitting-room, where he had come to fetch some string.

It was after ten o'clock. A furious gust of wind rattled the windows as though to hurry him up, and he thought with pity of the poor Londoners whose Christmas would be spent in such a climate, whilst he was skimming over snowy slopes in bright sunshine, and dancing in the evening with rosy-cheeked girls—Ah! that reminded him; he must put in his dancing-pumps and evening socks. He crossed over from his sitting-room to the cupboard on the landing where he kept his linen.

And as he did so he heard some one coming softly up the stairs.

He stood still a moment on the landing to listen. It was Mrs. Monks's step, he thought; she must be coming up with the last post. But then the steps ceased suddenly, and he heard no more. They were at least two flights down, and he came to the conclusion they were too heavy to be those of his bibulous landlady. No doubt they belonged to a late lodger who had mistaken his floor. He went into his bedroom and packed his pumps and dress-shirts as best he could.

The kit-bag by this time was two-thirds full, and stood upright on its own base like a sack of flour. For the first time he noticed that it was old and dirty, the canvas faded and worn, and that it had obviously been subjected to rather rough treatment. It was not a very nice bag to have sent him—certainly not a new one, or one that his chief valued. He gave the matter a passing thought, and went on with his packing. Once or twice, however, he caught himself wondering who it could have been wandering down below, for Mrs. Monks had not come up with letters, and the floor was empty and unfurnished. From time to time, moreover, he was almost certain he heard a soft tread of some one padding about over the bare boards—cautiously, stealthily, as silently as possible—and, further, that the sounds had been lately coming distinctly nearer.

For the first time in his life he began to feel a little creepy. Then, as though to emphasise this feeling, an odd thing happened: as he left the bedroom, having just packed his recalcitrant white shirts, he noticed that the top of the kit-bag lopped over towards him with an extraordinary resemblance to a human face. The canvas fell into a fold like a nose and forehead, and the brass rings for the padlock just filled the position of the eyes. A shadow—or was it a travel stain? for he could not tell exactly—looked like hair. It gave him rather a turn, for it was so absurdly, so outrageously, like the face of John Turk, the murderer.

He laughed, and went into the front room, where the light was stronger.

'That horrid case has got on my mind,' he thought; 'I shall be glad of a change of scene and air.' In the sitting-room, however, he was not pleased to hear again that stealthy tread upon the stairs, and to realise that it was much closer than before, as well as unmistakably real. And this time he got up and went out to see who it could be creeping about on the upper staircase at so late an hour.

But the sound ceased; there was no one visible on the stairs. He went to the floor below, not without trepidation, and turned on the electric light to make sure that no one was hiding in the empty rooms of the unoccupied suite. There was not a stick of furniture large enough to hide a dog. Then he called over the banisters to Mrs. Monks, but there was no answer, and his voice echoed down into the dark vault of the house, and was lost in the roar of the gale that howled outside. Everyone was in bed and asleep—everyone except himself and the owner of this soft and stealthy tread.

'My absurd imagination, I suppose,' he thought. 'It must have been the wind after all, although—it seemed so *very* real and close, I thought.' He went back to his packing. It was by this time getting on towards midnight. He drank his coffee up and lit another pipe—the last before turning in.

It is difficult to say exactly at what point fear begins, when the causes of that fear are not plainly before the eyes. Impressions gather on the surface of the mind, film by film, as ice gathers upon the surface of still water, but often so lightly that they claim no definite recognition from the consciousness. Then a point is reached where the accumulated impressions become a definite emotion, and the mind realises that something has happened. With something of a start, Johnson suddenly recognised that he felt nervous—oddly nervous; also, that for some time past the causes of this feeling had been gathering slowly in his mind, but that he had only just reached the point where he was forced to acknowledge them.

It was a singular and curious malaise that had come over him, and he hardly knew what to make of it. He felt as though he were doing something that was strongly objected to by another person, another person, moreover, who had some right to object. It was a most disturbing and disagreeable feeling, not unlike the persistent promptings of conscience: almost, in fact, as if he were doing something he knew to be wrong. Yet, though he searched vigorously and honestly in his mind, he could nowhere lay his finger upon the secret of this growing uneasiness, and it perplexed him. More, it distressed and frightened him.

'Pure nerves, I suppose,' he said aloud with a forced laugh. 'Mountain air will cure all that! Ah,' he added, still speaking to himself, 'and that reminds me—my snow-glasses.'

He was standing by the door of the bedroom during this brief soliloquy, and as he passed quickly towards the sitting-room to fetch them from the cupboard he saw out of the corner of his eye the indistinct outline of a figure standing on the stairs, a few feet from the top. It was someone in a stooping position, with one hand on the banisters, and the face peering up towards the landing. And at the same moment he heard a shuffling footstep. The person who had been creeping about below all this time had at last come up to his own floor. Who in the world could it be? And what in the name of Heaven did he want?

Johnson caught his breath sharply and stood stock still. Then, after a few seconds' hesitation, he found his courage, and turned to investigate. The stairs, he saw to his utter amazement, were empty; there was no one. He felt a series of cold shivers run over him, and something about the muscles of his legs gave a little and grew weak. For the space of several minutes he peered steadily into the shadows that congregated about the top of the staircase where he had seen the figure, and then he walked fast—almost ran, in fact—into the light of the front room; but hardly had he passed inside the doorway when he heard someone come up the stairs behind him with a quick bound and go swiftly into his bedroom. It was a heavy, but at the same time a stealthy footstep—the tread of somebody who did not wish to be seen. And it was at this precise moment that the nervousness he had hitherto experienced leaped the boundary line, and entered the state of fear, almost of acute, unreasoning fear. Before it turned into terror there was a further boundary to cross, and beyond that again lay the region of pure horror. Johnson's position was an unenviable one.

'By Jove! That *was* someone on the stairs, then,' he muttered, his flesh crawling all over; 'and whoever it was has now gone into my bedroom.' His delicate, pale face turned absolutely white, and for some minutes he hardly knew what to think or do. Then he realised intuitively that delay only set a premium upon fear; and he crossed the landing boldly and went straight into the other room, where, a few seconds before, the steps had disappeared.

'Who's there? Is that you, Mrs. Monks?' he called aloud, as he went, and heard the first half of his words echo down the empty stairs, while the second half fell dead against the curtains in a room that apparently held no other human figure than his own.

'Who's there?' he called again, in a voice unnecessarily loud and that only just held firm. 'What do you want here?'

The curtains swayed very slightly, and, as he saw it, his heart felt as if it almost missed a beat; yet he dashed forward and drew them aside with a rush. A window, streaming with rain, was all that met his gaze. He continued his search, but in vain; the cupboards held nothing but rows of clothes, hanging motionless; and under the bed there was no sign of anyone hiding. He stepped backwards into the middle of the room, and, as he did so, something all but tripped him up. Turning with a sudden spring of alarm he saw— the kit-bag.

'Odd!' he thought. 'That's not where I left it!' A few moments before it had surely been on his right, between the bed and the bath; he did not remember having moved it. It was very curious. What in the world was the matter with everything? Were all his senses gone queer? A terrific gust of wind tore at the windows, dashing the sleet against the glass with the force of a small gun-shot, and then fled away howling dismally over the waste of Bloomsbury roofs. A sudden vision of the Channel next day rose in his mind and recalled him sharply to realities.

'There's no-one here at any rate; that's quite clear!' he exclaimed aloud. Yet at the time he uttered them he knew perfectly well that his words were not true and that he did not believe them himself. He felt exactly as though someone was hiding close about him, watching all his movements, trying to hinder his packing in some way. 'And two of my senses,' he added, keeping up the pretence, 'have played me the most absurd tricks: the steps I heard and the figure I saw were both entirely imaginary.'

He went back to the front room, poked the fire into a blaze, and sat down before it to think. What impressed him more than anything else was the fact that the kit-bag was no longer where he had left it. It had been dragged nearer to the door.

What happened afterwards that night happened, of course, to a man already excited by fear, and was perceived by a mind that had not the full and proper control, therefore, of the senses. Outwardly, Johnson remained calm and master of himself to the end, pretending to the very last that everything he witnessed had a natural explanation, or was merely delusions of his tired nerves. But inwardly, in his very heart, he knew all along that someone had been hiding downstairs in the empty suite when he came in, that this person had watched his opportunity and then stealthily made his way up to the bedroom, and that all he saw and heard afterwards, from the moving of the kit-bag to—well, to the other things this story has to tell—were caused directly by the presence of this invisible person.

And it was here, just when he most desired to keep his mind and thoughts controlled, that the vivid pictures received day after day upon the mental plates exposed in the court-room of the Old Bailey, came strongly to light and developed themselves in the dark room of his inner vision. Unpleasant, haunting memories have a way of coming to life again just when the mind least desires them—in the silent watches of the night, on sleepless pillows, during the lonely hours spent by sick and dying beds. And so now, in the same way, Johnson saw nothing but the dreadful face of John Turk, the murderer, lowering at him from every corner of his mental field of vision; the white skin, the evil eyes, and the fringe of black hair low over the forehead. All the pictures of those ten days in court crowded back into his mind unbidden, and very vivid.

'This is all rubbish and nerves,' he exclaimed at length, springing with sudden energy from his chair. 'I shall finish my packing and go to bed. I'm overwrought, overtired. No doubt, at this rate I shall hear steps and things all night!'

But his face was deadly white all the same. He snatched up his field-glasses and walked across to the bedroom, humming a music-hall song as he went—a trifle too loud to be natural; and the instant he crossed the threshold and stood within the room something turned cold about his heart, and he felt that every hair on his head stood up.

The kit-bag lay close in front of him, several feet nearer to the door than he had left it, and just over its crumpled top he saw a head and face slowly sinking down out of sight as though someone were crouching behind it to hide, and at the same moment a sound like a long-drawn sigh was distinctly audible in the still air about him between the gusts of the storm outside.

Johnson had more courage and will-power than the girlish inde-cision of his face indicated; but at first such a wave of terror came over him that for some seconds he could do nothing but stand and stare. A violent trembling ran down his back and legs, and he was conscious of a foolish, almost an hysterical, impulse to scream aloud. That sigh seemed in his very ear, and the air still quivered with it. It was unmistakably a human sigh.

'Who's there?' he said at length, finding his voice; but though he meant to speak with loud decision, the tones came out instead in a faint whisper, for he had partly lost the control of his tongue and lips.

He stepped forward, so that he could see all round and over the kit-bag. Of course there was nothing there, nothing but the faded carpet and the bulging canvas sides. He put out his hands and threw open the mouth of the sack where it had fallen over, being only three parts full, and then he saw for the first time that round the inside, some six inches from the top, there ran a broad smear of dull crimson. It was an old and faded blood stain. He uttered a scream, and drew back his hands as if they had been burnt. At the same moment the kit-bag gave a faint, but unmistakable, lurch forward towards the door.

Johnson collapsed backwards, searching with his hands for the support of something solid, and the door, being farther behind him than he realised, received his weight just in time to prevent his falling, and shut to with a resounding bang. At the same moment the swinging of his left arm accidentally touched the electric switch, and the light in the room went out.

It was an awkward and disagreeable predicament, and if Johnson had not been possessed of real pluck he might have done all manner of foolish things. As it was, however, he pulled himself together, and groped furiously for the little brass knob to turn the light on again. But the rapid closing of the door had set the coats hanging on it a-swinging, and his fingers became entangled in a confusion of sleeves and pockets, so that it was some moments before he found the switch. And in those few moments of bewilderment and terror two things happened that sent him beyond recall over the boundary into the region of genuine horror—he distinctly heard the kit-bag shuffling heavily across the floor in jerks, and close in front of his face sounded once again the sigh of a human being.

In his anguished efforts to find the brass button on the wall he nearly scraped the nails from his fingers, but even then, in those frenzied moments of alarm—so swift and alert are the impressions of a mind keyed up by a vivid emotion—he had time to realise that he dreaded the return of the light, and that it might be better for him to stay hidden in the merciful screen of darkness. It was but the impulse of a moment, however, and before he had time to act upon it he had yielded automatically to the original desire, and the room was flooded again with light.

But the second instinct had been right. It would have been better for him to have stayed in the shelter of the kind darkness. For there, close before him, bending over the half-packed kit-bag, clear as life in the merciless glare of the electric light, stood the figure of John Turk, the murderer. Not three feet from him the man stood, the fringe of black hair marked plainly against the pallor of the forehead, the whole horrible presentment of the scoundrel, as vivid as he had seen him day after day in the Old Bailey, when he stood there in the dock, cynical and callous, under the very shadow of the gallows.

In a flash Johnson realised what it all meant: the dirty and much-used bag; the smear of crimson within the top; the dreadful stretched condition of the bulging sides. He remembered how the victim's body had been stuffed into a canvas bag for burial, the ghastly, dis-membered fragments forced with lime into this very bag; and the bag itself produced as evidence—it all came back to him as clear as day...

Very softly and stealthily his hand groped behind him for the handle of the door, but before he could actually turn it the very thing that he most of all dreaded came about, and John Turk lifted his devil's face and looked at him. At the same moment that heavy sigh passed through the air of the room, formulated somehow into words: 'It's my bag. And I want it.'

Johnson just remembered clawing the door open, and then fall-ing in a heap upon the floor of the landing, as he tried frantically to make his way into the front room.

He remained unconscious for a long time, and it was still dark when he opened his eyes and realised that he was lying, stiff and bruised, on the cold boards. Then the memory of what he had seen rushed back into his mind, and he promptly fainted again. When he woke the second time the wintry dawn was just beginning to peep in at the windows, painting the stairs a cheerless, dismal grey, and he managed to crawl into the front room, and cover himself with an overcoat in the armchair, where at length he fell asleep.

A great clamour woke him. He recognised Mrs. Monks's voice, loud and voluble.

'What! You ain't been to bed, sir! Are you ill, or has anything 'appened? And there's an urgent gentleman to see you, though, it ain't seven o'clock yet, and—'

'Who is it?' he stammered. 'I'm all right, thanks. Fell asleep in my chair, I suppose.'

'Someone from Mr. Wilb'rim's, and he says he ought to see you quick before you go abroad, and I told him—'

'Show him up, please, at once,' said Johnson, whose head was whirling, and his mind was still full of dreadful visions.

Mr. Wilbraham's man came in with many apologies, and explained briefly and quickly that an absurd mistake had been made, and that the wrong kit-bag had been sent over the night before.

'Henry somehow got hold of the one that came over from the court-room, and Mr. Wilbraham only discovered it when he saw his own lying in his room, and asked why it had not gone to you,' the man said.

'Oh!' said Johnson stupidly.

'And he must have brought you the one from the murder case instead, sir, I'm afraid,' the man continued, without the ghost of an expression on his face. 'The one John Turk packed the dead body in. Mr. Wilbraham's awful upset about it, sir, and told me to come over first thing this morning with the right one, as you were leaving by the boat.'

He pointed to a clean-looking kit-bag on the floor, which he had just brought. 'And I was to bring the other one back, sir,' he added casually.

For some minutes Johnson could not find his voice. At last he pointed in the direction of his bedroom. 'Perhaps you would kindly unpack it for me. Just empty the things out on the floor.'

The man disappeared into the other room, and was gone for five minutes. Johnson heard the shifting to and fro of the bag, and the rattle of the skates and boots being unpacked.

'Thank you, sir,' the man said, returning with the bag folded over his arm. 'And can I do anything more to help you, sir?'

'What is it?' asked Johnson, seeing that he still had something he wished to say.

The man shuffled and looked mysterious. 'Beg pardon, sir, but knowing your interest in the Turk case, I thought you'd maybe like to know what's happened—'

'Yes.'

'John Turk killed himself last night with poison immediately on getting his release, and he left a note for Mr. Wilbraham saying as he'd be much obliged if they'd have him put away, same as the woman he murdered, in the old kit-bag.'

'What time—did he do it?' asked Johnson.

'Ten o'clock last night, sir, the warder says.'

THE STORY OF A DISAPPEARANCE
AND AN APPEARANCE

M. R. James

First published in the *Cambridge Review*, 4 June 1913

Montague Rhodes 'Monty' James (1862–1936) was one of the greatest and most influential writers of ghost stories in the twentieth century. An academic and manuscripts expert at Cambridge University for much of his life, in 1893 James started a tradition of writing ghost stories to read to friends at Christmas. His narratives are infused with his own interest in antiquarianism and often feature the motif of a found manuscript or other artefact which unleashes a ghost or demon onto the unsuspecting academic who studies it. Although his stories were always read at Christmas, hardly any of them have a Christmas setting. This is a rare exception.

T HE LETTERS WHICH I NOW PUBLISH WERE SENT TO ME recently by a person who knows me to be interested in ghost stories. There is no doubt about their authenticity. The paper on which they are written, the ink, and the whole external aspect put their date beyond the reach of question.

The only point which they do not make clear is the identity of the writer. He signs with initials only, and as none of the envelopes of the letters are preserved, the surname of his correspondent—obviously a married brother—is as obscure as his own. No further preliminary explanation is needed, I think. Luckily the first letter supplies all that could be expected.

LETTER I

GREAT CHRISHALL, DEC. 22, 1837

MY DEAR ROBERT,—It is with great regret for the enjoyment I am losing, and for a reason which you will deplore equally with myself, that I write to inform you that I am unable to join your circle for this Christmas: but you will agree with me that it is unavoidable when I say that I have within these few hours received a letter from Mrs. Hunt at B——, to the effect that our Uncle Henry has suddenly and mysteriously disappeared, and begging me to go down there immediately and join the search that is being made for him. Little as I, or you either, I think, have ever seen of Uncle, I naturally feel that this is not a request that can be regarded lightly, and accordingly I propose to go to B——— by this afternoon's mail, reaching it late in the evening. I shall not go to the Rectory, but put up at the King's Head, and to which you may address letters. I enclose a small draft, which you will please make use of for the benefit of the young people. I shall write you daily (supposing me to be detained more than a single day) what goes on, and you may be sure, should the business be cleared up in time to permit of my coming to the Manor after all, I shall present myself. I have but a few minutes at disposal. With cordial greetings to you all, and many regrets, believe me, your affectionate Bro.,

W.R.

LETTER II

KING'S HEAD, DEC. 23, '37

MY DEAR ROBERT,—In the first place, there is as yet no news of Uncle H., and I think you may finally dismiss any idea—I won't say hope—that I might after all 'turn up' for Xmas. However, my thoughts will be with you, and you have my best wishes for a really festive day. Mind that none of my nephews or nieces expend any fraction of their guineas on presents for me.

Since I got here I have been blaming myself for taking this affair of Uncle H. too easily. From what people here say, I gather that there is very little hope that he can still be alive; but whether it is accident or design that carried him off I cannot judge. The facts are these. On Friday the 19th, he went as usual shortly before five o'clock to read evening prayers at the Church; and when they were over the clerk brought him a message, in response to which he set off to pay a visit to a sick person at an outlying cottage the better part of two miles away. He paid the visit, and started on his return journey at about half-past six. This is the last that is known of him. The people here are very much grieved at his loss; he had been here many years, as you know, and though, as you also know, he was not the most genial of men, and had more than a little of the *martinet* in his composition, he seems to have been active in good works, and unsparing of trouble to himself.

Poor Mrs. Hunt, who has been his housekeeper ever since she left Woodley, is quite overcome: it seems like the end of the world to her. I am glad that I did not entertain the idea of taking quarters at the Rectory; and I have declined several kindly offers of hospitality from people in the place, preferring as I do to be independent, and finding myself very comfortable here.

You will, of course, wish to know what has been done in the way of inquiry and search. First, nothing was to be expected from investigation at the Rectory; and to be brief, nothing has transpired. I asked Mrs. Hunt—as others had done before—whether there was either any unfavourable symptom in her master such as might portend a sudden stroke, or attack of illness, or whether he had ever had reason to apprehend any such thing: but both she, and also his medical man, were clear that this was not the case. He was quite in his usual health. In the second place, naturally, ponds and streams have been dragged, and fields in the neighbourhood which he is known to have visited last, have been searched—without result. I have myself talked to the parish clerk and—more important—have been to the house where he paid his visit.

There can be no question of any foul play on these people's part. The one man in the house is ill in bed and very weak: the wife and the children of course could do nothing themselves, nor is there the shadow of a probability that they or any of them should have agreed to decoy poor Uncle H. out in order that he might be attacked on the way back. They had told what they knew to several other inquirers already, but the woman repeated it to me. The Rector was looking just as usual: he wasn't very long with the sick man—'He ain't,' she said, 'like some what has a gift in prayer; but there, if we was all that way, 'owever would the chapel people get their living?' He left some money when he went away, and one of the children saw him cross the stile into the next field. He was dressed as he always was: wore his bands—I gather he is nearly the last man remaining who does so—at any rate in this district.

You see I am putting down everything. The fact is that I have nothing else to do, having brought no business papers with me; and, moreover, it serves to clear my own mind, and may suggest points which have been overlooked. So I shall continue to write all that passes, even to conversations if need be—you may read or not as you please, but pray keep the letters. I have another reason for writing so fully, but it is not a very tangible one.

You may ask if I have myself made any search in the fields near the cottage. Something—a good deal—has been done by others, as I mentioned; but I hope to go over the ground tomorrow. Bow Street has now been informed, and will send down by tonight's coach, but I do not think they will make much of the job. There is no snow, which might have helped us. The fields are all grass. Of course I was on the *qui vive* for any indication today both going and returning; but there was a thick mist on the way back, and I was not in trim for wandering about unknown pastures, especially on an evening when bushes looked like men, and a cow lowing in the distance might have been the last trump. I assure you, if Uncle Henry had stepped out from among the trees in a little copse which borders the path at one place, carrying his head under his arm, I should have been very little more uncomfortable than I was. To tell you the truth, I was rather expecting something of the kind. But I must drop my pen for the moment: Mr. Lucas, the curate, is announced.

Later. Mr. Lucas has been, and gone, and there is not much beyond the decencies of ordinary sentiment to be got from him. I can see that he has given up any idea that the Rector can be alive, and that, so far as he can be, he is truly sorry. I can also discern that even in a more emotional person than Mr. Lucas, Uncle Henry was not likely to inspire strong attachment.

Besides Mr. Lucas, I have had another visitor in the shape of my Boniface—mine host of the 'King's Head'—who came to see whether I had everything I wished, and who really requires the pen of a Boz to do him justice. He was very solemn and weighty at first. 'Well, sir,' he said, 'I suppose we must bow our 'ead beneath the blow, as my poor wife had used to say. So far as I can gather there's been neither hide nor yet hair of out late respected incumbent scented out as yet; not that he was what the Scripture terms a hairy man in any sense of the word.'

I said—as well as I could—that I supposed not, but could not help adding that I had heard he was sometimes a little difficult to deal with. Mr. Bowman looked at me sharply for a moment, and then passed in a flash from solemn sympathy to impassioned declamation. 'When I think,' he said, 'of the language that man see fit to employ to me in this here parlour over no more a matter than a cask of beer—such a thing as I told him might happen any day of the week to a man with a family—though as it turned out he was quite under a mistake, and that I knew at the time, only I was that shocked to hear him I couldn't lay my tongue to the right expression.'

He stopped abruptly and eyed me with some embarrassment. I only said, 'Dear me, I'm sorry to hear you had any little differences: I suppose my uncle will be a good deal missed in the parish?' Mr.

Bowman drew a long breath. 'Ah, yes!' he said; 'your uncle! You'll understand me when I say that for the moment it had slipped my remembrance that he was a relative; and natural enough, I must say, as it should, for as to you bearing any resemblance to—to him, the notion of any such a thing is clean ridiculous. All the same, 'ad I 'ave bore it in my mind, you'll be among the first to feel, I'm sure, as I should have abstained my lips, or rather I should *not* have abstained my lips with no such reflections.'

I assured him that I quite understood, and was going to have asked him some further questions, but he was called away to see after some business. By the way, you need not take it into your head that he has anything to fear from the inquiry into poor Uncle Henry's disappearance—though, no doubt, in the watches of the night it will occur to him that *I* think he has, and I may expect explanations tomorrow.

I must close this letter: it has to go by the late coach.

LETTER III

DEC. 25, '37

MY DEAR ROBERT,—This is a curious letter to be writing on Christmas Day, and yet after all there is nothing much in it. Or there may be— you shall be the judge. At least, nothing decisive. The Bow Street men practically say that they have no clue. The length of time and the weather conditions have made all tracks so faint as to be quite useless: nothing that belonged to the dead man—I'm afraid no other word will do—has been picked up.

As I expected, Mr. Bowman was uneasy in his mind this morning; quite early I heard him holding forth in a very distinct voice—purposely so, I thought—to the Bow Street officers in the bar, as to the loss that the town had sustained in their Rector, and as to the necessity of leaving no stone unturned (he was very great on this phrase) in order to come at the truth. I suspect him of being an orator of repute at convivial meetings.

When I was at breakfast he came to wait on me, and took an opportunity when handling a muffin to say in a low tone, 'I 'ope, sir, you recognise as my feelings towards your relative is not actuated by any taint of what you may call melignity—you can leave the room, Eliza, I will see the gentleman 'as all he requires with my own hands—I ask your pardon, sir, but you must be well aware a man is not always master of himself: and when that man has been 'urt in his mind by the application of expressions which I will go so far as to say 'ad not ought to have been made use of (his voice was rising all this time and his face growing redder); no, sir; and 'ere, if you will permit of it, I should like to explain to you in a very few words the exact state of the bone of contention. This cask—I might more truly call it a firkin—of beer—'

I felt it was time to interpose, and said that I did not see that it would help us very much to go into that matter in detail. Mr. Bowman acquiesced, and resumed more calmly:

'Well, sir, I bow to your ruling, and as you say, be that here or be it there, it don't contribute a great deal, perhaps, to the present question. All I wish you to understand is that I am as prepared as you are yourself to lend every hand to the business we have afore us, and as I took the opportunity to say as much to the Orficers not three-quarters of an hour ago—to leave no stone unturned as may throw even a spark of light on this painful matter.'

In fact, Mr. Bowman did accompany us on our exploration, but though I am sure his genuine wish was to be helpful, I am afraid he did not contribute to the serious side of it. He appeared to be under the impression that we were likely to meet either Uncle Henry or the person responsible for his disappearance, walking about the fields, and did a great deal of shading his eyes with his hand and calling our attention, by pointing with his stick, to distant cattle and labourers. He held several long conversations with old women whom we met, and was very strict and severe in his manner, but on each occasion returned to our party saying, 'Well, I find she don't seem to 'ave no connexion with this sad affair. I think you may take it from me, sir, as there's little or no light to be looked for from that quarter; not without she's keeping somethink back intentional.'

We gained no appreciable result, as I told you at starting; the Bow Street men have left the town, whether for London or not I am not sure.

This evening I had company in the shape of a bagman, a smartish fellow. He knew what was going forward, but though he has been on the roads for some days about here, he had nothing to tell of suspicious characters—tramps, wandering sailors or gipsies. He was very full of a capital Punch and Judy Show he had seen this same day at W——, and asked if it had been here yet, and advised me by no means to miss it if it does come. The best Punch and the best Toby dog, he said, he had ever come across. Toby dogs, you know, are the last new thing in the shows. I have only seen one myself, but before long all the men will have them.

Now why, you will want to know, do I trouble to write all this to you? I am obliged to do it, because it has something to do with another absurd trifle (as you will inevitably say), which in my present state of rather unquiet fancy—nothing more, perhaps—I have to put down. It is a dream, sir, which I am going to record, and I must say it is one of the oddest I have had. Is there anything in it beyond what the bagman's talk and Uncle Henry's disappearance could have suggested? You, I repeat, shall judge: I am not in a sufficiently cool and judicial frame to do so.

It began with what I can only describe as a pulling aside of curtains: and I found myself seated in a place—I don't know whether indoors or out. There were people—only a few—on either side of me, but I did not recognise them, or indeed think much about them. They never spoke, but, so far as I remember, were all grave and pale-faced and looked fixedly before them. Facing me there was a Punch and Judy Show, perhaps rather larger than the ordinary ones, painted with black figures on a reddish-yellow ground. Behind it and on each side was only darkness, but in front there was a sufficiency of light. I was 'strung up' to a high degree of expectation and looked every moment to hear the pan-pipes and the Roo-too-too-it. Instead of that there came suddenly an enormous—I can use no other word—an enormous single toll of a bell, I don't know from how far off—somewhere behind. The little curtain flew up and the drama began.

I believe someone once tried to re-write Punch as a serious tragedy; but whoever he may have been, this performance would have suited him exactly. There was something Satanic about the hero. He varied his methods of attack: for some of his victims he lay in wait, and to see his horrible face—it was yellowish white, I may remark—peering round the wings made me think of the Vampyre in Fuseli's foul sketch. To others he was polite and carneying—particularly to the unfortunate alien who can only say *Shallabalah*—though what Punch said I never could catch. But with all of them I came to dread the moment of death. The crack of the stick on their skulls, which in the ordinary way delights me, had here a crushing sound as if the bone was giving way, and the victims quivered and kicked as they lay. The baby—it sounds more ridiculous as I go on—the baby, I am sure, was alive. Punch wrung its neck, and if the choke or squeak which it gave were not real, I know nothing of reality.

The stage got perceptibly darker as each crime was consummated, and at last there was one murder which was done quite in the dark, so that I could see nothing of the victim, and took some time to effect. It was accompanied by hard breathing and horrid muffled sounds, and after it Punch came and sat on the footboard and fanned himself and looked at his shoes, which were bloody, and hung his head on one side, and sniggered in so deadly a fashion that I saw some of those beside me cover their faces, and I would gladly have done the same. But in the meantime the scene behind Punch was clearing, and showed, not the usual house front, but something more ambitious—a grove of trees and the gentle slope of a hill, with a very natural—in fact, I should say a real—moon shining on it. Over this there rose slowly an object which I soon perceived to be a human figure with something peculiar about the head—what, I was unable at first to see. It did not stand on its feet, but began creeping or dragging itself across the middle distance towards Punch, who still sat back to it; and by this time, I may remark (though it did not occur to me at the moment) that all pretence of this being a puppet show had vanished. Punch was still Punch, it is true, but, like the others, was in some sense a live creature, and both moved themselves at their own will.

When I next glanced at him he was sitting in malignant reflection; but in another instant something seemed to attract his attention, and he first sat up sharply and then turned round, and evidently caught sight of the person that was approaching him and was in fact now very near. Then, indeed, did he show unmistakable signs of terror: catching up his stick, he rushed towards the wood, only just eluding the arm of his pursuer, which was suddenly flung out to intercept him.

It was with a revulsion which I cannot easily express that I now saw more or less clearly what this pursuer was like. He was a sturdy figure clad in black, and, as I thought, wearing bands: his head was covered with a whitish bag.

The chase which now began lasted I do not know how long, now among the trees, now along the slope of the field, sometimes both figures disappearing wholly for a few seconds, and only some uncertain sounds letting one know that they were still afoot. At length there came a moment when Punch, evidently exhausted, staggered in from the left and threw himself down among the trees. His pursuer was not long after him, and came looking uncertainly from side to side. Then, catching sight of the figure on the ground, he too threw himself down—his back was turned to the audience—with a swift motion twitched the covering from his head, and thrust his face into that of Punch. Everything on the instant grew dark.

There was one long, loud, shuddering scream, and I awoke to find myself looking straight into the face of—what in all the world do you think? but—a large owl, which was seated on my window-sill immediately opposite my bed-foot, holding up its wings like two shrouded arms. I caught the fierce glance of its yellow eyes, and then it was gone. I heard the single enormous bell again—very likely, as you are saying to yourself, the church clock; but I do not think so— and then I was broad awake.

All this, I may say, happened within the last half-hour. There was no probability of my getting to sleep again, so I got up, put on clothes enough to keep me warm, and am writing this rigmarole in the first hours of Christmas Day. Have I left out anything? Yes; there was no Toby dog, and the names over the front of the Punch and Judy booth were Kidman and Gallop, which were certainly not what the bagman told me to look out for.

By this time, I feel a little more as if I could sleep, so this shall be sealed and wafered.

LETTER IV

DEC. 26, '37

MY DEAR ROBERT,—All is over. The body has been found. I do not make excuses for not having sent off my news by last night's mail, for the simple reason that I was incapable of putting pen to paper. The events that attended the discovery bewildered me so completely that I needed what I could get of a night's rest to enable me to face the situation at all. Now I can give you my journal of the day, certainly the strangest Christmas Day that ever I spent or am likely to spend.

The first incident was not very serious. Mr. Bowman had, I think, been keeping Christmas Eve, and was a little inclined to be captious: at least, he was not on foot very early, and to judge from what I could hear, neither men or maids could do anything to please him. The latter were certainly reduced to tears; nor am I sure that Mr. Bowman succeeded in preserving a manly composure. At any rate, when I came downstairs, it was in a broken voice that he wished me the compliments of the season, and a little later on, when he paid his visit of ceremony at breakfast, he was far from cheerful: even Byronic, I might almost say, in his outlook on life.

'I don't know,' he said, 'if you think with me, sir; but every Christmas as comes round the world seems a hollerer thing to me. Why, take an example now from what lays under my own eye. There's my servant Eliza—been with me now for going on fifteen years. I thought I could have placed my confidence in Eliza, and yet this very morning—Christmas morning too, of all the blessed days in the year—with the bells a ringing and—and—all like that—I say, this very morning, had it not have been for Providence watching over us all, that girl would have put—indeed I may go so far to say, 'ad put the cheese on your breakfast-table—' He saw I was about to speak, and waved his hand at me. 'It's all very well for you to say, "Yes, Mr. Bowman, but you took away the cheese and locked it up in the cupboard," which I did, and have the key here, or if not the actual key, one very much about the same size. That's true enough, sir, but what do you think is the effect of that action on me? Why, it's no exaggeration for me to say that the ground is cut from under my feet. And yet when I said as much to Eliza, not nasty, mind you, but just firm-like, what was my return? "Oh," she says: "well," she says, "there wasn't no bones broke, I suppose." Well, sir, it 'urt me, that's all I can say: it 'urt me, and I don't like to think of it now.'

There was an ominous pause here, in which I ventured to say something like, 'Yes, very trying,' and then asked at what hour the church service was to be. 'Eleven o'clock,' Mr. Bowman said with a heavy sigh. 'Ah, you won't have no such discourse from poor Mr. Lucas as what you would have done from our late Rector. Him and me may have had our little differences, and did do, more's the pity.'

I could see that a powerful effort was needed to keep him off the vexed question of the cask of beer, but he made it. 'But I will say this, that a better preacher, nor yet one to stand faster by his rights, or what he considered to be his rights—however, that's not the question now—I for one, never set under. Some might say, "Was he an eloquent man?" and to that my answer would be: "Well, there you've a better right per'aps to speak of your own uncle than what I have." Others might ask, "Did he keep a hold of his congregation?" and there again I should reply, "That depends." But as I say—yes,

Eliza, my girl, I'm coming—eleven o'clock, sir, and you inquire for the King's Head pew.' I believe Eliza had been very near the door, and shall consider it in my vail.

The next episode was church: I felt Mr. Lucas had a difficult task in doing justice to Christmas sentiments, and also to the feeling of disquiet and regret which, whatever Mr. Bowman might say, was clearly prevalent. I do not think he rose to the occasion. I was uncomfortable. The organ wolved—you know what I mean: the wind died—twice in the Christmas Hymn, and the tenor bell, I suppose owing to some negligence on the part of the ringers, kept sounding faintly about once in a minute during the sermon. The clerk sent up a man to see to it, but he seemed unable to do much. I was glad when it was over. There was an odd incident, too, before the service. I went in rather early, and came upon two men carrying the parish bier back to its place under the tower. From what I overheard them saying, it appeared that it had been put out by mistake, by someone who was not there. I also saw the clerk busy folding up a moth-eaten velvet pall—not a sight for Christmas Day.

I dined soon after this, and then, feeling disinclined to go out, took my seat by the fire in the parlour, with the last number of *Pickwick*, which I had been saving up for some days. I thought I could be sure of keeping awake over this, but I turned out as bad as our friend Smith. I suppose it was half-past two when I was roused by a piercing whistle and laughing and talking voices outside in the market-place. It was a Punch and Judy—I had no doubt the one that my bagman had seen at W——. I was half delighted, half not—the latter because my unpleasant dream came back to me so vividly; but, anyhow, I determined to see it through, and I sent Eliza out with a crown-piece to the performers and a request that they would face my window if they could manage it.

The show was a very smart new one; the names of the proprie-
tors, I need hardly tell you, were Italian, Foresta and Calpigi. The
Toby dog was there, as I had been led to expect. All B—— turned
out, but did not obstruct my view, for I was at the large first-floor
window and not ten yards away.

The play began on the stroke of a quarter to three by the church
clock. Certainly it was very good; and I was soon relieved to find that
the disgust my dream had given me for Punch's onslaughts on his
ill-starred visitors was only transient. I laughed at the demise of the
Turncock, the Foreigner, the Beadle, and even the baby. The only
drawback was the Toby dog's developing a tendency to howl in the
wrong place. Something had occurred, I suppose, to upset him, and
something considerable: for, I forget exactly at what point, he gave
a most lamentable cry, leapt off the footboard, and shot away across
the market-place and down a side street. There was a stage-wait, but
only a brief one. I suppose the men decided that it was no good going
after him, and that he was likely to turn up again at night.

We went on. Punch dealt faithfully with Judy, and in fact with all
comers; and then came the moment when the gallows was erected,
and the great scene with Mr. Ketch was to be enacted. It was now
that something happened of which I can certainly not yet see the
import fully. You have witnessed an execution, and know what the
criminal's head looks like with the cap on. If you are like me, you
never wish to think of it again, and I do not willingly remind you of
it. It was just such a head as that, that I, from my somewhat higher
post, saw in the inside of the showbox; but at first the audience did
not see it. I expected it to emerge into their view, but instead of
that there slowly rose for a few seconds an uncovered face, with an
expression of terror upon it, of which I have never imagined the like.
It seemed as if the man, whoever he was, was being forcibly lifted,

with his arms somehow pinioned or held back, towards the little gibbet on the stage. I could just see the nightcapped head behind him. Then there was a cry and a crash. The whole showbox fell over backwards; kicking legs were seen among the ruins, and then two figures—as some said; I can only answer for one—were visible running at top speed across the square and disappearing in a lane which leads to the fields.

Of course everybody gave chase. I followed; but the pace was killing, and very few were in, literally, at the death. It happened in a chalk pit: the man went over the edge quite blindly and broke his neck. They searched everywhere for the other, until it occurred to me to ask whether he had ever left the market-place. At first everyone was sure that he had; but when we came to look, he was there, under the showbox, dead too.

But in the chalk pit it was that poor Uncle Henry's body was found, with a sack over the head, the throat horribly mangled. It was a peaked corner of the sack sticking out of the soil that attracted attention. I cannot bring myself to write in greater detail.

I forgot to say the men's real names were Kidman and Gallop. I feel sure I have heard them, but no one here seems to know anything about them.

I am coming to you as soon as I can after the funeral. I must tell you when we meet what I think of it all.

BOXING NIGHT

E. F. Benson

First published in *The Tatler*, 30 November 1923

Edward Frederic Benson (1867–1940) was studying Classics at King's College, Cambridge, when he met M. R. James and became inspired to start writing ghost stories of his own. After short periods working in Athens and Egypt he became a prolific writer of fiction, publishing stories in a number of magazines, as well as at least 93 books. In addition to his supernatural stories he wrote the popular social satirical series known as 'Mapp and Lucia', set in a fictionalised version of Rye in East Sussex, where he lived from 1918 till his death. He never married and critics have often inferred from his writings that he was something of a misogynist.

HUGH GRANGER WAS SPENDING CHRISTMAS WITH US, AND, AS usually happens when he is present, the talk turned on the topics that concern the invisible world, which, though it is sundered from our material plane, sometimes cuts across it, and makes its presence perceived by strange and inexplicable manifestations. He held that his evidence of its existence, communications from the unseen to our mortal sense, were established beyond any doubt.

'Ghosts, clairvoyant visions, true presentiments, and dreams are all glimpses of the unseen,' he said. 'Such messages and messengers come from we know not where, and we know not how they come, but certainly they do come. Often the very act of communication appears difficult: those beyond the ken of our normal perceptions find it hard to get into touch with us, and often the messages get distorted or bungled in transit.'

'So as to be quite trivial or meaningless,' said someone.

'That is so,' said he. 'But, again, sometimes the message seems to be rendered more convincing by the very errors it contains. Error is so likely in such a tremendous transmission. I heard a story at first-hand the other day which illustrates that very aptly.'

There was an encouraging murmur of invitation, and Hugh drew from a drawer in the writing-table a sheaf of manuscript.

'I heard it in considerable detail,' he said, 'and I have only turned it into narrative form. It just happened like this.'

He sat down by the lamp, and read to us.

Woollard's Farm lay remote and solitary in the green lap of the Romney Marsh. Not a house stood within a mile of it as a bird would travel, and the curve of the farm road following the big drainage dyke made that distance half again as long for wheeled traffic. For a foot passenger, a couple of railed plank bridges crossed the dyke, and by cutting off the curve made a directer route, but now, in mid-winter, the flood water was high and the foot-bridges awash; deep pools lay in the intervening pastures, and any who would go into Rye must make the longer circuit before he struck the high road.

The farm took its name from the family which for two hundred years, so the tombstones in the Brooklands churchyard testified, had once owned its ample acres. Today these acres were sorely dwindled, and dwindled, too, was the yeoman stock which had once more prosperously tilled it. The last proprietor of the diminishing line had begotten no son, and though one at least of his two daughters to whom he had left it had a masculine grip in her efficient management, they were both unmarried and middle-aged, and no doubt, at their death Woollard's Farm, though it might retain its patronymic style, would pass into the hands of strangers. They knew of no other paternal relation except their Uncle Alfred, who was a town-bred man and would surely, if he survived them, sell this marsh-land property. There was more than an off-chance of this, for, twenty years younger than their father, he was but little their senior, and a gnarled, robust fellow. Often, indeed, had he urged his nieces to make the sale themselves, for houses such as theirs, with its spacious parlours, its solid oak floors and staircases, its pleasant brick-walled garden, were fetching high prices in the market. There had been several enquiries lately at his house-agent's office in Rye for just such a property, and he promised them a fine bid for it, and himself, no doubt, a fine percentage on the transaction. He was considerably in need of some such piece of business, for times were bad and money scarce with him.

But his hectoring persuasions had hitherto failed to convince his nieces; as long as they could get a livelihood out of the place, their affection for their home was impregnable to such suggestions. As for the loneliness of it, they were self-sufficient women, neither making friends nor needing them, undesirous of chatting neighbours, and content to get through the day's work and be ready for the next. Lately affairs had gone very well with them: market-days at Rye and New Romney had enabled Ellen Woollard to amass a fat sheaf of notes from the sale of pigs and poultry, and a wallet, with a hundred and fifty pounds in it was, on this evening of Christmas day, safely stowed in the secret cupboard in the panelling of the parlour at the farm. Next week there were substantial purchases to be made at the Ashford market, and for that reason she had not paid her notes into the County Bank at Rye. Ready money, to be paid down then and there, made the best bargaining at a market, and to deposit and draw out again from the bank meant a half-day twice occupied with the excursion.

The two sisters lived with the utmost simplicity: they kept no servant, except a girl whom they had allowed to go for two days of Christmas holiday to her family in Rye; she, with Rebecca Woollard, the younger of the sisters, did the cooking and the house-work, while Ellen was busy all day with outdoor affairs. In general, they ate and sat in the big lattice-panel kitchen, but tonight, in honour of the festival, Rebecca had made ready the parlour, and here, after their supper, when doors were locked and windows curtained, they spent the evening among the Christmas tokens of holly and evergreens with which she had decked the room. On other evenings she would be busy with sewing and household mendings, while Ellen, tired with her outdoor activities, dozed by the fire, but tonight a cheerful, talkative idleness occupied them, the sober glow of past memories, and, in spite of the shadows of middle age, optimistic gleams for the future.

'Yes, that was a rare good sale last week at New Romney,' said Ellen. 'There'll be enough and to spare for the new linen you say you want.'

Rebecca held up her thin hands to the blaze; pretty hands they were, but weak and irresolute.

'Well, I like that!' she said. 'Fancy talking of the new linen I say I want! Why, there's more patches in the tablecloth than weaving, and as for the sheets, I only ask you, Ellen, to look at them before you get into bed. Not that it's any good to ask you to do that, for I'm sure you're half asleep always before you turn your bedclothes down.'

'And you've been sleeping better lately, Rebecca, haven't you?' said her sister.

'I've certainly lain awake less. But such dreams as I have now all night long! They fairly scare me sometimes, and I think I'd sooner lie tossing and turning and hearing the weary clock striking than go through such adventures.'

Ellen laughed.

'Dreams are all a pack of rubbish,' she said, 'fit to smile about and forget as you dress in the morning. I can dream, too, if it comes to that, for it was only last night as I thought Uncle Alfred came here with a couple of bailiffs and told us we must quit, for we couldn't pay our taxes; we were sold up and he'd bought the place. Why, if there's any sense in dreams, they go by the opposite. If I paid any heed to them, I should say that meant that the farm would prosper next year as it never did before. The thought of all that good money in the cupboard there was what made me dream so contrarily.'

Rebecca pursed her lips with a gloomy shake of her head.

'I see a deal of truth in your dream, sister,' she said. 'Certain and sure it is that if Uncle Alfred had a chance he'd turn us out of the farm, be the means foul or fair.'

'Maybe, but that wasn't my dream, Rebecca. I dreamed he did turn us out, and there's little likelihood of that with all going so well. But he's a disagreeable man, that's sure. Such an answer as he sent me when I asked him to take his Christmas dinner with us today, and bide over the holiday.'

'I wonder at your asking him year after year like that,' said Rebecca. 'He don't want to come, and the Lord knows we don't want him. Would you be the happier if Uncle Alfred was sitting with us now, finding fault with this, and scolding at that, and wanting us to be quit of the farm, and go to live in some mucky town where there's not a breath of fresh air from year's end to year's end, and never a fresh egg to eat, and the washing coming back all chawed up and yellow, and nothing but the gabble of neighbours all day? No, give me Uncle Alfred's room sooner than his company, and thank you kindly.'

The mention of Uncle Alfred always made Rebecca rage; Ellen was ready to have done with the obnoxious subject.

'Well, we won't bother with him, nor he with us,' she said. 'But he's father's brother, Rebecca, and it is but decent to bid him spend Christmas with us. To be sure there are pleasanter things to talk about. Your house linen, now; twenty pounds you shall have to lay out on it, and any bits of things you want, and that will leave me with enough to get such pigs and hens as the farm hasn't been stocked with for the last five years. And who knows that before the year turns out there won't come along some bright young fellow to court you—'

This was a long-standing joke, that, like sound wine, seemed to improve with years. It set Rebecca laughing, for, indeed, she was no more of a marrying sort than her sister, and presently afterwards they made the fire safe with regard to flying sparks, and went up to the raftered bedchamber, where they slept together.

Ellen, as usual, was the first to be down next morning, and, with the girl away, she lit the kitchen fire and put the kettle to boil, while she prepared the feed for the chickens. It was very dark still, for though the sun was risen, the sky was thick with leaden clouds, moving heavily in a bitter north-east wind, and promising snow. Her face was worried and troubled; she looked sharply from time to time into the dark corners of the room and out of the latticed panes, for despite the scornful incredulity she had expressed last night on the subject of dreams, a vision so hideously and acutely real had torn her from her sleep that even now she was up and dressed and actively engaged she could not shake herself free from the horrid clutch of it.

She had dreamed that she and her sister were sitting in the parlour after nightfall on Boxing Day when a tapping came at the front door, and going to open it she had found on the threshold a soldier dressed in khaki, who begged a night's lodging, for outside a hurricane of snow was raging, and he had lost his way. In he came, pushing by her before she had bidden him to enter, and he walked straight down the passage and into the parlour. She followed him, and already he was breaking in with the butt of his rifle the panelled door of the cupboard which contained her money. It crashed inwards beneath his blows, and he put the fat wallet of notes into his pocket. 'Now we'll have no witnesses,' he cried, and next moment, with a swing of his rifle, which he held by the barrel, he had felled Rebecca with a terrific blow on the head, and there she lay bloody and battered on the floor. Then true nightmare began, for Ellen, trying to flee, found she could stir neither hand nor foot. She gave a thin, strangled cry as once more the murderous weapon was swung for the blow which she knew would crash down on her head, and with the shock of that mortal agony she awoke.

Busy herself as she might, Ellen could not shake off the convincing reality of the nightmare. It was not of dream-texture at all; it was on another plane, vivid and actual as the fire she had just lit or the bitter wind that whistled and rattled the panes. The thing had never happened, but it was of the solid stuff of reality. It was in vain that she reasoned with herself, and snapped an unconvinced finger: just here by the door she stood and saw the tall figure framed against the driving snow, and if none of this had happened, fulfilment would come to it... Then a foot on the stairs recalled her, and here was Rebecca coming down to prepare their breakfast on the morning of Boxing Day. It would never do to speak of this to her sister; it would scare her silly.

Rebecca went about her work in silence, laying the table and cutting the rashers. She had no spoken word for Ellen's greeting, but only a mumbling movement of her lips, and her hands were a-tremble. She bent over her work, so that Ellen got no clear sight of her face, and it was not till they were seated at the table, with a candle burning there, that she got a comprehensive look at it. And what she saw made her lay down her knife and fork.

'Goodsakes, what's the matter, Rebecca?' she asked.

Rebecca raised her eyes; there sat in them some nameless and abject terror.

'Nothing,' she said; 'it would only make you laugh at me if I told you.'

Ellen gave her a cheerful face.

'Well, I should like a laugh on this dark morning,' she said. 'One of your dreams, maybe?'

'Yes, that's right enough,' said Rebecca, 'but such a dream as I've never had before.'

In spite of the growing heat of the fire, it must have been still very cold in the kitchen, for suddenly, from head to foot, an icy shiver ran through Ellen.

'Tell me then,' she said. 'Get rid of it.'

Rebecca caught that shudder, and violently trembling, pushed her plate from her.

'I'll tell you,' she said, 'for, sure, I can't bear it alone. It wasn't a dream; it wasn't of that stuff that makes dreams... I thought it was the evening of Boxing Day, the day that's dawned now—'

She told her dream. It was identical down to the minutest detail with Ellen's, except that it was she herself who had gone to the door, and that she had seen her sister battered down by a blow, and waited in the catalepsy of nightmare for the stroke that would follow.

Even to Ellen's practical and unfanciful mind, the coincidence—if coincidence it was—was overwhelming; the sanest and least fantastical could not but see in this double vision a warning that it would be foolhardy to disregard, and within an hour the two of them had locked up the house, and were in the pony-cart on the way to Rye. As it was Boxing Day, the bank would be shut, and their plan was to entrust their money to their uncle for safe keeping till tomorrow. They had agreed not to tell him the true cause of their expedition; it was reasonable enough that two women in a place so remote should not care to be keeping so large a sum in the house. Tomorrow one of them would call again and deposit it at the bank. They found him already at the whisky bottle, and acid and disagreeable as ever.

'Well, what brings you two here?' he said. 'Compliments of the season, or some such rubbish?'

They explained their errand.

'A pack of nonsense!' said he. 'I'll not have aught to do with your money. Supposing my house was broken into before tomorrow morning, and your notes taken, you'd have the law on me for their recovery. And I tell you that that's a deal more likely to happen in a town than that a thief should go trapezing half-a-dozen miles out into the marsh on the chance of finding a packet of bank-notes at a lonely farmhouse!'

He got up, beat the ashes out of his pipe, and filled it again, frowning and muttering to himself.

'Burglars, indeed, at Woollard's Farm,' he said. 'I never heard of such a crazy notion! If I had a bit of money in the house here— worse luck I haven't—it would be a deal more reasonable of me to ask you to take care of it. Who ever heard of a burglary at a house like yours? The man would be daft who tramped halfway across the marsh, and in a snowstorm, too—for there'll be snow before night, unless I'm much mistaken—on such a chance. Who's to know that you've got the worth of a penny piece in the house?—for I warrant you've told nobody.'

'Uncle Alfred, you might be kind and keep it for us,' said Ellen. 'It's only till tomorrow.'

'I might, might I?' he sneered. 'Well, I tell you I mightn't, and more than that, I won't. You've got safe places enough. Where do you keep it?'

'In the panel-cupboard in the parlour,' said Ellen.

'Aye, and a good place, too,' said he. 'I remember that cupboard; your father always kept his brass there. And do you figure a burglar smashing in all your panelling in hopes of finding a cupboard there, and when he's hit on that, thinking to discover a wallet with bank-notes in it? A couple of dreamy, timorous women—that's what you are. I wouldn't keep your money in my house, not if you paid me ten per cent. of it for my trouble. Where should I be if it got stolen? Be off with you both, and don't bother me with your Christmas invitations!'

It was no manner of good to spend time and persuasions on the crusty fellow, and there was no one else whom they knew sufficiently well to approach on so unusual an errand. By midday the two were back again at the farm, glad to be indoors on this morning of shrewd snowy blasts, and the money, since assuredly there was no better hiding place than this concealed cupboard in the panelling, was back once more in the *caché*. Sullen and snarling as Uncle Alfred had been, there was certainly good sense in his view that this remote homestead was about the unlikeliest possible place for a burglar to choose for his operations, and Ellen, with more success than in the cold dawn, could reason herself out of her alarm. A dream was no more than a dream when all was said and done, and it was not for a sensible woman to heed such things. It was singular to be sure that the same vision had torn Rebecca from her sleep, but tomorrow by this time she would be laughing at the fears which had sent her twittering into Rye this morning.

Before the close of the short winter day the snow had begun to fall in earnest, and by the time the chickens and pigs were fed and made secure, and the thick curtains drawn, they could hear the thick insistent flurry of it as the wind drove it against the panes. But now that doors were locked and windows bolted, the squeal of the tempest shrill above the soft tapping of the snow-flakes only intensified the comfort of the swept hearth and the log fire that glowed in the open grate. Once again, as last night, they sat in the parlour, with the dark panelled walls gleaming sombrely in the firelight and the flames leaping as the wind bugled in the chimney. Eight o'clock, and nine, and ten sounded on the chimes of the grandfather clock, and as the last hour struck Ellen got up. The tranquil passage of the evening had quite restored the grip of her common sense, and she could even joke about her vanished apprehensions.

'Well, I reckon it's no use our sitting up for that soldier of yours, Rebecca,' she said. 'He's missed his connection, you might say, and I shall be off to bed, for tomorrow's a work-day again—'

Her sentence hung suspended and unfinished. There came a rap at the front door at the end of the passage, and the bell tingled. Rebecca rose to her feet with hands up to her ears, as if to shut out the sound.

'Who can it be at this time of night?' whispered Ellen.

Rebecca came close to her, white and palsied with fear.

'It's he,' she said. 'I know it's he. We must keep still, for there's no light showing, and perhaps he may go away. Dear God, let him go!'

A rattling at the latch had succeeded the knocking, and then all was quiet. Presently it began again, and again the bell repeated its summons.

Then Ellen lit a hand-lamp; anything was better than this unbearable suspense; besides if their visitor was some strayed wayfarer—

'I'm going to the door,' she said. 'It may be someone who has lost his way in the snow and the darkness, and on such a night he might well perish of cold before he found shelter. What should you and I feel, Rebecca, if tomorrow a woman, or a girl maybe, was found stiff and stark nigh the house, or drowned in the big dyke? That would be worse stuff than any dream.'

Trembling with fright but with unshakeable courage, and disregarding her sister's appeals, she went straight to the front door, drew back the heavy bolts, and opened it. On the threshold, framed against the fast-falling snow, stood a man in khaki. In the flickering light from her lamp she could not distinctly see his face, but over his shoulder was a rifle, of which he grasped the butt.

'I'm lost in the marsh, ma'am,' he said, 'trying for a short cut to Rye, but I knew there was a farm hereabouts, and thank God I've found it. I ask you for a lodging till dawn, for on a night like this there's death out there.'

'I can give you no lodging,' she said shortly. 'Follow the farm-road and you'll strike the highway.'

'But there's no seeing your hand before your face,' he said, 'and I'm half perished with cold already. Any outhouse will do for me, just shelter and a wisp of straw to wrap me in.'

The strangle of her nightmare was on her. Rebecca had crept along the passage, and in her ashen face Ellen saw her own heart mirrored.

'You can get no lodging here,' she said. 'Them as walk at night must get tramping.'

For answer he held out his rifle to her.

'Here, take that, ma'am,' he said. 'You're scared of me, I can see, but if I meant you harm would I give you my gun? I'll take off my boots, too, and my belt with its bayonet; a footsore man without boots or weapons can't harm you, and you may lock me into any cupboard or shed you please.'

His hands and face were bleached with the cold, and dream or no dream, she could not shut a man out in the cold of this impenetrable night.

'Come in,' she said. 'Take off your boots, and get you into the kitchen. Come what may, it's sheer death tonight in the marsh.'

At her bidding he walked into the kitchen while she had a whispered word with Rebecca.

'We can't do different, Rebecca,' she said, 'though strange it is about your dream and mine, and if it's God's will we be clubbed to death, it's His will. But what's not His will is that we should let a man die on our doorstep because we were afraid. Why should he give me his gun, besides, if he meant ill to us? So now I'll give him his bite of supper, for he's clemmed with cold and hunger, and then lock him into the kitchen. Meantime you take the money from the cupboard and hide it between your mattresses or mine. Why that's the finish of our dreaming already if you do that, for by the dream it should be from the cupboard in the parlour that he took it.'

Indeed, she needed heartening herself, so strangely had their dream found fulfilment, but taking hold on her courage, she walked into the kitchen, while Rebecca went upstairs. But she could not bear to remain solitary there, and she came back and helped her sister to get a bite of supper for the man.

The food and warmth revived him, and presently, leaving him stretched on two chairs in front of the drowsy fire, they turned the key of the kitchen door on him and went to their room.

Neither of them undressed, but with locked doors and light burning they lay on their beds to pass the vigil till day. The wind had fallen by midnight, the driven snow no longer pattered on the panes, and the stillness sang in their ears. Ellen's bed was nearest to the window, and presently after she sat up to listen more intently, without alarming her sister, to a noise that ever so faintly overscored the silence. There it was again; someone was rattling the sash of the window immediately below, the window of the passage along the front of the house which led to the kitchen. Rebecca heard also, and like a ghost she slid across to her sister's bed.

'There's someone outside,' she whispered. 'That's his fellow, Ellen; there are two of them now, one within and the other outside. He'll go round to the kitchen presently, and the man we left there will let him in. Sister, why did you suffer him to come in? We're done for now; ah, we're done for, and naught can save us!'

Ellen's heart sank. The interpretation seemed only too terribly probable. She drew her sister towards her and kissed her.

'You must try to forgive me, Rebecca,' she said, 'if I've brought your death upon you. But God knows I couldn't do different if I hoped for salvation. It's the money they've come for, and the dream is true. Ah, where is it? Give it to me, and I'll go down to the fellow in the kitchen and offer it to him, and swear to let him go scot free if he'll only take it and spare our lives. We'll lay no information to identify him; we'll let it be known we've just been robbed, and there's the end of it. And yet, why did he give me his rifle and off with his boots? That was a strange thing for him to do.'

Rebecca sat huddled on the bed.

'Strange or no,' she said, 'it's all over with us. There's no help nor succour for us.'

She was half distraught with terror; there was no reasoning with, and Ellen, leaving the rifle she had brought upstairs with her sister, took the wallet containing the notes in her hand and went forth on her midnight and unconjecturable errand. At the bottom of the stairs she must pass the window where they had heard the stir of movement, and now outside there was the grating and grinding of some tool against the glass, and she guessed that whoever was outside was cutting the pane.

She unlocked the kitchen door and entered. The man she had fed and sheltered was awake and standing on his feet. There she was quite defenceless, with her money in her hand, and yet he did not close with her nor push her to get into touch with his accomplice. Instead he came close to her and whispered:

'There's someone moving outside and round about the house,' he said. 'A while ago he was at the kitchen window here. I couldn't come to you and warn you, for you had locked me in.'

She held out the wallet.

'I know the manner of man you are,' she said. 'You came to rob and murder us, and that's your confederate outside. A strange warning came to us, but out of compassion I didn't heed it. Here, then, is the money; spare our lives, and take it and begone, for that was your plan, and I swear we'll not set the police on you.'

He looked at her narrowly.

'What are you telling of?' he said. 'I'm neither robber nor murderer. But waste no more time, ma'am; there's someone at the window now, and he's after no good. He'd have knocked at the door if he'd been a lost wayfarer like me. Now I'm here to help you, for you took me in, and we'll catch him. Where's my rifle?'

For one moment, at the thought of restoring that to him nightmare clutched her again, and she envisaged Rebecca clubbed to death, with herself to follow. But then some ray of hope gleamed in her, some confidence born out of his speech and his mien.

'I'll fetch it for you,' she said.

She went swiftly upstairs and returned with it, and together they stood by the curtained window, while Rebecca nursed a candle on the stairs to give a glimmer of light. He had picked up his belt with his bayonet, and now, as they waited, he fitted it into its catch and drew on his boots. There he was, now armed again, and she defenceless, and in silence they waited.

Presently the scratching at the pane outside ceased, and a current of cold air poured in, making the curtain belly in the draught. It was clear that the burglar had detached a pane of glass and withdrawn it. Then the curtains were thrust aside from without, and a hand entered, feeling for the catch of the window. At that her companion laid down his rifle, and took a step forward, and seized it by the wrist. But it slipped from him, and snatching up his rifle, he ran to the door, and unbolted and opened it.

'We'll catch him yet though,' he called to her. 'Lock the door after me, and let none in unless you hear my voice,' and he vanished into the snowflecked blackness of the night.

Rebecca came down to her, and together they went into the kitchen to wait for what might come out of the night to them. It was no longer possible to doubt the good faith of their visitor, for there on the table lay the wallet with the money untouched. Presently they heard a knock at the door, and his voice calling to them to open. The snow shrouded him in white, and for the second time the soldier of their dream stood on the threshold.

'There was no finding him,' he said, 'for it's dark as the pit, and the snow is like a solid thing. Once I heard him close, and I called on him to stop else I would run my bayonet through him. Not a word did I get, and I thrust at the noise of his running and there was a squeal as the point pierced something, but he shook free again and I heard no more of him. I took him in the arm I reckon. Let's see what the steel can tell us.'

The bayonet confirmed this impression; in the scooped sides of it were runnels of melted snow red with the deeper dye of the blood which for not more than an inch covered the point of it. A flesh wound probably had been inflicted, which had not prevented him from making his escape. With that, there was no more to be done that night, and soon the two sisters were back in their room again, and their guest, with the kitchen door locked no longer, lay down to sleep again. Tomorrow, if no more snow fell, they might perhaps trace and identify the fugitive.

All three were early astir next morning. The snow had ceased and a frosty sun gleamed on the whiteness of the fields. While they were at breakfast the servant-girl, returning from her holiday, came running into the kitchen, breathless and wide-eyed with excitement and alarm.

'There's something in the great dyke, mistress,' she said. 'It's like the body of a man caught among the reeds below the foot-bridge.'

They ran out, and it was easy to follow certain half-obliterated tracks in the frozen snow that led from under the window in the passage to the edge of the dyke. From there, in the deep water by the half-submerged foot-bridge the body had drifted but a few yards into the shallows by the reed-bed, where, with head-downwards, it had been caught and anchored. A couple of long poles soon towed it to the shore, and turning it over, his nieces looked on the face of Alfred Woollard. His coat-sleeve was torn just below the right shoulder, and the ragged edges were stained with blood.

THE PRESCRIPTION

Marjorie Bowen

First published in *The London Magazine*, January 1929

Margaret Gabrielle Vere Campbell Long (1885–1952) had a tragic life. Her parents separated when she was a small child and she lived with her mother in poverty. She had artistic talent but various attempts to attend art college went badly due to her lack of money, and she turned to writing. Her first novel, *The Viper of Milan*, was published in 1906—it was a success and Graham Greene later credited it with inspiring him to become an author. She was married twice, her first husband dying of tuberculosis after less than four years of marriage, and her first baby died of meningitis. She wrote under several different pseudonyms—Marjorie Bowen, George Preedy, John Winch, Robert Paye and Joseph Shearling—and wrote historical romances, children's books, gothic stories and crime dramas. Her success as a novelist eventually gave her the financial stability she had lacked in her early life.

JOHN CUMING COLLECTED GHOST STORIES; HE ALWAYS DECLARED that this was the best that he knew, although it was partially second-hand and contained a mystery that had no reasonable solution, while most really good ghost stories allow of a plausible explanation, even if it is one as feeble as a dream, excusing all; or an hallucination or a crude deception. Cuming told the story rather well. The first part of it at least had come under his own observation and been carefully noted by him in the flat green book which he kept for the record of all curious cases of this sort. He was a shrewd and trained observer; he honestly restrained his love of drama from leading him into embellishing facts. Cuming told the story to us all on the most suitable occasion—Christmas Eve—and prefaced it with a little homily.

'You all know the good old saw—"The more it changes the more it is the same thing"—and I should like you to notice that this extremely up-to-date ultra-modern ghost story is really almost exactly the same as one that might have puzzled Babylonian or Assyrian sages. I can give you the first start of the tale in my own words, but the second part will have to be in the words of someone else. They were, however, most carefully and scrupulously taken down. As for the conclusion, I must leave you to draw that for yourselves—each according to your own mood, fancy, and temperament; it may be that you will all think of the same solution, it may be that you will each think of a different one, and it may be that every one will be left wondering.'

Having thus enjoyed himself by whetting our curiosity, Cuming settled himself down comfortably in his deep arm-chair and unfolded his tale.

'It was about five years ago. I don't wish to be exact with time, and of course I shall alter names—that's one of the first rules of the game, isn't it? Well, whenever it was, I was the guest of a—Mrs. Janey we will call her—who was, to some extent, a friend of mine; an intelligent, lively, rather bustling sort of woman who had the knack of gathering interesting people about her. She had lately taken a new house in Buckinghamshire. It stood in the grounds of one of those large estates which are now so frequently being broken up. She was very pleased with the house, which was quite new and had only been finished a year, and seemed, according to her own rather excited imagination, in every way desirable. I don't want to emphasise anything about the house except that it *was* new and did stand on the verge, as it were, of this large old estate, which had belonged to one of those notable English families now extinct and completely forgotten. I am no antiquarian or connoisseur in architecture, and the rather blatant modernity of the house did not offend me. I was able to appreciate its comfort and to enjoy what Mrs. Janey rather maddeningly called "the old-world gardens," which were really a section of the larger gardens of the vanished mansion which had once commanded this domain. Mrs. Janey, I should tell you, knew nothing about the neighbourhood nor anyone who lived there, except that for the first it was very convenient for town, and for the second she believed that they were all "*nice*" people, not likely to bother one. I was slightly disappointed with the crowd she had gathered together at Christmas. They were all people whom either I knew too well or whom I didn't wish to know at all, and at first the party showed signs of being extremely flat. Mrs. Janey seemed to perceive this too, and with rather nervous haste produced, on Christmas Eve, a trump card in the way of amusement—a professional medium, called Mrs. Mahogany, because that could not possibly have been her name. Some of us "believed in," as the saying goes, mediums, and some didn't; but we were all willing to be diverted by the experiment. Mrs. Janey continually lamented that a certain Dr. Dilke would not be present. He was going to be one of the party, but had been detained in town and would not reach Verrall, which was the name of the house, until later, and the medium, it seemed, could not stay; for she, being a personage in great demand, must go on to a further engagement. I, of course, like every one else possessed of an intelligent curiosity and a certain amount of leisure, had been to mediums before. I had been slightly impressed, slightly disgusted, and very much bewildered, and on the whole had decided to let the matter alone, considering that I really preferred the more direct and old-fashioned method of getting in touch with what we used to call "The Unseen." This sitting in the great new house seemed rather banal. I could understand in some haunted old manor that a clairvoyant, or a clairaudient, or a trance-medium might have found something interesting to say, but what was she going to get out of Mrs. Janey's bright, brilliant, and comfortable dwelling?

'Mrs. Mahogany was a nondescript sort of woman—neither young nor old, neither clever nor stupid, neither dark nor fair, placid, and not in the least self-conscious. After an extremely good luncheon (it was a gloomy, stormy afternoon) we all sat down in a circle in the cheerful drawing-room; the curtains were pulled across the dreary prospect of grey sky and grey landscape, and we had merely the light of the fire. We sat quite close together in order to increase "the power," as Mrs. Mahogany said, and the medium sat in the middle, with no special precautions against trickery; but we all knew that trickery would have been really impossible, and we were quite prepared to be tremendously impressed and startled if any manifestations took place. I think we all felt rather foolish, as we did not know each other very well, sitting round there, staring at this very ordinary, rather common, stout little woman, who kept nervously pulling a little tippet of grey wool over her shoulders, closing her eyes and muttering, while she twisted her fingers together. When we had sat silent for about ten minutes Mrs. Janey announced in a rather raw whisper that the medium had gone into a trance. "Beautifully," she added. I thought that Mrs. Mahogany did not look at all beautiful. Her communication began with a lot of rambling talk which had no point at all, and a good deal of generalisation under which I think we all became a little restive. There was too much of various spirits who had all sorts of ordinary names, just regular Toms, Dicks, and Harrys of the spirit world, floating round behind us, their arms full of flowers and their mouths of goodwill, all rather pointless. And though, occasionally, a Tom, Dick, or a Harry was identified by some of us, it wasn't very convincing, and, what was worse, not very interesting. We got, however, our surprise and our shock, because Mrs. Mahogany began suddenly to writhe into ugly contortions and called out in a loud voice, quite different from the one that she had hitherto used:

"'Murder!'"

'This word gave us all a little thrill, and we leant forward eagerly to hear what further she had to say. With every sign of distress and horror Mrs. Mahogany began to speak:

"'He's murdered her. Oh, how dreadful. Look at him! Can't somebody stop him? It's so near here, too. He tried to save her. He was sorry, you know. Oh, how dreadful! Look at him—he's borne it as long as he can, and now he's murdered her! I see him mixing it in a glass. Oh, isn't it awful that no one could have saved her—and he was so terribly remorseful afterwards. Oh, how dreadful! How horrible!"

'She ended in a whimpering of fright and horror, and Mrs. Janey, who seemed an adept at this sort of thing, leant forward and asked eagerly:

'"Can't you get the name—can't you find out who it is? Why do you get that here?"

'"I don't know," muttered the medium, "it's somewhere near here—a house, an old dark house, and there are curtains of mauve velvet—do you call it mauve?, a kind of blue red—at the windows. There's a garden outside with a fishpond and you go through a low doorway and down stone steps."

'"It isn't near here," said Mrs. Janey decidedly, "all the houses are new."

'"The house is near here," persisted the medium. "I am walking through it now; I can see the room, I can see that poor, poor woman, and a glass of milk—"

'"I wish you'd get the name," insisted Mrs. Janey, and she cast a look, as I thought not without suspicion, round the circle. "You can't be getting this from my house, you know, Mrs. Mahogany," she added decidedly, "it must be given out by someone here—something they've read or seen, you know," she said, to reassure us that our characters were not in dispute.

'But the medium replied drowsily, "No, it's somewhere near here. I see a light dress covered with small roses. If he could have got help he would have gone for it, but there was no one; so all his remorse was useless…"

'No further urging would induce the medium to say more; soon afterwards she came out of the trance, and all of us, I think, felt that she had made rather a stupid blunder by introducing this vague piece of melodrama, and if it was, as we suspected, a cheap attempt to give a ghostly and mysterious atmosphere to Christmas Eve, it was a failure.

'When Mrs. Mahogany, blinking round her, said brightly, "Well, here I am again! I wonder if I said anything that interested you?" we all replied rather coldly, "Of course it has been most interesting, but there hasn't been anything definite." And I think that even Mrs. Janey felt that the sitting had been rather a disappointment, and she suggested that if the weather was really too horrible to venture out of doors we should sit round the fire and tell old-fashioned ghost stories. "The kind," she said brightly, "that are about bones and chairs and shrouds. I really think that is the most thrilling kind after all." Then, with some embarrassment, and when Mrs. Mahogany had left the room, she suggested that not one of us should say anything about what the medium had said in her trance.

'"It really was rather absurd," said our hostess, "and it would make me look a little foolish if it got about; you know some people think these mediums are absolute fakes, and anyhow, the whole thing, I am afraid, was quite stupid. She must have got her contacts mixed. There is no old house about here and never has been since the original Verrall was pulled down, and that's a good fifty years ago, I believe, from what the estate agent told me; and as for a murder, I never heard the shadow of any such story."

'We all agreed not to mention what the medium had said, and did this with the more heartiness as we were, not any one of us, impressed. The feeling was rather that Mrs. Mahogany had been obliged to say something and had said that…

'Well,' said Cuming comfortably, 'that is the first part of my story, and I daresay you'll think it's dull enough. Now we come to the second part.

'Lateish that evening Dr. Dilke arrived. He was not in any way a remarkable man, just an ordinary successful physician, and I refuse to say that he was suffering from overwork or nervous strain; you

know that is so often put into this kind of story as a sort of excuse for
what happens afterwards. On the contrary, Dr. Dilke seemed to be
in the most robust of health and the most cheerful frame of mind,
and quite prepared to make the most of his brief holiday. The car
that fetched him from the station was taking Mrs. Mahogany away,
and the doctor and the medium met for just a moment in the hall.
Mrs. Janey did not trouble to introduce them, but without waiting
for this Mrs. Mahogany turned to the doctor, and looking at him
fixedly, said, "You're very psychic, aren't you?" And upon that Mrs.
Janey was forced to say hastily: "This is Mrs. Mahogany, Dr. Dilke,
the famous medium."

'The physician was indifferently impressed: "I really don't know,"
he answered smiling, "I have never gone in for that sort of thing.
I shouldn't think I am what you call 'psychic' really; I have had a
hard, scientific training, and that rather knocks the bottom out of
fantasies."

'"Well, you are, you know," said Mrs. Mahogany; "I felt it at once;
I shouldn't be at all surprised if you had some strange experience
one of these days."

'Mrs. Mahogany left the house and was duly driven away to the
station. I want to make the point very clear that she and Dr. Dilke
did not meet again and that they held no communication except
those few words in the hall spoken in the presence of Mrs. Janey. Of
course Dr. Dilke got twitted a good deal about what the medium
had said; it made quite a topic of conversation during dinner and
after dinner, and we all had queer little ghost stories or incidents of
what we considered "psychic" experiences to trot out and discuss. Dr.
Dilke remained civil, amused, but entirely unconvinced. He had what
he called a material, or physical, or medical explanation for almost
everything that we said, and, apart from all these explanations he

added, with some justice, that human credulity was such that there was always some one who would accept and embellish anything, however wild, unlikely, or grotesque it was.

'"I should rather like to hear what you would say if such an experience happened to you," Mrs. Janey challenged him; "whether you use the ancient terms of 'ghost,' 'witches,' 'black magic,' and so on, or whether you speak in modern terms like 'medium,' 'clairvoyance,' 'psychic contacts,' and all the rest of it; well, it seems one is in a bit of a tangle anyhow, and if any queer thing ever happens to you—"

'Dr. Dilke broke in pleasantly: "Well, if it ever does I will let you all know about it, and I dare say I shall have an explanation to add at the end of the tale."

'When we all met again the next morning we rather hoped that Dr. Dilke *would* have something to tell us—some odd experience that might have befallen him in the night, new as the house was, and banal as was his bedroom. He told us, of course, that he had passed a perfectly good night.

'We most of us went to the morning service in the small church that had once been the chapel belonging to the demolished mansion, and which had some rather curious monuments inside and in the churchyard. As I went in I noticed a mortuary chapel with niches for the coffins to be stood upright, now whitewashed and used as a sacristy. The monuments and mural tablets were mostly to the memory of members of the family of Verrall—the Verralls of Verrall Hall, who appeared to have been people of little interest or distinction. Dr. Dilke sat beside me, and I, having nothing better to do through the more familiar and monotonous portions of the service, found myself idly looking at the mural table beyond him. This was a large slab of black marble deeply cut with a very worn Latin inscription which I found, unconsciously, I was spelling out. The stone, it seemed, commemorated a woman who had been, of course, the possessor of all the virtues; her name was Philadelphia Carwithen, and I rather pleasantly sampled the flavour of that ancient name—Philadelphia. Then I noticed a smaller inscription at the bottom of the slab, which indicated that the lady's husband also rested in the vault; he had died suddenly about six months after her—of grief at her loss, no doubt, I thought, scenting out a pretty romance.

'As we walked home across the frost-bitten fields and icy lanes Dr. Dilke, who walked beside me, as he had sat beside me in church, began to complain of cold; he said he believed that he had caught a chill. I was rather amused to hear this old-womanish expression on the lips of so distinguished a physician, and I told him that I had been taught in my more enlightened days that there was no such thing as "catching a chill." To my surprise he did not laugh at this, but said:

'"Oh, yes, there is, and I believe I've got it—I keep on shivering; I think it was that slab of black stone I was sitting next. It was as cold as ice, for I touched it, and it seemed to me exuding moisture—some of that old stone does, you know, it's always, as it were, sweating; and I felt exactly as if I were sitting next a slab of ice from which a cold wind was blowing; it was really as if it penetrated my flesh."

'He looked pale, and I thought how disagreeable it would be for us all, and particularly for Mrs. Janey, if the good man was to be taken ill in the midst of her already not too successful Christmas party. Dr. Dilke seemed, too, in that ill-humour which so often presages an illness; he was quite peevish about the church and the service, and the fact that he had been asked to go there.

'"These places are nothing but charnel-houses, after all," he said fretfully; "one sits there among all those rotting bones, with that damp marble at one's side…"

"'It is supposed to give you 'atmosphere,'" I said. "The atmosphere of an old-fashioned Christmas... Did you notice who your black stone was erected 'to the memory of'?" I asked, and the doctor replied that he had not.

"'It was to a young woman—a young woman, I took it, and her husband: 'Philadelphia Carwithen,' I noticed that, and of course there was a long eulogy of her virtues, and then underneath it just said that he had died a few months afterwards. As far as I could see it was the only example of that name in the church—all the rest were Verralls. I suppose they were strangers here."

"'What was the date?" asked the doctor, and I replied that really I had not been able to make it out, for where the roman figures came the stone had been very worn.

'The day ambled along somehow, with games, diversions, and plenty of good food and drink, and towards the evening we began to feel a little more satisfied with each other and our hostess. Only Dr. Dilke remained a little peevish and apart, and this was remarkable in one who was obviously of a robust temperament and an even temper. He still continued to talk of a "chill," and I did notice that he shuddered once or twice, and continually sat near the large fire which Mrs. Janey had rather laboriously arranged in imitation of what she would call "the good old times."

'That evening, the evening of Christmas Day, there was no talk whatever of ghosts or psychic matters; our discussions were entirely topical and of mundane matters, in which Dr. Dilke, who seemed to have recovered his spirits, took his part with ability and agreeableness. When it was time to break up I asked him, half in jest, about his mysterious chill, and he looked at me with some surprise and appeared to have forgotten that he had ever said he had got such a thing; the impression, whatever it was, which he had received in the church, had evidently been effaced from his mind. I wish to make that quite clear.

'The next morning Dr. Dilke appeared very late at the breakfast table, and when he did so his looks were matter for hints and comment; he was pale, distracted, troubled, untidy in his dress, absent in his manner, and I, at least, instantly recalled what he had said yesterday, and feared he was sickening for some illness.

'On Mrs. Janey putting to him some direct question as to his looks and manner, so strange and so troubled, he replied rather sharply, "Well, I don't know what you can expect from a fellow who's been up all night. I thought I came down here for a rest."

'We all looked at him as he dropped into his place and began to drink his coffee with eager gusto; I noticed that he continually shivered. There was something about this astounding statement and his curious appearance which held us all discreetly silent. We waited for further developments before committing ourselves; even Mrs. Janey, whom I had never thought of as tactful, contrived to say casually:

'"Up all night, doctor. Couldn't you sleep, then? I'm so sorry if your bed wasn't comfortable."

'"The bed was all right," he answered, "that made me the more sorry to leave it. Haven't you got a local doctor who can take the local cases?" he added.

'"Why, of course we have; there's Dr. Armstrong and Dr. Fraser—I made sure about that before I came here."

'"Well, then," demanded Dr. Dilke angrily, "why on earth couldn't one of them have gone last night?"

'Mrs. Janey looked at me helplessly, and I, obeying her glance, took up the matter.

'"What do you mean, doctor? Do you mean that you were called out of your bed last night to attend a case?" I asked deliberately.

'"Of course I was—I only got back with the dawn."

'Here Mrs. Janey could not forbear breaking in.

'"But whoever could it have been? I know nobody about here yet, at least, only one or two people by name, and they would not be aware that you were here. And how did you get out of the house? It's locked every night."

'Then the doctor gave his story in rather, I must confess, a confused fashion, and yet with an earnest conviction that he was speaking the simple truth. It was broken up a good deal by ejaculations and comments from the rest of us, but I give it you here shorn of all that and exactly as I put it down in my notebook afterwards.

'"I was awoken by a tap at the door. I was instantly wide awake and I said, 'Come in.' I thought immediately that probably someone in the house was ill—a doctor, you know, is always ready for these emergencies. The door opened at once, and a man entered holding a small ordinary storm-lantern. I noticed nothing peculiar about the man. He had a dark greatcoat on, and appeared extremely anxious. 'I am sorry to disturb you,' he said at once, 'but there is a young woman dangerously ill. I want you to come and see her.' I, somehow, did not think of arguing or of suggesting that there were other medical men in the neighbourhood, or of asking how it was he knew of my presence at Verrall. I dressed myself quickly and accompanied him out of the house. He opened the front door without any trouble, and it did not occur to me to ask him how it was he had obtained either admission or egress. There was a small carriage outside the door, such a one as you may still see in isolated country places, but such a one as I was certainly surprised to see here. I could not very well make out either the horse or the driver, for, though the moon was high in the heavens, it was frequently obscured by clouds. I got into the carriage and noticed, as I have often noticed before in these

ancient vehicles, a most repulsive smell of decay and damp. My companion got in beside me. He did not speak a word during the whole
of the journey, which was, I have the impression, extremely long. I
had also the sense that he was in the greatest trouble, anguish, and
almost despair; I do not know why I did not question him. I should
tell you that he had drawn down the blinds of the carriage and we
travelled in darkness, yet I was perfectly aware of his presence and
seemed to see him in his heavy dark greatcoat turned up round the
chin, his black hair low on his forehead, and his anxious, furtive dark
eyes. I think I may have gone to sleep in the carriage, I was tired and
cold. I was aware, however, when it stopped, and of my companion
opening the door and helping me out. We went through a garden,
down some steps and past a fishpond; I could see by the moonlight
the silver and gold shapes of fishes slipping in and out of the black
water. We entered the house by a side-door—I remember that very
distinctly—and went up what seemed to be some secret or seldom-
used stairs, and into a bedroom. I was, by now, quite alert, as one is
when one gets into the presence of the patient, and said to myself,
'What a fool I've been, I've brought nothing with me,' and I tried to
remember, but could not quite do so, whether or not I had brought
anything with me—my cases and so on—to Verrall. The room was
very badly lit, but a certain illumination—I could not say whether it
came from any artificial light within the room or merely from the
moonlight through the open window, draped with mauve velvet
curtains—fell on the bed, and there I saw my patient. She was a
young woman, who, I surmised, would have been, when in health,
of considerable though coarse charm. She was now in great suffering,
twisted and contorted with agony, and in her struggles of anguish had
pulled and torn the bedclothes into a heap. I noticed that she wore a
dress of some light material spotted with small roses, and it occurred

to me at once that she had been taken ill during the daytime and must have lain thus in great pain for many hours, and I turned with some reproach to the man who had fetched me and demanded why help had not been sought sooner. For answer he wrung his hands—a gesture that I do not remember having noticed in any human being before; one hears a great deal of hands being wrung, but one does not so often see it. This man, I remember distinctly, wrung his hands, and muttered, 'Do what you can for her—do what you can!' I feared that this would be very little. I endeavoured to make an examination of the patient, but owing to her half-delirious struggles this was very difficult; she was, however, I thought, likely to die, and of what malady I could not determine. There was a table nearby on which lay some papers—one I took to be a will—and a glass in which there had been milk. I do not remember seeing anything else in the room—the light was so bad. I endeavoured to question the man, whom I took to be the husband, but without any success. He merely repeated his monotonous appeal for me to save her. Then I was aware of a sound outside the room—of a woman laughing, perpetually and shrilly laughing. 'Pray stop that,' I cried to the man; 'who have you got in the house—a lunatic?' But he took no notice of my appeal, merely repeating his own hushed lamentations. The sick woman appeared to hear that demoniacal laughter outside, and raising herself on one elbow said, 'You have destroyed me and you may well laugh.'

"'I sat down at the table on which were the papers and the glass half full of milk, and wrote a prescription on a sheet torn out of my notebook. The man snatched it eagerly. 'I don't know when and where you can get that made up,' I said, 'but it's the only hope.' At this he seemed wishful for me to depart, as wishful as he had been for me to come. 'That's all I want,' he said. He took me by the arm and led me out of the house by the same back stairs. As I descended I still heard those two dreadful sounds—the thin laughter of the woman I had not seen, and the groans, becoming every moment fainter, of the young woman whom I had seen. The carriage was waiting for me, and I was driven back by the same way I had come. When I reached the house and my room I saw the dawn just breaking. I rested till I heard the breakfast gong. I suppose some time had gone by since I returned to the house, but I wasn't quite aware of it; all through the night I had rather lost the sense of time."

'When Dr. Dilke had finished his narrative, which I give here baldly—but, I hope, to the point—we all glanced at each other rather uncomfortably, for who was to tell a man like Dr. Dilke that he had been suffering from a severe hallucination? It was, of course, quite impossible that he could have left the house and gone through the peculiar scenes he had described, and it seemed extraordinary that he could for a moment have believed that he had done so. What was even more remarkable was that so many points of his story agreed with what the medium, Mrs. Mahogany, had said in her trance. We recognised the frock with the roses, the mauve velvet curtains, the glass of milk, the man who had fetched Dr. Dilke sounded like the murderer, and the unfortunate woman writhing on the bed sounded like the victim; but how had the doctor got hold of these particulars? We all knew that he had not spoken to Mrs. Mahogany, and each suspected the other of having told him what the medium had said, and that this having wrought on his mind he had the dream, vision, or hallucination he had just described to us. I must add that this was found afterwards to be wholly false; we were all reliable people and there was not a shadow of doubt we had all kept our counsel about Mrs. Mahogany. In fact, none of us had been alone with Dr. Dilke the previous day for more than a moment or so save myself, who had walked with him from the church, when we had certainly spoken of nothing except the black stone in the church and the chill which he had said emanated from it... Well, to put the matter as briefly as possible, and to leave out a great deal of amazement and wonder, explanation, and so on, we will come to the point when Dr. Dilke was finally persuaded that he had not left Verrall all the night. When his story was taken to pieces and put before him, as it were, in the raw, he himself recognised many absurdities: How could the man have come straight to his bedroom? How could he have left the house?—the doors were locked every night, there was no doubt about that. Where did the carriage come from and where was the house to which he had been taken? And who could possibly have known of his presence in the neighbourhood? Had not, too, the scene in the house to which he was taken all the resemblance of a nightmare? Who was it laughing in the other room? What was the mysterious illness that was destroying the young woman? Who was the black-browed man who had fetched him? And, in these days of telephone and motor-cars, people didn't go out in the old-fashioned one-horse carriages to fetch doctors from miles away in the case of dangerous illness.

'Dr. Dilke was finally silenced, uneasy, but not convinced. I could see that he disliked intensely the idea that he had been the victim of an hallucination and that he equally intensely regretted the impulse which had made him relate his extraordinary adventure of the night. I could only conclude that he must have done so while still, to an extent, under the influence of his delusion, which had been so strong that never for a moment had he questioned the reality of it. Though he was forced at last to allow us to put the whole thing down as a most remarkable dream, I could see that he did not intend to let the matter rest there, and later in the day (out of good manners we had eventually ceased discussing the story) he asked me if I would accompany him on some investigation in the neighbourhood.

'"I think I should know the house," he said, "even though I saw it in the dark. I was impressed by the fishpond and the low doorway through which I had to stoop in order to pass without knocking my head."

'I did not tell him that Mrs. Mahogany had also mentioned a fishpond and a low door.

'We made the excuse of some old brasses we wished to discover in a nearby church to take my car and go out that afternoon on an investigation of the neighbourhood in the hope of discovering Dr. Dilke's dream house.

'We covered a good deal of distance and spent a good deal of time without any success at all, and the short day was already darkening when we came upon a row of almshouses in which, for no reason at all that I could discern, Dr. Dilke showed an interest and insisted on stopping before them. He pointed out an inscription cut in the centre gable, which said that there had been built by a certain Richard Carwithen in memory of Philadelphia, his wife.

'"The people whose tablet you sat next in the church," I remarked.

'"Yes," murmured Dr. Dilke, "when I felt the chill," and he added, "when I *first* felt the chill. You see, the date is 1830. That would be about right."

'We stopped in the little village, which was a good many miles from Verrall, and after some tedious delays because everything was shut up for the holiday, we did discover an old man who was willing to tell us something about the almshouses, though there was nothing much to be said about them. They had been founded by a certain Mr. Richard Carwithen with his wife's fortune. He had been a poor man, a kind of adventurer, our informant thought, who had married a wealthy woman; they had not been at all happy. There had been quarrels and disputes, and a separation (at least, so the gossip went, as his father had told it to him); finally, the Carwithens had taken a house here in this village of Sunford—a large house it was and it still stood. The Carwithens weren't buried in this village though, but at Verrall; she had been a Verrall by birth—perhaps that's why they came to this neighbourhood—it was the name of a great family in those days, you know… There was another woman in the old story, as it went, and she got hold of Mr. Carwithen and was for making him put his wife aside; and so, perhaps, he would have done, but the poor lady died suddenly, and there was some talk about it, having the other woman in the house at the time, and it being so convenient for both of them… But he didn't marry the other woman, because he died six months after his wife… By his will he left all his wife's money to found these almshouses.

'Dr. Dilke asked if he could see the house where the Carwithens had lived.

'"It belongs to a London gentleman," the old man said, "who never comes here. It's going to be pulled down and the land sold in building lots; why, it's been locked up these ten years or more. I don't suppose it's been inhabited since—no, not for a hundred years."

'"Well, I'm looking for a house round about here. I don't mind spending a little money on repairs if that house is in the market."

'The old man didn't know whether it was in the market or not, but kept repeating that the property was to be sold and broken up for building lots.

'I won't bother you with all our delays and arguments, but merely tell you that we did finally discover the lodgekeeper of the estate, who gave us the key. It was not such a very large estate, nothing to be compared to Verrall, but had been, in its time, of some pretension.

Builders' boards had already been raised along the high road frontage. There were some fine old trees, black and bare, in a little park. As we turned in through the rusty gates and motored towards the house it was nearly dark, but we had our electric torches and the power-ful headlamps of the car. Dr. Dilke made no comment on what we had found, but he reconstructed the story of the Carwithens whose names were on that black stone in Verrall church.

'"They were quarrelling over money, he was trying to get her to sign a will in his favour; she had some little sickness perhaps—brought on probably by rage—he had got the other woman in the house, remember; I expect he was no good. There was some sort of poison about—perhaps for a face-wash, perhaps as a drug. He put it in the milk and gave it to her."

'Here I interrupted: "How do you know it was in the milk?"

'The doctor did not reply to this. I had now swung the car round to the front of the ancient mansion—a poor, pretentious place, sin-ister in the half-darkness.

'"And then, when he had done it," continued Dr. Dilke, mount-ing the steps of the house, "he repented most horribly; he wanted to fly for a doctor to get some antidote for the poison with the idea in his head that if he could have got help he could have saved her himself. The other woman kept on laughing. He couldn't forgive her that—that she could laugh at a moment like that; he couldn't get help! He couldn't find a doctor. His wife died. No one suspected foul play—they seldom did in those days as long as the people were respectable; you must remember the state in which medical knowledge was in 1830. He couldn't marry the other woman, and he couldn't touch the money; he left it all to found the almshouses; then he died himself, six months afterwards, leaving instructions that his name should be added to that black stone. I dare say he died by his own hand. Probably he loved her through it all, you know—it was only the money, that cursed money, a fortune just within his grasp, but which he couldn't take."

'"A pretty romance," I suggested, as we entered the house; "I am sure there is a three-volume novel in it of what Mrs. Janey would call 'the good old-fashioned' sort."

'To this Dr. Dilke answered: "Suppose the miserable man can't rest? Supposing he is still searching for a doctor?"

'We passed from one room to another of the dismal, dusty, dismantled house. Dr. Dilke opened a damaged shutter which concealed one of the windows at the back, and pointed out in the waning light a decayed garden with stone steps and a fishpond; and a low gateway to pass through which a man of his height would have had to stoop. We could just discern this in the twilight. He made no comment. We went upstairs.'

Here Cuming paused dramatically to give us the full flavour of the final part of his story. He reminded us, rather unnecessarily, for somehow he had convinced us that this was all perfectly true.

'I am not romancing; I won't answer for what Dr. Dilke said or did, or his adventure of the night before, or the story of the Carwithens as he constructed it, but *this* is actually what happened… We went upstairs by the wide main stairs. Dr. Dilke searched about for and found a door which opened on to the back stairs, and then he said: "This must be the room." It was entirely devoid of any furniture, and stained with damp, the walls stripped of panelling and cheaply covered with decayed paper, peeling, and in parts fallen.

'"What's this?" said Dr. Dilke.

'He picked up a scrap of paper that showed vivid on the dusty floor and handed it to me. It was a prescription. He took out his notebook and showed me the page where this fitted in.

'"This page I tore out last night when I wrote that prescription in this room. The bed was just there, and there was the table on which were the papers and the glass of milk."

'"But you couldn't have been here last night," I protested feebly, "the locked doors—the whole thing!…"

'Dr. Dilke said nothing. After a while neither did I. "Let's get out of this place," I said. Then another thought struck me. "What is your prescription?" I asked.

'He said: "A very uncommon kind of prescription, a very desperate sort of prescription, one that I've never written before, nor I hope shall again—an antidote for severe arsenical poisoning."

'I leave you,' smiled Cuming, 'to your various attitudes of incredulity or explanation.'

THE SNOW

Hugh Walpole

First published in *Shudders*, edited by Cynthia Asquith, 1929

Sir Hugh Seymour Walpole (1884–1941) was born in Auckland, New Zealand to English parents, and spent his childhood in New York and at various English boarding schools. He was related to two important Gothic writers—Horace Walpole, who wrote the first Gothic novel *The Castle of Otranto* in 1764, and Richard Harris Barham, author of *The Ingoldsby Legends*. He became a prolific novelist himself, publishing his most famous book *Rogue Herries*, a historical novel set near his home in Cumbria, in 1930. He was shocked that same year when his friend Somerset Maugham included a satirical portrait of him in the novel *Cakes and Ale*, saying 'I could think of no one among my contemporaries who had achieved so considerable a position on so little talent.' This shook his confidence and he wrote sadly in his diary in 1935, 'shall I have any lasting reputation? Like every author in history who has seriously tried to be an artist, I sometimes consider the question. Fifty years from now I think the Lake stories will still be read locally, otherwise I shall be mentioned in a small footnote to my period in literary history.' However, he was admired by writers including Arnold Bennett, Clemence Dance, J. B. Priestley and Joseph Conrad, and he was a close friend of Virginia Woolf. He was in a long term relationship until his death with a former policeman called Harold Cheevers who was known officially as his chauffeur.

THE SECOND MRS. RYDER WAS A YOUNG WOMAN NOT EASILY frightened, but now she stood in the dusk of the passage leaning back against the wall, her hand on her heart, looking at the grey-faced window beyond which the snow was steadily falling against the lamplight.

The passage where she was led from the study to the dining-room, and the window looked out onto the little paved path that ran at the edge of the Cathedral green. As she stared down the passage she couldn't be sure whether the woman were there or no. How absurd of her! She knew the woman was not there. But if the woman was not, how was it that she could discern so clearly the old-fashioned grey cloak, the untidy grey hair and the sharp outline of the pale cheek and pointed chin? Yes, and more than that, the long sweep of the grey dress, falling in folds to the ground, the flash of a gold ring on the white hand. No. No. NO. This was madness. There was no one and nothing there. Hallucination…

Very faintly a voice seemed to come to her: 'I warned you. This is for the last time…'

The nonsense! How far now was her imagination to carry her? Tiny sounds about the house, the running of a tap somewhere, a faint voice from the kitchen, these and something more had translated themselves into an imagined voice. 'The last time…'

But her terror was real. She was not normally frightened by anything. She was young and healthy and bold, fond of sport, hunting, shooting, taking any risk. Now she was truly *stiffened* with terror—she could not move, could not advance down the passage as she wanted to and find light, warmth, safety in the dining-room. All the time the snow fell steadily, stealthily, with its own secret purpose, maliciously, beyond the window in the pale glow of the lamplight.

Then unexpectedly there was noise from the hall, opening of doors, a rush of feet, a pause and then in clear beautiful voices the well-known strains of 'Good King Wenceslas.' It was the Cathedral choir boys on their regular Christmas round. This was Christmas Eve. They always came just at this hour on Christmas Eve.

With an intense, almost incredible relief she turned back into the hall. At the same moment her husband came out of the study. They stood together smiling at the little group of mufflered, becoated boys who were singing, heart and soul in the job, so that the old house simply rang with their melody.

Reassured by the warmth and human company, she lost her terror. It had been her imagination. Of late she had been none too well. That was why she had been so irritable. Old Doctor Bernard was no good: he didn't understand her case at all. After Christmas she would go to London and have the very best advice...

Had she been well she could not, half an hour ago, have shown such miserable temper over nothing. She knew that it was over nothing and yet that knowledge did not make it any easier for her to restrain herself. After every bout of temper she told herself that there should never be another—and then Herbert said something irritating, one of his silly muddle-headed stupidities, and she was off again!

She could see now as she stood beside him at the bottom of the staircase, that he was still feeling it. She had certainly half an hour ago said some abominably rude personal things—things that she had not at all meant—and he had taken them in his meek, quiet way. Were he not so meek and quiet, did he only pay her back in her own coin, she would never lose her temper. Of that she was sure. But who wouldn't be irritated by that meekness and by the only reproachful thing that he ever said to her: 'Elinor understood me better, my dear.' To throw the first wife up against the second! Wasn't that the most tactless thing that a man could possibly do? And Elinor, that old, worn elderly woman, the very opposite of her own gay, bright, amusing self? That was why Herbert had loved her, because she was gay and bright and young. It was true that Elinor had been devoted, that she had been so utterly wrapped up in Herbert that she lived only for him. People were always recalling her devotion, which was sufficiently rude and tactless of them.

Well, she could not give anyone that kind of old-fashioned sugary devotion; it wasn't in her, and Herbert knew it by this time.

Nevertheless she loved Herbert in her own way, as he must know, know it so well that he ought to pay no attention to the bursts of temper. She wasn't well. She would see a doctor in London…

The little boys finished their carols, were properly rewarded, and tumbled like feathery birds out into the snow again. They went into the study, the two of them, and stood beside the big open log-fire. She put her hand up and stroked his thin beautiful cheek.

'I'm so sorry to have been cross just now, Bertie. I didn't mean half I said, you know.'

But he didn't, as he usually did, kiss her and tell her that it didn't matter. Looking straight in front of him, he answered:

'Well, Alice, I do wish you wouldn't. It hurts, horribly. It upsets me more than you think. And it's growing on you. You make me miserable. I don't know what to do about it. And it's all about nothing.'

Irritated at not receiving the usual commendation for her sweetness in making it up again, she withdrew a little and answered:

'Oh, all right. I've said I'm sorry. I can't do any more.'

'But tell me,' he insisted, 'I want to know. What makes you so angry, so suddenly?—and about nothing at all.'

She was about to let her anger rise, her anger at his obtuseness, obstinacy, when some fear checked her, a strange unanalysed fear, as though someone had whispered to her, 'Look out! This is the last time!'

'It's not altogether my own fault,' she answered, and left the room.

She stood in the cold hall, wondering where to go. She could feel the snow falling outside the house and shivered. She hated the snow, she hated the winter, this beastly, cold dark English winter that went on and on, only at last to change into a damp, soggy English spring.

It had been snowing all day. In Polchester it was unusual to have so heavy a snowfall. This was the hardest winter that they had known for many years.

When she urged Herbert to winter abroad—which he could quite easily do—he answered her impatiently; he had the strongest affection for this poky dead-and-alive Cathedral town. The Cathedral seemed to be precious to him; he wasn't happy if he didn't go and see it every day! She wouldn't wonder if he didn't think more of the Cathedral than he did of herself. Elinor had been the same; she had even written a little book about the Cathedral, about the Black Bishop's Tomb and the stained glass and the rest...

What was the Cathedral after all? Only a building! She was standing in the drawing-room looking out over the dusky ghostly snow to the great hulk of the Cathedral that Herbert said was like a flying ship, but to herself was more like a crouching beast licking its lips over the miserable sinners that it was forever devouring.

As she looked and shivered, feeling that in spite of herself her temper and misery were rising so that they threatened to choke her, it seemed to her that her bright and cheerful fire-lit drawing-room was suddenly open to the snow. It was exactly as though cracks had appeared everywhere, in the ceiling, the walls, the windows, and that through these cracks the snow was filtering, dribbling in little tracks of wet down the walls, already perhaps making pools of water on the carpet.

This was of course imagination, but it was a fact that the room was most dreadfully cold although a great fire was burning and it was the cosiest room in the house.

Then, turning, she saw the figure standing by the door. This time there could be no mistake. It was a grey shadow, and yet a shadow with form and outline—the untidy grey hair, the pale face like a moon-lit leaf, the long grey clothes, and something obstinate, vindictive, terribly menacing in its pose.

She moved and the figure was gone; there was nothing there and the room was warm again, quite hot in fact. But young Mrs. Ryder, who had never feared anything in all her life save the vanishing of her youth, was trembling so that she had to sit down, and even then her trembling did not cease. Her hand shook on the arm of her chair.

She had created this thing out of her imagination of Elinor's hatred of her and her own hatred of Elinor. It was true that they had never met, but who knew but that the spiritualists were right, and Elinor's spirit, jealous of Herbert's love for her, had been there driving them apart, forcing her to lose her temper and then hating her for losing it? Such things might be! But she had not much time for speculation. She was preoccupied with her fear. It was a definite, positive fear, the kind of fear that one has just before one goes into an operation. Someone or something was threatening her. She clung to her chair as though to leave it were to plunge into disaster. She looked around her everywhere; all the familiar things, the pictures, the books, the little tables, the piano were different now, isolated, strange, hostile, as though they had been won over by some enemy power.

She longed for Herbert to come and protect her; she felt most kindly to him. She would never lose her temper with him again—and at that same moment some cold voice seemed to whisper in her ear: 'You had better not. It will be for the last time.'

At length she found courage to rise, cross the room and go up to dress for dinner. In her bedroom courage came to her once more. It was certainly very cold, and the snow, as she could see when she looked between her curtains, was falling more heavily than ever, but she had a warm bath, sat in front of her fire and was sensible again.

For many months this odd sense that she was watched and accompanied by someone hostile to her had been growing. It was the stronger perhaps because of the things that Herbert told her about Elinor; she was the kind of woman, he said, who, once she loved anyone, would never relinquish her grasp; she was utterly faithful. He implied that her tenacious fidelity had been at times a little difficult.

'She always said,' he added once, 'that she would watch over me until I rejoined her in the next world. Poor Elinor!' he sighed. 'She had a fine religious faith, stronger than mine, I fear.'

It was always after one of her tantrums that young Mrs. Ryder had been most conscious of this hallucination, this dreadful discomfort of feeling that someone was near you who hated you—but it was only during the last week that she began to fancy that she actually saw anyone, and with every day her sense of this figure had grown stronger.

It was of course only nerves, but it was one of those nervous afflictions that became tiresome indeed if you did not rid yourself of it. Mrs. Ryder, secure now in the warmth and intimacy of her bedroom, determined that henceforth everything should be sweetness and light. No more tempers! Those were the things that did her harm.

Even though Herbert were a little trying, was not that the case with every husband in the world? And was it not Christmas time? Peace and Good Will to men! Peace and Good Will to Herbert!

They sat down opposite to one another in the pretty little dining-room hung with Chinese woodcuts, the table gleaming and the amber curtains richly dark in the firelight.

But Herbert was not himself. He was still brooding, she supposed, over their quarrel of the afternoon. Weren't men children? Incredible the children that they were!

So when the maid was out of the room she went over to him, bent down and kissed his forehead.

'Darling... you're still cross, I can see you are. You mustn't be. Really you mustn't. It's Christmas time and, if I forgive you, you must forgive me.'

'You forgive me?' he asked, looking at her in his most aggravating way. 'What have you to forgive me for?'

Well, that was really too much. When she had taken all the steps, humbled her pride.

She went back to her seat, but for a while could not answer him because the maid was there. When they were alone again she said, summoning all her patience:

'Bertie dear, do you really think that there's anything to be gained by sulking like this? It isn't worthy of you. It isn't really.'

He answered her quietly.

'Sulking? No, that's not the right word. But I've got to keep quiet. If I don't I shall say something I'm sorry for.' Then, after a pause, in a low voice, as though to himself: 'These constant rows are awful.'

Her temper was rising again; another self that had nothing to do with her real self, a stranger to her and yet a very old familiar friend.

'Don't be so self-righteous,' she answered, her voice trembling a little. 'These quarrels are entirely my own fault, aren't they?'

'Elinor and I never quarrelled,' he said, so softly that she scarcely heard him.

'No! Because Elinor thought you perfect. She adored you. You've often told me. I don't think you perfect. I'm not perfect either. But we've both got faults. I'm not the only one to blame.'

'We'd better separate,' he said, suddenly looking up. 'We don't get on now. We used to. I don't know what's changed everything. But, as things are, we'd better separate.'

She looked at him and knew that she loved him more than ever, but because she loved him so much she wanted to hurt him, and because he had said that he thought he could get on without her she was so angry that she forgot all caution. Her love and her anger helped one another. The more angry she became the more she loved him.

'I know why you want to separate,' she said. 'It's because you're in love with someone else.' ('How funny,' something inside her said. 'You don't mean a word of this.') 'You've treated me as you have, and then you leave me.'

'I'm not in love with anyone else,' he answered her steadily, 'and you know it. But we are so unhappy together that it's silly to go on… silly… The whole thing has failed.'

There was so much unhappiness, so much bitterness, in his voice that she realised that at last she had truly gone too far. She had lost him.

She had not meant this. She was frightened and her fear made her so angry that she went across to him.

'Very well then... I'll tell everyone... what you've been. How you've treated me.'

'Not another scene,' he answered wearily. 'I can't stand any more. Let's wait. Tomorrow is Christmas Day...'

He was so unhappy that her anger with herself maddened her. She couldn't bear his sad, hopeless disappointment with herself, their life together, everything.

In a fury of blind temper she struck him; it was as though she were striking herself. He got up and without a word left the room. There was a pause, and then she heard the hall door close. He had left the house.

She stood there, slowly coming to her control again. When she lost her temper it was as though she sank under water. When it was all over she came once more to the surface of life, wondering where she'd been and what she had been doing. Now she stood there, bewildered, and then at once she was aware of two things, one that the room was bitterly cold and the other that someone was in the room with her.

This time she did not need to look around her. She did not turn at all, but only stared straight at the curtained windows, seeing them very carefully, as though she were summing them up for some future analysis, with their thick amber folds, gold rod, white lines—and beyond them the snow was falling.

She did not need to turn, but, with a shiver of terror, she was aware that that grey figure who had, all these last weeks, been approaching ever more closely, was almost at her very elbow. She heard quite clearly: 'I warned you. That was the last time.'

At the same moment Onslow the butler came in. Onslow was broad, fat and rubicund—a good faithful butler with a passion for church music. He was a bachelor and, it was said, disappointed of women. He had an old mother in Liverpool to whom he was greatly attached.

In a flash of consciousness she thought of all these things when he came in. She expected him also to see the grey figure at her side. But he was undisturbed, his ceremonial complacency clothed him securely.

'Mr. Fairfax has gone out,' she said firmly. Oh, surely he must see something, feel something.

'Yes, Madam!' Then, smiling rather grandly: 'It's snowing hard. Never seen it harder here. Shall I build up the fire in the drawing-room, Madam?'

'No, thank you. But Mr. Fairfax's study…'

'Yes, Madam. I only thought that as this room was so warm you might find it chilly in the drawing-room.'

This room warm, when she was shivering from head to foot; but holding herself lest he should see… She longed to keep him there, to implore him to remain; but in a moment he was gone, softly closing the door behind him.

Then a mad longing for flight seized her, and she could not move. She was rooted there to the floor, and even as, wildly trying to cry, to scream, to shriek the house down, she found that only a little whisper would come, she felt the cold touch of a hand on hers.

She did not turn her head: her whole personality, all her past life, her poor little courage, her miserable fortitude were summoned to meet this sense of approaching death which was as unmistakable as a certain smell, or the familiar ringing of a gong. She had dreamt in nightmares of approaching death and it had always been like this, a fearful constriction of the heart, a paralysis of the limbs, a choking sense of disaster like an anaesthetic.

'You were warned,' something said to her again.

She knew that if she turned she would see Elinor's face, set, white, remorseless. The woman had always hated her, been vilely jealous of her, protecting her wretched Herbert.

A certain vindictiveness seemed to release her. She found that she could move, her limbs were free.

She passed to the door, ran down the passage, into the hall. Where would she be safe? She thought of the Cathedral, where tonight there was a carol service. She opened the hall door and just as she was, meeting the thick, involving, muffling snow, she ran out.

She started across the green towards the Cathedral door. Her thin black slippers sank in the snow. Snow was everywhere—in her hair, her eyes, her nostrils, her mouth, on her bare neck, between her breasts.

'Help! Help! Help!' she wanted to cry, but the snow choked her. Lights whirled about her. The Cathedral rose like a huge black eagle and flew towards her.

She fell forward, and even as she fell a hand, far colder than the snow, caught her neck. She lay struggling in the snow and as she struggled there two hands of an icy fleshless chill closed about her throat.

Her last knowledge was of the hard outline of a ring pressing into her neck. Then she lay still, her face in the snow, and the flakes eagerly, savagely, covered her.

SMEE

A. M. Burrage

First published in *Nash's Pall Mall Magazine*, December 1929

Alfred McLelland Burrage (1889–1956) came from a family dependent on the magazine industry. Both his father and his uncle were
writers—his father wrote mainly adventure stories for periodicals
aimed at boys. His father died when Burrage was still at school and
he quickly began submitting his own stories to magazines, probably
in an attempt to keep the family solvent. He fought in World War I,
continuing to send stories home for publication, although this was
awkward as mail was censored and understandably the army was not
keen on having to get through sheaves of pages of fiction in addition
to conventional letters. His works were mainly either romance/
adventure hybrids, or ghost stories.

'NO,' SAID JACKSON, WITH A DEPRECATORY SMILE, 'I'M SORRY. I don't want to upset your game. I shan't be doing that because you'll have plenty without me. But I'm not playing any games of hide-and-seek.'

It was Christmas Eve, and we were a party of fourteen with just the proper leavening of youth. We had dined well; it was the season for childish games, and we were all in the mood for playing them—all, that is, except Jackson. When somebody suggested hide-and-seek there was rapturous and almost unanimous approval. His was the one dissentient voice.

It was not like Jackson to spoil sport or refuse to do as others wanted. Somebody asked him if he were feeling seedy.

'No,' he answered. 'I feel perfectly fit, thanks. But,' he added with a smile which softened without retracting the flat refusal, 'I'm not playing hide-and-seek.'

One of us asked him why not. He hesitated for some seconds before replying.

'I sometimes go and stay at a house where a girl was killed through playing hide-and-seek in the dark. She didn't know the house very well. There was a servant's staircase with a door to it. When she was pursued she opened the door and jumped into what she must have thought was one of the bedrooms—and she broke her neck at the bottom of the stairs.'

We all looked concerned, and Mrs. Fernley said:

'How awful! And you were there when it happened?'

Jackson shook his head very gravely. 'No,' he said, 'but I was there when something else happened. Something worse.'

'I shouldn't have thought anything could be worse.'

'This was,' said Jackson, and shuddered visibly. 'Or so it seemed to me.'

I think he wanted to tell the story and was angling for encouragement. A few requests which may have seemed to him to lack urgency, he affected to ignore and went off at a tangent.

'I wonder if any of you have played a game called "Smee". It's a great improvement on the ordinary game of hide-and-seek. The name derives from the ungrammatical colloquialism, "It's me." You might care to play if you're going to play a game of that sort. Let me tell you the rules.

'Every player is presented with a sheet of paper. All the sheets are blank except one, on which is written "Smee". Nobody knows who is "Smee" except "Smee" himself—or herself, as the case may be. The lights are then turned out and "Smee" slips from the room and goes off to hide, and after an interval the other players go off in search, without knowing whom they are actually in search of. One player meeting another challenges with the word "Smee" and the other player, if not the one concerned, answers "Smee".

'The real "Smee" makes no answer when challenged, and the second player remains quietly by him. Presently they will be discovered by a third player, who, having challenged and received no answer, will link up with the first two. This goes on until all the players have formed a chain, and the last to join is marked down for a forfeit. It's a good noisy, romping game, and in a big house it often takes a long time to complete the chain. You might care to try it; and I'll pay my forfeit and smoke one of Tim's excellent cigars here by the fire until you get tired of it.'

I remarked that it sounded a good game and asked Jackson if he had played it himself.

'Yes,' he answered; 'I played it in the house I was telling you about.'

'And *she* was there? The girl who broke—'

'No, no,' Mrs. Fernley interrupted. 'He told us he wasn't there when it happened.'

Jackson considered. 'I don't know if she was there or not. I'm afraid she was. I know that there were thirteen of us and there ought only to have been twelve. And I'll swear that I didn't know her name, or I think I should have gone clean off my head when I heard that whisper in the dark. No, you don't catch me playing that game, or any other like it, any more. It spoiled my nerve quite a while, and I can't afford to take long holidays. Besides, it saves a lot of trouble and inconvenience to own up at once to being a coward.'

Tim Vouce, the best of hosts, smiled around at us, and in that smile there was a meaning which is sometimes vulgarly expressed by the slow closing of an eye. 'There's a story coming,' he announced.

'There's certainly a story of sorts,' said Jackson, 'but whether it's coming or not—' He paused and shrugged his shoulders.

'Well, you're going to pay a forfeit instead of playing?'

'Please. But have a heart and let me down lightly. It's not just a sheer cussedness on my part.'

'Payment in advance,' said Tim, 'insures honesty and promotes good feeling. You are therefore sentenced to tell the story here and now.'

And here follows Jackson's story, unrevised by me and passed on without comment to a wider public:—

*   *   *

Some of you, I know, have run across the Sangstons. Christopher Sangston and his wife, I mean. They're distant connections of mine—at least, Violet Sangston is. About eight years ago they bought a house between the North and South Downs on the Surrey and Sussex border, and five years ago they invited me to come and spend Christmas with them.

It was a fairly old house—I couldn't say exactly of what period—and it certainly deserved the epithet 'rambling'. It wasn't a particularly big house, but the original architect, whoever he may have been, had not concerned himself with economising in space, and at first you could get lost in it quite easily.

Well, I went down for that Christmas, assured by Violet's letter that I knew most of my fellow-guests and that the two or three who might be strangers to me were all 'lambs'. Unfortunately, I'm one of the world's workers, and I couldn't get away until Christmas Eve, although the other members of the party had assembled on the preceding day. Even then I had to cut it rather fine to be there for dinner on my first night. They were all dressing when I arrived and I had to go straight to my room and waste no time. I may even have kept dinner waiting a bit, for I was last down, and it was announced within a minute of my entering the drawing-room. There was just time to say 'hullo' to everybody I knew, to be briefly introduced to the two or three I didn't know, and then I had to give my arm to Mrs. Gorman.

I mention this as the reason why I didn't catch the name of a tall dark, handsome girl I hadn't met before. Everything was rather hurried and I am always bad at catching people's names. She looked cold and clever and rather forbidding, the sort of girl who gives the impression of knowing all about men and the more she knows of them the less she likes them. I felt that I wasn't going to hit it off with this particular 'lamb' of Violet's, but she looked interesting all the same, and I wondered who she was. I didn't ask, because I was pretty sure of hearing somebody address her by name before very long.

Unluckily, though, I was a long way off her at table, and as Mrs. Gorman was at the top of her form that night I soon forgot to worry about who she might be. Mrs. Gorman is one of the most amusing women I know, an outrageous but quite innocent flirt, with a very sprightly wit which isn't always unkind. She can think half a dozen moves ahead in conversation just as an expert can in a game of chess. We were soon sparring, or, rather, I was 'covering' against the ropes, and I quite forgot to ask her in an undertone the name of the cold, proud beauty. The lady on the other side of me was a stranger, or had been until a few minutes since, and I didn't think of seeking information in that quarter.

There was a round dozen of us, including the Sangstons themselves, and we were all young or trying to be. The Sangstons themselves were the oldest members of the party and their son Reggie, in his last year at Marlborough, must have been the youngest. When there was talk of playing games after dinner it was he who suggested 'Smee'. He told us how to play it just as I've described it to you.

His father chipped in as soon as we all understood what was going to be required of us. 'If there are any games of that sort going on in the house,' he said, 'for goodness' sake be careful of the back stairs on the first-floor landing. There's a door to them and I've often meant to take it down. In the dark anybody who doesn't know the house very well might think they were walking into a room. A girl actually did break her neck on those stairs about ten years ago when the Ainsties lived here.'

I asked how it happened.

'Oh,' said Sangston, 'there was a party here one Christmas time and they were playing hide-and-seek as you propose doing. This girl was one of the hiders. She heard somebody coming, ran along the passage to get away, and opened the door of what she thought was a bedroom, evidently with the intention of hiding behind it while her pursuer went past. Unfortunately it was the door leading to the back stairs, and that staircase is as straight and almost as steep as the shaft of a pit. She was dead when they picked her up.'

We all promised for our own sakes to be careful. Mrs. Gorman said that she was sure nothing could happen to her, since she was insured by three different firms, and her next-of-kin was a brother whose consistent ill-luck was a byword in the family. You see, none of us had known the unfortunate girl, and as the tragedy was ten years old there was no need to pull long faces about it.

Well, we started the game almost immediately after dinner. The men allowed themselves only five minutes before joining the ladies, and then young Reggie Sangston went round and assured himself that the lights were out all over the house except in the servants' quarters and in the drawing-room where we were assembled. We then got busy with twelve sheets of paper which he twisted into pellets and shook up between his hands before passing them round. Eleven of them were blank, and 'Smee' was written on the twelfth. The person drawing the latter was the one who had to hide. I looked and saw that mine was a blank. A moment later out went the electric lights, and in the darkness I heard somebody get up and creep to the door.

After a minute or so somebody gave a signal and we made a rush for the door. I for one hadn't the least idea which of the party was 'Smee'. For five or ten minutes we were all rushing up and down passages and in and out of rooms challenging one another and answering, '*Smee?—Smee!*'

After a bit the alarums and excursions died down, and I guessed that 'Smee' was found. Eventually I found a chain of people all sitting still and holding their breath on some narrow stairs leading up to a row of attics. I hastily joined it, having challenged and been answered with silence, and presently two more stragglers arrived, each racing the other to avoid being last. Sangston was one of them, indeed it was he who was marked down for a forfeit, and after a little while he remarked in an undertone, 'I think we're all here now, aren't we?'

He struck a match; looked up the shaft of the staircase, and began to count. It wasn't hard, although we just about filled the staircase, for we were sitting each a step or two above the next, and all our heads were visible.

'...nine, ten, eleven, twelve—*thirteen*,' he concluded, and then laughed. 'Dash it all, that's one too many!'

The match had burned out and he struck another and began to count. He got as far as twelve, and then uttered an exclamation.

'There are thirteen people here!' he exclaimed. 'I haven't counted myself yet.'

'Oh, nonsense!' I laughed. 'You probably began with yourself, and now you want to count yourself twice.'

Out came his son's electric torch, giving a brighter and steadier light and we all began to count. Of course we numbered twelve.

Sangston laughed.

'Well', he said, 'I could have sworn I counted thirteen twice.'

From halfway up the stairs came Violet Sangston's voice with a little nervous trill in it. 'I thought there was somebody sitting two steps above me. Have you moved up, Captain Ransome?'

Ransome said that he hadn't: He also said that he thought there was somebody sitting between Violet and himself. Just for a moment

there was an uncomfortable Something in the air, a little cold ripple
which touched us all. For that little moment it seemed to all of us,
I think, that something odd and unpleasant had happened and was
liable to happen again. Then we laughed at ourselves and at one
another and were comfortable once more. There *were* only twelve
of us, and there *could* only have been twelve of us, and there was no
argument about it. Still laughing we trooped back to the drawing-
room to begin again.

This time I was 'Smee', and Violet Sangston ran me to earth
while I was still looking for a hiding-place. That round didn't last
long, and we were a chain of twelve within two or three minutes.
Afterwards there was a short interval. Violet wanted a wrap fetched
for her, and her husband went up to get it from her room. He was
no sooner gone than Reggie pulled me by the sleeve. I saw that he
was looking pale and sick.

'Quick!' he whispered, 'while father's out of the way. Take me
into the smoke room and give me a brandy or a whisky or something.'

Outside the room I asked him what was the matter, but he didn't
answer at first, and I thought it better to dose him first and question
him afterward. So I mixed him a pretty dark-complexioned brandy
and soda which he drank at a gulp and then began to puff as if he
had been running.

'I've had rather a turn,' he said to me with a sheepish grin.

'What's the matter?'

'I don't know. You were "Smee" just now, weren't you? Well, of
course I didn't know who "Smee" was, and while mother and the
others ran into the west wing and found you, I turned east. There's
a deep clothes cupboard in my bedroom—I'd marked it down as
a good place to hide when it was my turn, and I had an idea that

"Smee" might be there. I opened the door in the dark, felt round, and touched somebody's hand. "Smee?" I whispered, and not getting any answer I thought I had found "Smee".

'Well, I don't know how it was, but an odd creepy feeling came over me, I can't describe it, but I felt that something was wrong. So I turned on my electric torch and there was nobody there. Now, I swear I touched a hand, and I was filling up the doorway of the cupboard at the time, so nobody could get out and past me.' He puffed again. 'What do you make of it?' he asked.

'You imagined that you had touched a hand,' I answered, naturally enough.

He uttered a short laugh. 'Of course I knew you were going to say that,' he said. 'I must have imagined it, mustn't I?' He paused and swallowed. 'I mean, it couldn't have been anything else *but* imagination, could it?'

I assured him that it couldn't, meaning what I said, and he accepted this, but rather with the philosophy of one who knows he is right but doesn't expect to be believed. We returned together to the drawing-room where, by that time, they were all waiting for us and ready to start again.

It may have been my imagination—although I'm almost sure it wasn't—but it seemed to me that all enthusiasm for the game had suddenly melted like a white frost in strong sunlight. If anybody had suggested another game I'm sure we should all have been grateful and abandoned 'Smee'. Only nobody did. Nobody seemed to like to. I for one, and I can speak for some of the others too, was oppressed with the feeling that there was something wrong. I couldn't have said what I thought was wrong, indeed I didn't think about it at all, but somehow all the sparkle had gone out of the fun, and hovering over my mind like a shadow was the warning of some sixth sense which told me that there was an influence in the house which was neither sane, sound nor healthy. Why did I feel like that? Because Sangston had counted thirteen of us instead of twelve, and his son had thought he had touched somebody in an empty cupboard. No, there was more in it than just that. One would have laughed at such things in the ordinary way, and it was just that feeling of something being wrong which stopped me from laughing.

Well, we started again, and when we went in pursuit of the unknown 'Smee', we were as noisy as ever, but it seemed to me that most of us were acting. Frankly, for no reason other than the one I've given you, we'd stopped enjoying the game. I had an instinct to hunt with the main pack, but after a few minutes, during which no 'Smee' had been found, my instinct to play winning games and be first if possible, set me searching on my own account. And on the first floor of the west wing following the wall which was actually the shell of the house, I blundered against a pair of human knees.

I put out my hand and touched a soft, heavy curtain. Then I knew where I was. There were tall, deeply-recessed windows with seats along the landing, and curtains over the recesses to the ground. Somebody was sitting in a corner of this window-seat behind the curtain. Aha, I had caught 'Smee!' So I drew the curtain aside, stepped in, and touched the bare arm of a woman.

It was a dark night outside, and, moreover, the window was not only curtained but a blind hung down to where the bottom panes joined up with the frame. Between the curtain and the window it was as dark as the plague of Egypt. I could not have seen my hand held six inches before my face, much less the woman sitting in the corner.

'Smee?' I whispered.

I had no answer. 'Smee' when challenged does not answer. So I sat down beside her, first in the field, to await the others. Then, having settled myself I leaned over to her and whispered:

'Who is it? What's your name, "Smee?"'

And out of the darkness beside me the whisper came back: 'Brenda Ford.'

I didn't know the name, but because I didn't know it I guessed at once who she was. The tall, pale, dark girl was the only person in the house I didn't know by name. Ergo my companion was the tall, pale, dark girl. It seemed rather intriguing to be there with her, shut in between a heavy curtain and a window, and I rather wondered whether she was enjoying the game we were all playing. Somehow she hadn't seemed to me to be one of the romping sort. I muttered one or two commonplace questions to her and had no answer.

'Smee' is a game of silence. 'Smee' and the person or persons who have found 'Smee' are supposed to keep quiet to make it hard for the others. But there was nobody else about, and it occurred to me that she was playing the game a little too much to the letter. I spoke again and got no answer, and then I began to be annoyed. She was of that cold, 'superior' type which affects to despise men; she didn't like me; and she was sheltering behind the rules of a game for children to be discourteous. Well, if she didn't like sitting there with me, I certainly didn't want to be sitting there with her! I half turned from her and began to hope that we should both be discovered without much more delay.

Having discovered that I didn't like being there alone with her, it was queer how soon I found myself hating it, and that for a reason very different from the one which had at first whetted my annoyance. The girl I had met for the first time before dinner, and seen diagonally across the table, had a sort of cold charm about her which had attracted while it had half angered me. For the girl who was with me, imprisoned in the opaque darkness between the curtain and the window, I felt no attraction at all. It was so very much the reverse that I should have wondered at myself if, after the first shock of the discovery that she had suddenly become repellent to me, I had no room in my mind for anything besides the consciousness that her close presence was an increasing horror to me.

It came upon me just as quickly as I've uttered the words. My flesh suddenly shrank from her as you see a strip of gelatine shrink and wither before the heat of a fire. That feeling of something being wrong had come back to me, but multiplied to an extent which turned foreboding into actual terror. I firmly believe that I should have got up and run if I had not felt that at my first movement she would have divined my intention and compelled me to stay, by some means of which I could not bear to think. The memory of having touched her bare arm made me wince and draw in my lips. I prayed that somebody else would come along soon.

My prayer was answered. Light footfalls sounded on the landing. Somebody on the other side of the curtain brushed against my knees. The curtain was drawn aside and a woman's hand, fumbling in the darkness, presently rested on my shoulder. 'Smee?' whispered a voice which I instantly recognised as Mrs. Gorman's.

Of course she received no answer. She came and settled down beside me with a rustle, and I can't describe the sense of relief she brought me.

'It's Tony, isn't it?' she whispered.

'Yes,' I whispered back.

'You're not "Smee" are you?'

'No, she's on my other side.'

She reached a hand across me, and I heard one of her nails scratch the surface of a woman's silk gown.

'Hullo, "Smee!" How are you? *Who* are you? Oh, is it against the rules to talk? Never mind, Tony, we'll break the rules. Do you know, Tony, this game is beginning to irk me a little. I hope they're not going to run it to death by playing it all the evening. I'd like to play some game where we can all be together in the same room with a nice bright fire.'

'Same here,' I agreed fervently.

'Can't you suggest something when we go down? There's something rather uncanny in this particular amusement. I can't quite shed the delusion that there's somebody in this game who oughtn't to be in it at all.'

That was just how I had been feeling, but I didn't say so. But for my part the worst of my qualms were now gone; the arrival of Mrs. Gorman had dissipated them. We sat on talking, wondering from time to time when the rest of the party would arrive.

I don't know how long elapsed before we heard a clatter of feet on the landing and young Reggie's voice shouting, 'Hullo! Hullo, there! Anybody there?'

'Yes,' I answered.

'Mrs. Gorman with you?'

'Yes.'

'Well, you're a nice pair! You've both forfeited. We've all been waiting for you for hours.'

'Why, you haven't found "Smee" yet,' I objected.

'*You* haven't, you mean. I happen to have been "Smee" myself.'

'But "Smee's" here with us,' I cried.

'Yes,' agreed Mrs. Gorman.

The curtain was stripped aside and in a moment we were blinking into the eye of Reggie's electric torch. I looked at Mrs. Gorman and then on my other side. Between me and the wall there was an empty space on the window seat. I stood up at once and wished I hadn't, for I found myself sick and dizzy.

'There *was* somebody there,' I maintained, 'because I touched her.'

'So did I,' said Mrs. Gorman in a voice which had lost its steadiness. 'And I don't see how she could have got up and gone without our knowing it.'

Reggie uttered a queer, shaken laugh. He, too, had had an unpleasant experience that evening. 'Somebody's been playing the goat,' he remarked. 'Coming down?'

We were not very popular when we arrived in the drawing-room. Reggie rather tactlessly gave it out that he had found us sitting on a window seat behind a curtain. I taxed the tall, dark girl with having pretended to be 'Smee' and afterwards slipping away. She denied it. After which we settled down and played other games. 'Smee' was done with for the evening, and I for one was glad of it.

Some long while later, during an interval, Sangston told me, if I wanted a drink, to go into the smoke room and help myself. I went, and he presently followed me. I could see that he was rather peeved with me, and the reason came out during the following minute or two. It seemed that, in his opinion, if I must sit out and flirt with Mrs. Gorman—in circumstances which would have been considered highly compromising in his young days—I needn't do it during a round game and keep everybody waiting for us.

'But there was somebody else there,' I protested, 'somebody pretending to be "Smee". I believe it was that tall, dark girl, Miss Ford, although she denied it. She even whispered her name to me.'

Sangston stared at me and nearly dropped his glass.

'Miss *Who*?' he shouted.

'Brenda Ford—she told me her name was.'

Sangston put down his glass and laid a hand on my shoulder.

'Look here, old man,' he said, 'I don't mind a joke, but don't let it go too far. We don't want all the women in the house getting hysterical. Brenda Ford is the name of the girl who broke her neck on the stairs playing hide-and-seek here ten years ago.'

THE DEMON KING

J. B. Priestley

First published in *The Strand Magazine*, January 1931

John Boynton Priestley (1894–1984) was born in Bradford, Yorkshire, to a mostly working-class family. After fighting in World War I he was able to obtain a grant to attend university, and went to Cambridge, where he was not very happy. He started writing in the 1920s and published novels, plays and social commentary. Probably his best known play *An Inspector Calls*, a socialist drama with a supernatural element, was finished in 1946 but was first performed in translation in Russia as no venue in London was initially interested. He is also known for writing an article in 1957 which inspired the creation of the Campaign for Nuclear Disarmament. He wrote only a few ghost stories, all to appear in magazines in the early 1930s and 1950s.

A MONG THE COMPANY ASSEMBLED FOR MR. TOM BURT'S GRAND Annual Pantomime at the old Theatre Royal, Bruddersford, there was a good deal of disagreement. They were not quite 'the jolly, friendly party' they pretended to be—through the good offices of 'Thespian'—to the readers of *The Bruddersford Herald* and *Weekly Herald Budget*. The Principal Boy told her husband and about fifty-five other people that she could work with anybody, was famous for being able to work with anybody, but that nevertheless the management had gone and engaged, as Principal Girl, the one woman in the profession who made it almost impossible for anybody to work with anybody. The Principal Girl told her friend, the Second Boy, that the Principal Boy and the Second Girl were spoiling everything and might easily ruin the show. The Fairy Queen went about pointing out that she did not want to make trouble, being notoriously easy-going, but that sooner or later the Second Girl would hear a few things that she would not like. Johnny Wingfield had been heard to declare that some people did not realise even yet that what audiences wanted from a panto was some good fast comedy work by the chief comedian, who had to have all the scope he required. Dippy and Doppy, the broker's men, hinted that even if there were two stages, Johnny Wingfield would want them both all the time.

But they were all agreed on one point, namely, that there was not a better demon in provincial panto than Mr. Kirk Ireton, who had been engaged by Mr. Tom Burt for this particular show. The pantomime was *Jack and Jill*, and those people who are puzzled to know what demons have to do with Jack and Jill, those innocent water-fetchers, should pay a visit to the nearest pantomime, which will teach them a lot they did not know about fairy tales. Kirk Ireton was not merely a demon, but the Demon King, and when the curtain first went up, you saw him on a darkened stage standing in front of a little chorus of attendant demons, made up of local baritones at ten shillings a night. Ireton looked the part, for he was tall and rather satanically featured and was known to be very clever with his make-up; and what was more important, he sounded the part too, for he had a tremendous bass voice, of most demonish quality. He had played Mephistopheles in *Faust* many times with a good touring opera company. He was, indeed, a man with a fine future behind him. If it had not been for one weakness, pantomime would never have seen him. The trouble was that for years now he had been in the habit of 'lifting the elbow' too much. That was how they all put it. Nobody said that he drank too much, but all agreed that he lifted the elbow. And the problem now was—would there be trouble because of this elbow-lifting?

He had rehearsed with enthusiasm, sending his great voice to the back of the empty, forlorn gallery in the two numbers allotted to him, but at the later rehearsals there had been ominous signs of elbow-lifting.

'Going to be all right, Mr. Ireton?' the stage-manager inquired anxiously.

Ireton raised his formidable and satanic eyebrows. 'Of course it is,' he replied, somewhat hoarsely. 'What's worrying you, old man?'

The other explained hastily that he wasn't worried. 'You'll go well here,' he went on. 'They'll eat those two numbers of yours. Very musical in these parts. But you know Bruddersford, of course. You've played here before.'

'I have,' replied Ireton grimly. 'And I loathe the damn' place. Bores me stiff. Nothing to do in it.'

This was not reassuring. The stage-manager knew only too well Mr. Ireton was already finding something to do in the town, and his enthusiastic description of the local golf courses had no effect. Ireton loathed golf too, it seemed. All very ominous.

They were opening on Boxing Day night. By the afternoon, it was known that Kirk Ireton had been observed lifting the elbow very determinedly in the smoke-room of The Cooper's Arms, near the theatre. One of the stage-hands had seen him: 'And by gow, he wor lapping it up an' all,' said this gentleman, no bad judge of any-body's power of suction. From there, it appeared, he had vanished, along with several other riotous persons, two of them thought to be Leeds men—and in Bruddersford they know what Leeds men are.

The curtain was due to rise at seven-fifteen sharp. Most members of the company arrived at the theatre very early. Kirk Ireton was not one of them. He was still absent at six-thirty, though he had to wear an elaborate make-up, with glittering tinselled eyelids and all the rest of it, and had to be on the stage when the curtain rose. A messenger was dispatched to his lodgings, which were not far from the theatre. Even before the messenger returned, to say that Mr. Ireton had not been in since noon, the stage-manager was desperately coaching one of the local baritones, the best of a stiff and stupid lot, in the part of the Demon King. At six-forty-five, no Ireton; at seven, no Ireton. It was hopeless.

'All right, that fellow's done for himself now,' said the great Mr. Burt, who had come to give his Grand Annual his blessing. 'He doesn't get another engagement from me as long as he lives. What's this local chap like?'

The stage-manager groaned and wiped his brow. 'Like nothing on earth except a bow-legged baritone from a Wesleyan choir.'

'He'll have to manage somehow. You'll have to cut the part.'

'Cut it, Mr. Burt! I've slaughtered it, and what's left of it, he'll slaughter.'

Mr. Tom Burt, like the sensible manager he was, believed in a pantomime opening in the old-fashioned way, with a mysterious dark scene among the supernaturals. Here it was a cavern in the hill beneath the Magic Well, and in these dismal recesses the Demon King and his attendants were to be discovered waving their crimson cloaks and plotting evil in good, round chest-notes. Then the Demon King would sing his number (which had nothing whatever to do with Jack and Jill or demonology either), the Fairy Queen would appear, accompanied by a white spotlight, there would be a little dialogue between them, and then a short duet.

The cavern scene was all set, the five attendant demons were in their places, while the sixth, now acting as King, was receiving a few last instructions from the stage-manager, and the orchestra, beyond the curtain, were coming to the end of the overture, when suddenly, from nowhere, there appeared on the dimly-lighted stage a tall and terrifically imposing figure.

'My God! There's Ireton,' cried the stage-manager, and bustled across, leaving the temporary Demon King abandoned, a pitiful makeshift now. The new arrival was coolly taking his place in the centre. He looked superb. The costume a skin-tight crimson affair touched with a baleful green, was far better than the one provided by the management. And the make-up was better still. The face had a greenish phosphorescent glow, and its eyes flashed between glittering lids. When he first caught sight of the face, the stage-manager felt a sudden idiotic tremor of fear, but being a stage-manager first and a human being afterwards (as all stage-managers have to be), he did not feel that tremor long, for it was soon chased away by a sense of elation. It flashed across his mind that Ireton must have gone running off to Leeds or somewhere in search of this stupendous costume and make-up. Good old Ireton! He had given them all a fright, but it had been worth it.

'All right, Ireton?' said the stage-manager quickly.

'All right,' replied the Demon King, with a magnificent, careless gesture.

'Well, you get back in the chorus then,' said the stage-manager to the Wesleyan baritone.

'That'll do me champion,' said the gentleman, with a sigh of relief. He was not ambitious.

'All ready.'

The violins began playing a shivery sort of music, and up the curtain went. The six attendant demons, led by the Wesleyan, who was in good voice now that he felt such a sense of relief, told the audience who they were and hailed their monarch in appropriate form. The Demon King, towering above them, dominating the scene superbly, replied in a voice of astonishing strength and richness. Then he sang the number allotted to him. It had nothing to do with Jack and Jill and very little to do with demons, being a rather commonplace bass song about sailors and shipwrecks and storms, with thunder and lightning effects supplied by the theatre. Undoubtedly this was the same song that had been rehearsed; the words were the same; the music was the same. Yet it all seemed different. It was really sinister. As you listened, you saw the great waves breaking over the doomed ships, and the pitiful little white faces disappearing in the dark flood. Somehow, the storm was much stormier. There was one great clap of thunder and flash of lightning that made all the attendant demons, the conductor of the orchestra, and a number of people in the wings, nearly jump out of their skins.

'And how the devil did you do that?' said the stage-manager, after running round to the other wing.

'That's what I said to 'Orace 'ere,' said the man in charge of the two sheets of tin and the cannon ball.

'Didn't touch a thing that time, did we, mate?' said Horace.

'If you ask me, somebody let off a firework, one o' them big Chinese crackers, for that one,' his mate continued. 'Somebody monkeying about, that's what it is.'

And now a white spotlight had found its way on to the stage, and there, shining in its pure ray, was Miss Dulcie Farrar, the Fairy Queen, who was busy waving a silver wand. She was also busy controlling her emotions, for somehow she felt unaccountably nervous. Opening night is opening night, of course, but Miss Farrar had been playing Fairy Queen for the last ten years (and Principal Girls for the ten years before them), and there was nothing in this part to worry her. She rapidly came to the conclusion that it was Mr. Ireton's sudden reappearance, after she had made up her mind that he was not turning up, that had made her feel so shaky, and this caused her to feel rather resentful. Moreover, as an experienced Fairy Queen who had had trouble with demons before, she was convinced that he was about to take more than his share of the stage. Just because he had hit upon such a good make-up! And it *was* a good make-up, there could be no question about that. That greenish face, those glittering eyes—really, it was awful. Overdoing it, she called it. After all, a panto *was* a panto.

Miss Farrar, still waving her wand, moved a step or two nearer, and cried:

'I know your horrid plot, you evil thing,
And I defy you, though you are the Demon King.'

'What, you?' he roared, contemptuously, pointing a long forefinger
at her.

Miss Farrar should have replied: 'Yes, I, the Queen of Fairyland,'
but for a minute she could not get out a word. As that horribly long
forefinger shot out at her, she had felt a sudden sharp pain and had
then found herself unable to move. She stood there, her wand held
out at a ridiculous angle, motionless, silent, her mouth wide open.
But her mind was active enough. 'Is it a stroke?' it was asking fever-
ishly. 'Like Uncle Edgar had that time at Greenwich. Oo, it must be.
Oo, whatever shall I do? Oo. Oo. Ooooo.'

'Ho-ho-ho-ho-ho.' The Demon King's sinister baying mirth
resounded through the theatre.

'Ha-ha-ha-ha-ha.' This was from the Wesleyan and his friends,
and was a very poor chorus of laughs, dubious, almost apologetic. It
suggested that the Wesleyan and his friends were out of their depth,
the depth of respectable Bruddersfordian demons.

Their king now made a quick little gesture with one hand, and
Miss Farrar found herself able to move and speak again. Indeed, the
next second, she was not sure that she had ever been *unable* to speak
and move. That horrible minute had vanished like a tiny bad dream.
She defied him again, and this time nothing happened beyond an
exchange of bad lines of lame verse. There were not many of these,
however, for there was the duet to be fitted in, and the whole scene
had to be played in as short a time as possible. The duet, in which
the two supernaturals only defied one another all over again, was
early Verdi by way of the local musical director.

After singing a few bars each, they had a rest while the musical director exercised his fourteen instrumentalists in a most imposing operatic passage. It was during this half that Miss Farrar, who was now quite close to her fellow-duettist, whispered: 'You're in great voice, tonight, Mr. Ireton. Wish I was. Too nervous. Don't know why, but I am. Wish I could get it out like you.'

She received, as a reply, a flash of those glittering eyes (it really was an astonishing make-up) and a curious little signal with the long forefinger. There was no time for more, for now the voice part began again.

Nobody in the theatre was more surprised by what happened then than the Fairy Queen herself. She could not believe that the marvellously rich soprano voice that came pealing and soaring belonged to her. It was tremendous. Covent Garden would have acclaimed it. Never before, in all her twenty years of hard vocalism, had Miss Dulcie Farrar sung like that, though she had always felt that *somewhere* inside her there was a voice of that quality only waiting the proper signal to emerge and then astonish the world. Now, in some fantastic fashion, it had received that signal.

Not that the Fairy Queen overshadowed her supernatural colleague. There was no overshadowing *him*. He trolled in a diapason bass, and with a fine fury of gesture. The pair of them turned that stolen and botched duet into a work of art and significance. You could hear Heaven and Hell at battle in it. The curtain came down on a good rattle of applause. They are very fond of music in Bruddersford, but unfortunately the people who attend the first night of the pantomime are not the people who are most fond of music, otherwise there would have been a furore.

'Great stuff that,' said Mr. Tom Burt, who was on the spot. 'Never mind, Jim. Let 'em take a curtain. Go on, you two, take the curtain.' And when they had both bowed their acknowledgements, Miss Farrar excited and trembling, the Demon King cool and amused, almost contemptuous, Mr. Burt continued: 'That would have stopped the show in some places, absolutely stopped the show. But the trouble here is, they won't applaud, won't get going easily.'

'That's true, Mr. Burt,' Miss Farrar observed. 'They take a lot of warming up here. I wish they didn't. Don't you, Mr. Ireton?'

'Easy to warm them,' said the tall crimson figure.

'Well, if anything could, that ought to have done,' the lady remarked.

'That's so,' said Mr. Burt condescendingly. 'You were great, Ireton. But they won't let themselves go.'

'Yes, they will.' The Demon King, who appeared to be taking his part very seriously, for he had not yet dropped into his ordinary tones, flicked his long fingers in the air, roughly in the direction of the auditorium, gave a short laugh, turned away, and then somehow completely vanished, though it was not difficult to do that in those crowded wings.

Half an hour later, Mr. Burt, his manager, and the stage-manager, all decided that something must have gone wrong with Bruddersford. Liquor must have been flowing like water in the town. That was the only explanation.

'Either they're all drunk or I am,' cried the stage-manager.

'I've been giving 'em pantomime here for five-and-twenty years,' said Mr. Burt, 'and I've never known it happen before.'

'Well, nobody can say they're not enjoying it.'

'Enjoying it! They're enjoying it too much. They're going daft. Honestly, I don't like it. It's too much of a good thing.'

The stage-manager looked at his watch. 'It's holding up the show, that's certain. God knows when we're going to get through at this rate. If they're going to behave like this every night, we'll have to cut an hour out of it.'

'Listen to 'em now,' said Mr. Burt. 'And that's one of the oldest gags in the show. Listen to 'em. Nay, dash it, they must be all half-seas over.'

What had happened? Why—this: that the audience had suddenly decided to let itself go in a fashion never known in Bruddersford before. The Bruddersfordians are notoriously difficult to please, not so much because their taste is so exquisite but rather because, having paid out money, they insist upon having their money's worth, and usually arrive at a place of entertainment in a gloomy and suspicious frame of mind. Really tough managers like to open a new show in Bruddersford, knowing very well that if it will go there, it will go anywhere. But for the last half-hour of this pantomime there had been more laughter and applause than the Theatre Royal had known for the past six months. Every entrance produced a storm of wel-come. The smallest and stalest gags set the whole house screaming, roaring, and rocking. Every song was determinedly encored. If the people had been specially brought out of jail for the performance, they could not have been more easily pleased.

'Here,' said Johnny Wingfield, as he made an exit as a Dame pursued by a cow, 'this is frightening me. What's the matter with 'em? Is this a new way of giving the bird?'

'Don't ask me,' said the Principal Boy. 'I wasn't surprised they gave me such a nice welcome when I went on, because I've always been a favourite here, as Mr. Burt'll tell you, but the way they're car-rying on now, making such a fuss over nothing, it's simply ridiculous. Slowing up the show, too.'

After another quarter of an hour of this monstrous enthusiasm, this delirium, Mr. Burt could be heard grumbling to the Principal Girl, with whom he was standing in that close proximity which Principal Girls somehow invite. 'I'll tell you what it is, Alice,' Mr. Burt was saying. 'If this goes on much longer, I'll make a speech from the stage, asking 'em to draw it mild. Never known 'em to behave like this. And it's a funny thing, I was only saying to somebody—now who was it that I said that to?—anyhow, I was only saying to somebody that I wished this audience would let themselves go a bit more. Well, now I wish they wouldn't. And that's that.'

There was a chuckle, not loud, but rich, and distinctly audible.

'Here,' cried Mr. Burt, 'who's that? What's the joke?'

It was obviously nobody in their immediate vicinity. 'It sounded like Kirk Ireton,' said the Principal Girl, 'judging by the voice.' But Ireton was nowhere to be seen. Indeed, one or two people who had been looking for him, both in his dressing-room and behind, had not been able to find him. But he would not be on again for another hour, and nobody had time to discover whether Ireton was drinking or not. The odd thing was, though, that the audience lost its wild enthusiasm just as suddenly as it had found it, and long before the interval had turned itself into the familiar stolid Bruddersford crowd, grimly waiting for its money's worth. The pantomime went on its way exactly as rehearsed, until it came to the time when the demons had to put in another appearance.

Jack, having found the magic water and tumbled down the hill, had to wander into the mysterious cavern and there rest awhile. At least, he declared that he would rest, but being played by a large and shapely female, and probably having that restless feminine temperament, what he did do was to sing a popular song with immense gusto. At the end of that song, when Jack once more declared that he would rest, the Demon King had to make a sudden appearance through a trapdoor. And it was reported from below, where a springboard was in readiness, that no Demon King had arrived to be shot on to the stage.

'Now where—oh, where—the devil has Ireton got to?' moaned the stage-manager, sending people right and left, up and down, to find him.

The moment arrived. Jack spoke his and her cue, and the stage-manager was making frantic signals to her from the wings.

'Ouh-wer,' screamed Jack, and produced the most realistic bit of business in the whole pantomime. For the stage directions read *shows fright*, and Jack undoubtedly did show fright, as well he (or she) might, for no sooner was the cue spoken than there came a horrible green flash, followed by a crimson glare, and standing before her, having apparently arrived from nowhere, was the Demon King. Jack was now in the power of the Demon King and would remain in those evil clutches until rescued by Jill and the Fairy Queen. And it seemed as if the Principal Boy had suddenly developed a capacity for acting (of which nobody had ever suspected her before), or else that she was thoroughly frightened, for now she behaved like a large rabbit in tights. The unrehearsed appearance of the Demon King seemed to have upset her, and now and then she sent uneasy glances into the wings.

It had been decided, after a great deal of talk and drinks round, to introduce a rather novel dancing scene into this pantomime, in the form of a sort of infernal ballet. The Demon King, in order to show his power and to impress his captive, would command his subjects to dance—that is, after he himself had indulged in a little singing, assisted by his faithful six. They talk of that scene yet in Bruddersford. It was only witnessed in its full glory on this one night, but that was enough, for it passed into civic history, and local landlords were often called in to settle bets about it in the pubs. First, the Demon King sang his second number, assisted by the Wesleyan and his friends. He made a glorious job of it too. Then the Demon King had to call for his dancing subjects, who were made up of the troupe of girls known as Tom Burt's Happy Yorkshire Lasses, daintily but demonishly tricked out in red and green. While the Happy Yorkshire Lasses pranced in the foreground, the six attendants were supposed to make a few rhythmical movements in the background, enough to suggest that, if they wanted to dance, they could dance, a suggestion that the stage-manager and the producer knew to be entirely false. The six, in fact, could not dance and would not try very hard, being not only wooden but also stubborn Bruddersford baritones.

But now, the Happy Yorkshire Lasses having tripped a measure, the Demon King sprang to his full height, which seemed to be about seven feet two inches, swept an arm along the Wesleyan six, and commanded them harshly to dance. And they did dance, they danced like men possessed. The King himself beat time for them, flashing an eye at the conductor now and again to quicken that gentleman's baton, and his faithful six, all with the most grotesque and puzzled expressions on their faces, cut the most amazing capers, bounding high into the air, tumbling over one another, flinging their arms and legs about in an ecstasy, and all in time to the music. The sweat shone on their faces; their eyes rolled forlornly; but still they did not stop, but went on in crazier and crazier fashion, like genuine demons at play.

'All dance!' roared the Demon King, cracking his long fingers like a whip, and it seemed as if something had inspired the fourteen cynical men in the orchestra pit, for they played like madmen grown tuneful, and on came the Happy Yorkshire Lasses again, to fling themselves into the wild sport, not as if they were doing something they had rehearsed a hundred times, but as if they, too, were inspired. They joined the orgy of the bounding six, and now, instead of there being only eighteen Happy Lasses in red and green, there seemed to be dozens and dozens of them. The very stage seemed to get bigger and bigger, to give space to all these whirling figures of demoniac revelry. And as they all went spinning, leaping, cavorting crazily, the audience, shaken at last out of its stolidity, cheered them on, and all was one wild insanity.

Yet when it was done, when the King cried, 'Stop!' and all was over, it was as if it had never been, as if everybody had dreamed it, so that nobody was ready to swear that it had really happened. The Wesleyan and the other five all felt a certain faintness but each was convinced that he had imagined all that wild activity while he was making a few sedate movements in the background. Nobody could be quite certain about anything. The pantomime went on its way; Jack was rescued by Jill and the Fairy Queen (who was now complaining of neuralgia); and the Demon King allowed himself to be foiled after which he quietly disappeared again. They were looking for him when the whole thing was over except for that grand entry of all the characters at the very end. It was his business to march in with the Fairy Queen, the pair of them dividing between them all the applause for the supernaturals. Miss Farrar, feeling very miserable with her neuralgia, delayed her entrance for him, but as he was not to be found, she climbed the little ladder at the back alone, to march solemnly down the steps towards the audience. And the extraordinary thing was then when she was actually making her entrance, at the top of those steps, she discovered that she was not alone, that her fellow-supernatural was there too, and that he must have slipped away to freshen his make-up. He was more demonish than ever.

As they walked down between the files of Happy Yorkshire Lasses, now armed to the teeth with tinsel spears and shields, Miss Farrar whispered: 'Wish I'd arranged for a bouquet. You never get anything here.'

'You'd like some flowers?' said the fantastic figure at her elbow.

'Think I would! So would everybody else.'

'Quite easy,' he remarked, bowing slowly to the footlights. He took her hand and led her to one side, and it is a fact—as Miss Farrar will tell you, within half an hour of your making her acquaintance—that the moment their hands met, her neuralgia completely vanished. And now came the time for the bouquets. Miss Farrar knew what they would be: there would be one for the Principal Girl, bought by the management, and one for the Principal Boy, bought by herself.

'Oo, look!' cried the Second Boy. 'My gosh!—Bruddersford's gone mad.'

The space between the orchestra pit and the front row of stalls had been turned into a hothouse. The conductor was so busy passing up bouquets that he was no longer visible. There were dozens of bouquets, and all of them beautiful. It was monstrous. Somebody must have spent a fortune on flowers. Up they came, while everybody cheered, and every woman with a part had at least two or three. Miss Farrar, pink and wide-eyed above a mass of orchids, turned to her colleague among the supernaturals, only to find that once again he had quietly disappeared. Down came the curtain for the last time, but everybody remained standing there, with arms filled with expensive flowers, chattering excitedly. Then suddenly somebody cried, 'Oo!' and dropped *their* flowers, until at last everybody who had had a bouquet had dropped it and cried, 'Oo!'

'Hot,' cried the Principal Girl, blowing on her fingers, 'hot as anything, weren't they? Burnt me properly. That's a nice trick.'

'Oo, look!' said the Second Boy, once more. 'Look at 'em all. Withering away.' And they were, every one of them, all shedding their colour and bloom, curling, writhing, withering away...

'Message come through for you, sir, an hour since,' said the door-keeper to the manager, 'only I couldn't get at yer. From the Leeds Infirmary, it is. Says Mr. Ireton was knocked down in Board Lane by a car this afternoon, but he'll be all right tomorrow. Didn't know who he was at first, so couldn't let anybody know.'

The manager stared at him, made a number of strange noises, then fled, singing various imaginary temperance pledges as he went.

'And another thing,' said the stage-hand to the stage-manager. 'That's where I saw the bloke last. He was there one minute and next minute he wasn't. And look at the place. All scorched.'

'That's right,' said his mate, 'and what's more, just you take a whiff—that's all, just take a whiff. Oo's started using brimstone in this the-ater? Not me nor you neither. But I've a good idea who it is.'

LUCKY'S GROVE

H. Russell Wakefield

First published in *The Clock Strikes Twelve*, London, 1940

Herbert Russell Wakefield (1888–1964) worked as an editor in the publishing house William Collins, but also wrote dozens of ghost stories which met with critical acclaim. By 1940, when this story was published, fiction periodicals were no longer so popular, and so Wakefield mainly published in story collections. John Betjeman thought highly of him, stating that 'M. R. James is the greatest master of the ghost story. Henry James, Sheridan Le Fanu and H. Russell Wakefield are equal seconds.'

'And Loki begat Hel, Goddess of the Grave, Fenris, the Great Wolf, and the Serpent, Nidnogg, who lives beneath The Tree.'

M R. BRAXTON STROLLED WITH HIS LAND-AGENT, CURTIS, INTO the Great Barn.

'There you are,' said Curtis, in a satisfied tone, 'the finest little fir I ever saw, and the kiddies will never set eyes on a lovelier Christmas tree.'

Mr. Braxton examined it; it stood twenty feet from huge green pot to crisp, straight peak, and was exquisitely sturdy, fresh and symmetrical.

'Yes, it's a beauty,' he agreed. 'Where did you find it?'

'In that odd little spinney they call Lucky's Grove in the long meadow near the river boundary.'

'Oh!' remarked Mr. Braxton uncertainly. To himself he was saying vaguely, 'He shouldn't have got it from there, of course he wouldn't realise it, but he shouldn't have got it from there.'

'Of course we'll replant it,' said Curtis, noticing his employer's diminished enthusiasm. 'It's a curious thing, but it isn't a young tree; it's apparently full-grown. Must be a dwarf variety, but I don't know as much about trees as I should like.'

Mr. Braxton was surprised to find there was one branch of country lore on which Curtis was not an expert; for he was about the best-known man at his job in the British Isles. Pigs, bees, chickens, cattle, crops, running a shoot, he had mastered them one and all. He paid him two thousand a year with house and car. He was worth treble.

'I expect it's all right,' said Mr. Braxton; 'it is just that Lucky's Grove is—is—well, "sacred" is perhaps too strong a word. Maybe I should have told you, but I expect it's all right.'

'That accounts for it then,' laughed Curtis. 'I thought there seemed some reluctance on the part of the men while we were yanking it up and getting it on the lorry. They handled it a bit gingerly; on the part of the older men, I mean; the youngsters didn't worry.'

'Yes, there would be,' said Mr. Braxton. 'But never mind, it'll be back in a few days and it's a superb little tree. I'll bring Mrs. Braxton along to see it after lunch,' and he strolled back into Abingdale Hall.

Fifty-five years ago Mr. Braxton's father had been a labourer on this very estate, and in that year young Percy, aged eight, had got an errand boy's job in Oxford. Twenty years later he'd owned one small shop. Twenty-five years after that fifty big shops. Now, though he had finally retired, he owned two hundred and eighty vast shops and was a millionaire whichever way you added it up. How had this happened? No one can quite answer such questions. Certainly he'd worked like a brigade of Trojans, but midnight oil has to burn in Aladdin's Lamp before it can transform ninepence into one million pounds. It was just that he asked no quarter from the unforgiving minute, but squeezed from it the fruit of others many hours. Those like Mr. Braxton seem to have their own time-scale; they just say the word and up springs a fine castle of commerce, but the knowledge of that word cannot be imparted; it is as mysterious as the Logos. But all through his great labours he had been moved by one fixed resolve—to avenge his father—that fettered spirit—for he had been an able, intelligent man who had had no earthly chance of revealing the fact to the world. Always the categorical determination had blazed in his son's brain, 'I will own Abingdale Hall, and, where my father sweated, I will rule and be lord.' And of course it had happened. Fate accepts the dictates of such men as Mr. Braxton, shrugs its shoulders, and leaves its revenge to Death. The Hall had come on the market just when he was about to retire, and with an odd delight, an obscure sense of homecoming, the native returned, and his riding boots, shooting boots, golf shoes, and all the many glittering guineas' worth, stamped in and obliterated the prints of his father's hob-nails.

That was the picture he often re-visualised, the way it amused him to 'put it to himself,' as he roamed his broad acres and surveyed the many glowing triumphs of his model husbandry.

Some credit was due to buxom, blithe and debonair Mrs. Braxton, kindly, competent and innately adaptable. She was awaiting him in the morning-room and they went in solitary state to luncheon. But it was the last peaceful lunch they would have for a spell—'The Families' were pouring in on the morrow.

As a footman was helping them to Sole Meunière Mr. Braxton said, 'Curtis has found a very fine Christmas tree. It's in the barn. You must come and look at it after lunch.'

'That *is* good,' replied his wife. 'Where did he get it from?'

Mr. Braxton hesitated for a moment.

'From Lucky's Grove.'

Mrs. Braxton looked up sharply.

'From the grove!' she said, surprised.

'Yes, of course he didn't realise—anyway it'll be all right, it's all rather ridiculous, and it'll be replanted before the New Year.'

'Oh, yes,' agreed Mrs. Braxton. 'After all it's only a clump of trees.'

'Quite. And it's just the right height for the ball-room. It'll be taken in there tomorrow morning and the electricians will work on it in the afternoon.'

'I heard from Lady Pounser just now,' said Mrs. Braxton. 'She's bringing six over, that'll make seventy-four; only two refusals. The presents are arriving this afternoon.'

They discussed the party discursively over the cutlets and Pêche Melba and soon after lunch walked across to the barn. Mr. Braxton waved to Curtis, who was examining a new tractor in the garage fifty yards away, and he came over.

Mrs. Braxton looked the tree over and was graciously delighted with it, but remarked that the pot could have done with another coat of paint. She pointed to several streaks, rust-coloured, running through the green. 'Of course it won't show when it's wrapped, but they didn't do a very good job.'

Curtis leant down. 'They certainly didn't,' he answered irritably. 'I'll see to it. I think it's spilled over from the soil; that copse is on a curious patch of red sand—there are some at Frilford too. When we pulled it up I noticed the roots were stained a dark crimson.' He put his hand down and scraped at the stains with his thumb. He seemed a shade puzzled.

'It shall have another coat at once,' he said. 'What did you think of Lampson and Colletts' scheme for the barn?'

'Quite good,' replied Mrs. Braxton, 'but the sketches for the chairs are too fancy.'

'I agree,' said Curtis, who usually did so in the case of unessentials, reserving his tactful vetoes for the others.

The Great Barn was by far the most aesthetically satisfying as it was the oldest feature of the Hall buildings: it was vast, exquisitely proportioned and mellow. That could hardly be said of the house itself, which the 4th Baron of Abingdale had rebuilt on the cinders of its predecessor in 1752.

This nobleman had travelled abroad extensively and returned with most enthusiastic, grandiose and indigestible ideas of architecture. The result was a gargantuan piece of rococo-jocoso which only an entirely humourless pedant could condemn. It contained forty-two bedrooms and eighteen reception rooms—so Mrs. Braxton had made it at the last recount. But Mr. Braxton had not repeated with the interior the errors of the 4th Baron. He'd briefed the greatest expert in Europe with the result that that interior was quite tasteful and sublimely comfortable.

'Ugh!' he exclaimed, as they stepped out into the air, 'it *is* getting nippy!'

'Yes,' said Curtis, 'there's a nor'-easter blowing up—may be snow for Christmas.'

On getting back to the house Mrs. Braxton went into a huddle with butler and housekeeper and Mr. Braxton retired to his study for a doze. But instead his mind settled on Lucky's Grove. When he'd first seen it again after buying the estate, it seemed as if fifty years had rolled away, and he realised that Abingdale was far more summed up to him in the little copse than in the gigantic barracks two miles away. At once he felt at home again. Yet, just as when he'd been a small boy, the emotion the Grove had aroused in him had been sharply tinged with awe, so it had been now, half a century later. He still had a sneaking dread of it. How precisely he could see it, glowing darkly in the womb of the fire before him, standing starkly there in the centre of the big, fallow field, a perfect circle; and first, a ring of holm-oaks and, facing east, a breach therein to the firs and past them on the west a gap to the yews. It had always required a tug at his courage—not always forthcoming—to pass through them and face the mighty Scotch fir, rearing up its great bole from the grass mound. And when he stood before it, he'd always known an odd longing to fling himself down and—well, worship—it was the only word—the towering tree. His father had told him his forebears had done that very thing, but always when alone and at certain seasons of the year; and that no bird or beast was ever seen there. A lot of traditional nonsense, no doubt, but he himself had absorbed the spirit of the place and knew it would always be so.

One afternoon in late November, a few weeks after they had moved in, he'd gone off alone in the drowsing misty dark; and when he'd reached the holm-oak bastion and seen the great tree surrounded by its sentinels, he'd known again that quick turmoil of confused emotions. As he'd walked slowly towards it, it had seemed to quicken and be aware of his coming. As he passed the shallow grassy fosse and entered the oak ring he felt there was something he ought to say, some greeting, password or prayer. It was the most aloof, silent little place under the sun, and oh, so old. He'd tiptoed past the firs and faced the barrier of yews. He'd stood there for a long musing minute, tingling with the sensation that he was being watched and regarded. At length he stepped forward and stood before the God— that mighty word came abruptly and unforeseen—and he felt a wild desire to fling himself down on the mound and do obeisance. And then he'd hurried home. As he recalled all this most vividly and minutely, he was seized with a sudden gust of uncontrollable anger at the thought of the desecration of the grove. He knew now that if he'd had the slightest idea of Curtis's purpose he'd have resisted and opposed it. It was too late now. He realised he'd 'worked himself up' rather absurdly. What could it matter! He was still a superstitious bumpkin at heart. Anyway it was no fault of Curtis. It was the finest Christmas tree anyone could hope for, and the whole thing was too nonsensical for words. The general tone of these cadentic conclusions did not quite accurately represent his thoughts—a very rare failing with Mr. Braxton.

About dinner-time the blizzard set furiously in, and the snow was flying.

'Chains on the cars tomorrow,' Mrs. Braxton told the head chauffeur.

'Boar's Hill'll be a beggar,' thought that person.

Mr. and Mrs. Braxton dined early, casually examined the presents, and went to bed. Mr. Braxton was asleep at once as usual, but was awakened by the beating of a blind which had slipped its moorings. Reluctantly he got out of bed and went to fix it. As he was doing so he became conscious of the frenzied hysterical barking of a dog. The sound, muffled by the gale, came, he judged, from the barn. He believed the underkeeper kept his whippet there. Scared by the storm, he supposed, and returned to bed.

The morning was brilliantly fine and cold, but the snowfall had been heavy.

'I heard a dog howling in the night, Perkins,' said Mr. Braxton to the butler at breakfast; 'Drake's I imagine. What's the matter with it?'

'I will ascertain, sir,' replied Perkins.

'It was Drake's dog,' he announced a little later, 'apparently something alarmed the animal, for when Drake went to let it out this morning, it appeared to be extremely frightened. When the barn door was opened, it took to its heels and, although Drake pursued it, it jumped into the river and Drake fears it was drowned.'

'Um,' said Mr. Braxton, 'must have been the storm; whippets are nervous dogs.'

'So I understand, sir.'

'Drake was so fond of it,' said Mrs. Braxton, 'though it always looked so naked and shivering to me.'

'Yes, madam,' agreed Perkins, 'it had that appearance.'

Soon after Mr. Braxton sauntered out into the blinding glitter. Curtis came over from the garage. He was heavily muffled up.

'They've got the chains on all the cars,' he said. 'Very seasonable and all that, but farmers have another word for it.' His voice was thick and hoarse.

'Yes,' said Mr. Braxton. 'You're not looking very fit.'

'Not feeling it. Had to get up in the night. Thought I heard someone trying to break into the house, thought I saw him, too.'

'Indeed,' said Mr. Braxton. 'Did you see what he was like?'

'No,' replied Curtis uncertainly. 'It was snowing like the devil. Anyway, I got properly chilled to the marrow, skipping around in my nightie.'

'You'd better get to bed,' said Mr. Braxton solicitously. He had affection and a great respect for Curtis.

'I'll stick it out today and see how I feel tomorrow. We're going to get the tree across in a few minutes. Can I borrow the two footmen? I want another couple of pullers and haulers.'

Mr. Braxton consented, and went off on his favourite little stroll across the sparkling meadows to the river and the pool where the big trout set their cunning noses to the stream.

Half an hour later Curtis had mobilised his scratch team of sleeve-rolled assistants and, with Perkins steering and himself breaking, they got to grips with the tree and bore it like a camouflaged battering-ram towards the ball-room, which occupied the left centre of the frenetic frontage of the ground floor. There was a good deal of bumping and boring and genial blasphemy before the tree was manoeuvred into the middle of the room and levered by rope and muscle into position. As it came up its pinnacle just cleared the ceiling. Sam, a cow-man, whose ginger mob had been buried in the foliage for some time, exclaimed tartly as he slapped the trunk, 'There ye are, ye old sod! Thanks for the scratches on me mug, ye old—!'

The next moment he was lying on his back, a livid weal across his right cheek.

This caused general merriment, and even Perkins permitted himself a spectral smile. There was more astonishment than pain on the face of Sam. He stared at the tree in a humble way for a moment, like a chastised and guilty dog, and then slunk from the room. The merriment of the others died away.

'More spring in these branches than you'd think,' said Curtis to Perkins.

'No doubt, sir, that is due to the abrupt release of the tension,' replied Perkins scientifically.

The 'Families' met at Paddington and travelled down together, so at five o'clock three car-loads drew up at the Hall. There were Jack and Mary with Paddy aged eight, Walter and Pamela with Jane and Peter, seven and five respectively, and George and Gloria with Gregory and Phyllis, ten and eight.

Jack and Walter were sons of the house. They were much of a muchness, burly, handsome and as dominating as their sire; a fine pair of commercial kings, entirely capable rulers, but just lacking that something which founds dynasties. Their wives conformed equally to the social type to which they belonged, good-lookers, smart dressers, excellent wives and mothers, but rather coolly colourless, spiritually. Their offspring were 'charming children,' flawless products of the English matrix, though Paddy showed signs of some obstreperous originality. 'George' was the Honourable George, Calvin, Roderick, et cetera Penables, and Gloria was Mr. and Mrs. Braxton's only daughter. George had inherited half a million and had started off at twenty-four to be something big in the City. In a sense he achieved his ambition, for two years later he was generally reckoned the biggest 'Something' in the City, from which he then withdrew, desperately clutching his last hundred thousand and vowing lachrymose repentance. He had kept his word and his wad, hunted and shot six days a week in the winter, and spent most of the summer wrestling with the two dozen devils in his golf bag. According to current jargon he was the complete extrovert, but what a relief are such, in spite of the pitying shrugs of those who for ever are peering into the septic recesses of their souls.

Gloria had inherited some of her father's force. She was rather overwhelmingly primed with energy and pep for her opportunities of releasing it. So she was always rather pent up and explosive, though maternity had kept the pressure down. She was dispassionately fond of George who had presented her with a nice little title and aristocratic background and two 'charming children.' Phyllis gave promise of such extreme beauty that, beyond being the cynosure of every press-camera's eye, and making a resounding match, no more was to be expected of her. Gregory, however, on the strength of some artistic precocity and a violent temper was already somewhat prematurely marked down as a genius to be.

Such were the 'Families.'

During the afternoon four engineers arrived from one of the Braxton factories to fix up the lighting of the tree. The fairy lamps for this had been specially designed and executed for the occasion. Disney figures had been grafted upon them and made to revolve by an ingenious mechanism; the effect being to give the tree, when illuminated, an aspect of whirling life meant to be very cheerful and pleasing.

Mr. Braxton happened to see these electricians departing in their lorry and noticed one of them had a bandaged arm and a rather white face. He asked Perkins what had happened.

'A slight accident, sir. A bulb burst and burnt him in some manner. But the injury is, I understand, not of a very serious nature.'

'He looked a bit white.'

'Apparently, sir, he got a fright, a shock of some kind, when the bulb exploded.'

After dinner the grown-ups went to the ball-room. Mr. Braxton switched on the mechanism and great enthusiasm was shown. 'Won't the kiddies love it,' said George, grinning at the kaleidoscope. 'Look at the Big Bad Wolf. He looks so darn realistic I'm not sure I'd give him a "U" certificate.'

'It's almost frightening,' said Pamela, 'they look incredibly real. Daddie, you really are rather bright, darling.'

It was arranged that the work of decoration should be tackled on the morrow and finished on Christmas Eve.

'All the presents have arrived,' said Mrs. Braxton, 'and are being unpacked. But I'll explain about them tomorrow.'

They went back to the drawing-room. Presently Gloria puffed and remarked.

'Papa, aren't you keeping the house rather too hot?'

'I noticed the same thing,' said Mrs. Braxton.

Mr. Braxton walked over to a thermometer on the wall. 'You're right,' he remarked, 'seventy.' He rang the bell.

'Perkins,' he asked, 'who's on the furnace?'

'Churchill, sir.'

'Well, he's overdoing it. It's seventy. Tell him to get it back to fifty-seven.'

Perkins departed and returned shortly after.

'Churchill informs me he has damped down and cannot account for the increasing warmth, sir.'

'Tell him to get it back to fifty-seven at once,' rapped Mr. Braxton.

'Very good, sir.'

'Open a window,' said Mrs. Braxton.

'It is snowing again, madam.'

'Never mind.'

'My God!' exclaimed Mary, when she and Jack went up to bed. 'That furnace-man is certainly stepping on it. Open all the windows.'

A wild flurry of snow beat against the curtains.

Mr. Braxton did what he very seldom did, woke up in the early hours. He awoke sweating from a furtive and demoralising dream. It had seemed to him that he had been crouching down in the fosse round Lucky's Grove and peering beneath the holm-oaks, and that there had been activity of a sort vaguely to be discerned therein, some quick, shadowy business. He knew a very tight terror at the thought of being detected at this spying, but he could not wrench himself away. That was all and he awoke still trembling and troubled. No wonder he'd had such a nightmare, the room seemed like a stokehold. He went to the windows and flung another open, and as he did so he glanced out. His room looked over the rock garden and down the path to the maze. Something moved just outside, it caught his eye. He thought he knew what it was, that big Alsatian which had been sheep-worrying in the neighbourhood. What an enormous brute. Or was it just because it was outlined against the snow? It vanished suddenly, apparently into the maze. He'd organise a hunt for it after Christmas; if the snow lay, it should be easy to track.

The first thing he did after breakfast was to send for Churchill, severely reprimand him and threaten him with dismissal from his ship. That person was almost tearfully insistent that he had obeyed orders and kept his jets low. 'I can't make it out, sir. It's got no right to be as 'ot as what it is.'

'That's nonsense!' said Mr. Braxton. 'The system has been perfected and cannot take charge, as you suggest. See to it. You don't want me to get an engineer down, do you?'

'No, sir.'

'That's enough, Get it to fifty-seven and keep it there.'

Shortly after Mrs. Curtis rang up to say her husband was quite ill with a temperature and that the Doctor was coming. Mr. Braxton asked her to ring him again after he'd been.

During the morning the children played in the snow. After a pitched battle in which the girls lost their tempers, Gregory organised the erection of a snow-man. He designed, the others fetched the material. He knew he had a reputation for brilliance to maintain and produce something Epsteinish, huge and squat. The other children regarded it with little enthusiasm, but, being Gregory, they supposed it must be admired. When it was finished Gregory wandered off by himself while the others went in to dry. He came in a little late for lunch during which he was silent and preoccupied. Afterwards the grown-ups sallied forth.

'Let's see your snow-man, Greg,' said Gloria, in a mother-of-genius tone.

'It isn't all his, we helped,' said Phyllis, voicing a point of view which was to have many echoes in the coming years.

'Why, he's changed it!' exclaimed a chorus two minutes later.

'What an ugly thing!' exclaimed Mary, rather pleased at being able to say so with conviction.

Gregory had certainly given his imagination its head, for now the squat, inert trunk was topped by a big wolf's head with open jaw and ears snarlingly laid back, surprisingly well modelled. Trailing behind it was a coiled, serpentine tail.

'Whatever gave you the idea for that?' asked Jack.

Usually Gregory was facile and eloquent in explaining his inspiration, but this time he refused to be drawn, bit his lip and turned away.

There was a moment's silence and then Gloria said with convincing emphasis, 'I think it's wonderful, Greg!'

And then they strolled off to examine the pigs and the poultry and the Suffolk punches.

They had just got back for tea when the telephone bell rang in Mr. Braxton's study. It was Mrs. Curtis. The patient was no better and Doctor Knowles had seemed rather worried, and so on. So Mr. Braxton rang up the doctor.

'I haven't diagnosed his trouble yet,' he said. 'And I'm going to watch him carefully and take a blood-test if he's not better tomorrow. He has a temperature of a hundred and two, but no other superficial symptoms, which is rather peculiar. By the way, one of your cow-men, Sam Colley, got a nasty wound on the face yesterday and shows signs of blood poisoning. I'm considering sending him to hospital. Some of your other men have been in to see me—quite a little outbreak of illness since Tuesday. However, I hope we'll have a clean bill again soon. I'll keep you informed about Curtis.'

Mr. Braxton was one of those incredible people who never have a day's illness—till their first and last. Consequently his conception of disease was unimaginative and mechanical. If one of his more essential human machines was running unsatisfactorily, there was a machine-mender called a doctor whose business it was to ensure that all the plug leads were attached firmly and that the manifold drain-pipe was not blocked. But he found himself beginning to worry about Curtis, and this little epidemic amongst his henchmen affected him disagreeably—there was something disturbing to his spirit about it. But just what and why, he couldn't analyse and decide.

After dinner, with the children out of the way, the business of decorating the tree was begun. The general scheme had been sketched out and coloured by one of the Braxton display experts and the company consulted this as they worked, which they did rather silently; possibly Mr. Braxton's palpable anxiety somewhat affected them.

Pamela stayed behind after the others had left the ball-room to put some finishing touches to her section of the tree. When she rejoined the others she was looking rather white and tight-lipped.

She said good night a shade abruptly and went to her room. Walter, a very, very good husband, quickly joined her.

'Anything the matter, old girl?' he asked anxiously.

'Yes,' replied Pamela, 'I'm frightened.'

'Frightened! What d'you mean?'

'You'll think it's all rot, but I'll tell you. When you'd all left the ball-room, I suddenly felt very uneasy—you know the sort of feeling when one keeps on looking round and can't concentrate. However, I stuck at it. I was a little way up the steps when I heard a sharp hiss from above me in the tree. I jumped back to the floor and looked up; now, of course, you won't believe me, but the trunk of the tree was moving—it was like the coils of a snake writhing upward, and there was something at the top of the tree, horrid-looking, peering at me. I know you won't believe me.'

Walter didn't, but he also didn't know what to make of it. 'I know what happened!' he improvised slightly. 'You'd been staring in at that trunk for nearly two hours and you got dizzy—like staring at the sun on the sea; and that snow dazzle this afternoon helped it. You've heard of snow-blindness—something like that, it still echoes form the retina or whatever…'

'You think it might have been that?'

'I'm sure of it.'

'And that horrible head?'

'Well, as George put it rather brightly, I don't think some of those figures on the lamps should get a "U" certificate. There's the wolf to which he referred, and the witch.'

'Which witch?' laughed Pamela a little hysterically. 'I didn't notice one.'

'I did. I was working just near it, at least, I suppose it's meant to be a witch. A figure in black squinting round from behind a tree. As a matter of fact fairies never seemed all fun and frolic to me, there's often something diabolical about them—or rather casually cruel. Disney knows that.'

'Yes, there is,' agreed Pamela. 'So you think that's all there was to it?'

'I'm certain. One's eyes can play tricks on one.'

'Yes,' said Pamela, 'I know what you mean, as if they saw what one knew wasn't there or was different. Though who would "one" be then?'

'Oh, don't ask me that sort of question!' laughed Walter. 'Probably Master Gregory will be able to tell you in a year or two.'

'He's a nice little boy, really,' protested Pamela. 'Gloria just spoils him and it's natural.'

'I know he is, it's not his fault, but they will *force* him. Look at that snow-man—and staying behind to do it. A foul-looking thing!'

'Perhaps his eyes played funny tricks with him,' said Pamela.

'What d'you mean by that?'

'I don't know why I said it,' said Pamela frowning. 'Sort of echo, I suppose. Let's go to bed.'

Walter kissed her gently but fervently, as he loved her. He was a one-lady's man and had felt a bit nervous about her for a moment or two.

Was the house a little cooler? wondered Mr. Braxton, as he was undressing, or was it that he was getting more used to it? He was now convinced there was something wrong with the installation; he'd get an expert down. Meanwhile they must stick it. He yawned, wondered how Curtis was, and switched off the light.

Soon all the occupants were at rest and the great house swinging silently against the stars. *Should* have been at rest, rather, for one and all recalled that night with reluctance and dread. Their dreams were harsh and unhallowed, yet oddly related, being concerned with dim, uncertain and yet somehow urgent happenings in and around the house, as though some thing or things were stirring while they slept and communicated their motions to their dreaming consciousness. They awoke tired with a sense of unaccountable malaise.

Mrs. Curtis rang up during breakfast and her voice revealed her distress. Timothy was delirious and much worse. The doctor was coming at 10.30.

Mr. and Mrs. Braxton decided to go over there, and sent for the car. Knowles was waiting just outside the house when they arrived.

'He's very bad,' he said quietly. 'I've sent for two nurses and Sir Arthur Galley; I want another opinion. Has he had some trouble with a tree?'

'Trouble with a tree!' said Mr. Braxton, his nerves giving a flick.

'Yes, it's probably just a haphazard, irrational idea of delirium, but he continually fusses about some tree.'

'How bad is he?' asked Mrs. Braxton.

The doctor frowned. 'I wish I knew. I'm fairly out of my depth. He's keeping up his strength fairly well, but he can't go on like this.'

'As bad as that!' exclaimed Mr. Braxton.

'I'm very much afraid so. I'm anxiously awaiting Sir Arthur's verdict. By the way, that cow-man is very ill indeed; I'm sending him into hospital.'

'What happened to him?' asked Mr. Braxton, absently, his mind on Curtis.

'Apparently a branch of your Christmas tree snapped back at him and struck his face. Blood poisoning set in almost at once.'

Mr. Braxton felt that tremor again, but merely nodded.

'I was just wondering if there might be some connection between the two, that Curtis is blaming himself for the accident. Seems an absurd idea, but judging from his ravings he appears to think he is lashed to some tree and that the great heat he feels comes from it.'

They went into the house and did their best to comfort and reassure Mrs. Curtis, instructed Knowles to ring up as soon as Sir Arthur's verdict was known, and then drove home.

The children had just come in from playing in the snow.

'Grandpa, the snow-man's melted,' said Paddy, 'did it thaw in the night?'

'Must have done,' replied Mr. Braxton, forcing a smile.

'Come and look, Grandpa,' persisted Paddy, 'there's nothing left of it.'

'Grandpa doesn't want to be bothered,' said Mary, noticing his troubled face.

'I'll come,' said Mr. Braxton. When he reached the site of the snow-man his thoughts were still elsewhere, but his mind quickly refocused itself, for he was faced with something a little strange. Not a vestige of the statue remained, though the snow was frozen crisp and crunched hard beneath their feet; and yet that snow-man was completely obliterated and where it had stood was a circle of bare, brown grass.

'It must have thawed in the night and then frozen again,' he said uncertainly.

'Then why—' began Paddy.

'Don't bother Grandpa,' said Mary sharply. 'He's told you what happened.'

They wandered off toward the heavy, hurrying river.

'Are those dog-paw marks?' asked Phyllis.

That reminded Mr. Braxton. He peered down. 'Yes,' he replied. 'And I bet they're those of that brute of an Alsatian; it must be a colossal beast.'

'And it must have paws like a young bear,' laughed Mary. 'They're funny dogs, sort of Jekyll and Hydes. I rather adore them.'

'You wouldn't adore this devil. He's all Hyde.' (I'm in the wrong mood for these festivities, he thought irritably.)

During the afternoon George and Walter took the kids to a cinema in Oxford; the others finished the decoration of the tree.

The presents, labelled with the names of their recipients, were arranged on tables round the room and the huge cracker, ten feet long and forty inches in circumference, was placed on its gaily-decorated trestle near the tree. Just as the job was finished, Mary did a three-quarters faint, but was quickly revived with brandy.

'It's the simply ghastly heat in the house!' exclaimed Gloria, who was not looking too grand herself. 'The installation must be completely diseased. Ours always works perfectly.' Mary had her dinner in bed and Jack came up to her immediately he had finished his.

'How are you feeling, darling?' he asked.

'Oh, I'm all right.'

'It *was* just the heat, of course?'

'Oh, yes,' replied Mary with rather forced emphasis.

'Scared you a bit, going off like that?' suggested Jack, regarding her rather sharply.

'I'm quite all right, thank you,' said Mary in the tone she always adopted when she'd had enough of a subject. 'I'd like to rest. Switch off the light.'

But when Jack had gone, she didn't close her eyes, but lay on her back staring up at the faint outline of the ceiling. She frowned and lightly chewed the little finger of her left hand, a habit of hers when unpleasantly puzzled. Mary, like most people of strong character and limited imagination, hated to be puzzled. Everything she considered ought to have a simple explanation if one tried hard enough to find it. But how could one explain this odd thing that had happened to her? Besides the grandiose gifts on the tables which bore a number, as well as the recipient's name, a small present for everyone was hung on the tree. This also bore a number, the same one as the lordly gift, so easing the Braxton's task of handing these out to the right people. Mary had just fixed Curtis's label to a cigarette lighter and tied it on the tree when it swung on its silk thread, so that the back of the card was visible; and on it was this inscription: 'Died, December 25th, 1938.' It spun away again and back and the inscription was no longer there.

Now Mary came of a family which rather prided itself on being unimaginative. Her father had confined his flights of fancy to the Annual Meeting of his Shareholders, while to her mother, imagination and mendacity were at least first cousins. So Mary could hardly credit the explanation that, being remotely worried about Mr. Curtis, she had subconsciously concocted that sinister sentence. On the other hand she knew poor Mr. Curtis was very ill and, therefore, perhaps, if her brain had played that malign little trick on her, it might have done so in 'tombstone writing.'

This was a considerable logical exercise for Mary, the effort tired her, the impression began to fade and she started wondering how much longer Jack was going to sit up. She dozed off and there, as if flashed on the screen 'inside her head' was 'Died, December 25th, 1938.' This, oddly enough, completely reassured her. There was 'nothing there' this time. There had been nothing that other time. She'd been very weak and imaginative even to think otherwise.

While she was deciding this, Dr. Knowles rang up. 'Sir Arthur has just been,' he said. 'And I'm sorry to say he's pessimistic. He says Curtis is very weak.'

'But what's the matter with him?' asked Mr. Braxton urgently.

'He doesn't know. He calls it P.U.O., which really means nothing.'

'But what's it stand for?'

'Pyrexia unknown origin. There are some fevers which cannot be described more precisely.'

'How ill is he really?'

'All I can say is, we must hope for the best.'

'My God!' exclaimed Mr. Braxton. 'When's Sir Arthur coming again?'

'At eleven tomorrow. I'll ring you up after he's been.'

Mr. Braxton excused himself and went to his room. Like many men of his dominating, sometimes ruthless type, he was capable of an intensity of feeling, anger, resolution, desire for revenge, but also affection and sympathy, unknown to more superficially Christian and kindly souls. He was genuinely attached to Curtis and his wife and very harshly and poignantly moved by this news which, he realised, could hardly have been worse. He would have to exercise all his will power if he was to sleep.

If on the preceding night the rest of the sleepers had been broken by influences which had insinuated themselves into their dreams, that which caused the night of that Christmas Eve to be unforgettable was the demoniacal violence of the elements. The northeaster had been waxing steadily all the evening and by midnight reached hurricane force, driving before it an almost impenetrable wall of snow. Not only so, but continually all through the night the wall was enflamed, and the roar of the hurricane silenced, by fearful flashes of lightning and claps of thunder. The combination was almost intolerably menacing. As the great house shook from the gale and trembled at the blasts and the windows blazed with strange polychromatic balls of flame, all were tense and troubled. The children fought or succumbed to their terror according to their natures; their parents soothed and reassured them.

Mr. Braxton was convinced the lightning conductors were struck three times within ten minutes, and he could imagine them recoiling from the mighty impacts and seething from the terrific charges. Not till a dilatory, chaotic dawn staggered up the sky did the storm temporarily lull. For a time the sky cleared and the frost came hard. It was a yawning and haggard company which assembled at breakfast. But determined efforts were made to engender a communal cheerfulness. Mr. Braxton did his best to contribute his quota of seasonal bonhomie, but his mind was plagued by thoughts of Curtis. Before the meal was finished the vicar rang up to say the church tower had been struck and almost demolished, so there could be no services. It rang again to say that Brent's farmhouse had been burnt to the ground.

While the others went off to inspect the Church Mr. Braxton remained in the study. Presently Knowles rang to say Sir Arthur had been and pronounced Curtis weaker, but his condition was not quite hopeless. One of the most ominous symptoms was the violence of the delirium. Curtis appeared to be in great terror and sedatives had no effect.

'How's that cow-man?' asked Mr. Braxton.

'He died in the night, I'm sorry to say.'

Whereupon Mr. Braxton broke one of his strictest rules by drinking a very stiff whisky with very little soda.

Christmas dinner was tolerably hilarious, and after it, the children, bulging and incipiently bilious, slept some of it off, while their elders put the final touches to the preparations for the party.

In spite of the weather, not a single 'cry-off' was telephoned. There was a good reason for this, Mr. Braxton's entertainments were justly famous.

So from four-thirty onwards the 'Cream of North Berkshire Society' came ploughing through the snow to the Hall; Lady Pounser and party bringing up the rear in her heirloom Rolls which was dribbling steam from its ancient and aristocratic beak. A tea of teas, not merely a high-tea, an Everest tea, towering, skyscraping, was then attacked by the already stuffed juveniles who, by the end of it, were almost livid with repletion, finding even the efforts of cracker-pulling almost beyond them.

They were then propelled into the library where rows of chairs had been provided for them. There was a screen at one end of the room, a projector at the other. Mr. Braxton had provided one of his famous surprises! The room was darkened and on the screen was flashed the sentence: 'The North Berks News Reel.'

During the last few weeks Mr. Braxton had had a sharp-witted and discreetly furtive camera-man at work shooting some of the guests while busy about their more or less lawful occasions.

For example, there was a sentence from a speech by Lord Gallen, the Socialist Peer: 'It is a damnable and calculated lie for our opponents to suggest we aim at a preposterous and essentially *inequitable* equalisation of income—' And then there was His Lordship just entering his limousine, and an obsequious footman, rug in hand, holding the door open for him.

His Lordship's laughter was raucous and vehement, though he *would* have liked to have said a few words in rebuttal.

And there was Lady Pounser's Rolls, locally known as 'the hippogriffe,' stuck in a snow-drift and enveloped in steam, with the caption, 'Oh, Mr. Mercury, *do* give me a start!' And other kindly, slightly sardonic japes at the expense of the North Berks Cream.

The last scene was meant as an appropriate prelude to the climax of the festivities. It showed Curtis and his crew digging up the tree from Lucky's Grove. Out they came from the holm-oaks straining under their load, but close observers noticed there was one who remained behind, standing menacing and motionless, a very tall, dark, brooding figure. There came a blinding lightning flash which seemed to blaze sparking round the room and a fearsome metallic bang. The storm had returned with rasping and imperious salute.

The lights immediately came on and the children were marshalled into the ball-room. As they entered and saw the high tree shining there and the little people so lively upon its branches a prolonged 'O—h!' of astonishment was exhorted from the blasé brats. But there was another wave of flame against the windows which rattled wildly at the ensuing roar, and the cries of delight were tinged with terror. And, indeed, the hard, blue glare flung a sinister glow on the tree and its whirling throng.

The grown-ups hastened to restore equanimity and, forming rings of children, circled round the tree.

Presently Mrs. Braxton exclaimed: 'Now then, look for your names on the cards and see what Father Christmas has brought you.'

Though hardly one of the disillusioned infants retained any belief in that superannuated Deliverer of Goods, the response was immediate. For they had sharp ears which had eagerly absorbed the tales of Braxton munificence. (At the same time it was noticeable that some approached the tree with diffidence, almost reluctance, and started back as a livid flare broke against the window-blinds and the dread peals shook the streaming snow from the eaves.)

Mary had just picked up little Angela Rayner so that she could reach her card, when the child screamed out and pulled away her hand.

'The worm!' she cried, and a thick, black-grey squirming maggot fell from her fingers to the floor and writhed away. George, who was near, put his shoe on it with a squish.

One of the Pounser tribe, whose card was just below the Big Bad Wolf, refused to approach it. No wonder, thought Walter, for it looked horribly hunting and alive. There were other mischances too. The witch behind the sombre tree seemed to pounce out at Clarissa Balder, so she tearfully complained, and Gloria had to pull off her card for her. Of course Gregory was temperamental, seeming to stare at a spot just below the taut peak of the tree, as if mazed and entranced. But the presents were wonderful and more than worth the small ordeal of finding one's card and pretending not to be frightened when the whole room seemed full of fiery hands and the thunder cracked against one's ear-drums and shook one's teeth. Easy to be afraid!

At length the last present had been bestowed and it was time for the *pièce de résistance*, the pulling of the great cracker. Long, silken cords streamed from each end with room among them for fifty chubby fists, and a great surprise inside, for sure. The languid, uneasy troop were lined up at each end and took a grip on the silken cords.

At that moment a footman came in and told Mr. Braxton he was wanted on the telephone.

Filled with foreboding he went to his study. He heard the voice of Knowles—

'I'm afraid I have very bad news for you…'

The chubby fists gripped the silken cords.

'Now pull!' cried Mrs. Braxton.

The opposing teams took the strain.

A leaping flash and a blasting roar. The children were hurled, writhing and screaming over each other.

Up from the middle of the cracker leapt a rosy shaft of flame which, as it reached the ceiling, seemed to flatten its peak so that it resembled a great snake of fire which turned and hurled itself against the tree in a blinding embrace. There was a fierce sustained 'Hiss,' the tree flamed like a torch, and all the fairy globes upon it burst and splintered. And then the roaring torch cast itself down amongst the screaming chaos. For a moment the great pot, swathed in green, was a carmine cauldron and its paint streamed like blood upon the floor. Then the big room was a dream of fire and those within it driven wildly from its heat.

Phil Tangler, whose farmhouse, on the early slopes of Missen Rise, overlooked both Lucky's Grove and the Hall, solemnly declared that at 7.30 on Christmas Day, 1938, he was watching from a window and marvelling at the dense and boiling race of snow, the bitter gale, and the wicked flame and fury of the storm, when he saw a high fist of fire form in a rift in the cloud-rack, a fist with two huge blazing fingers, one of which speared down on the Hall, another touched and kindled the towering fir in Lucky's Grove, as though saluting it. Five minutes later he was racing through the hurricane to join in a vain night-long fight to save the Hall, already blazing from stem to stern.